VOICE OF THE DEAD

Book 2
Between Worlds Series

TRACEE FORD

VOICE OF THE DEAD
BETWEEN WORLDS SERIES
BOOK 2

CoverArt: Select-O-Graphics/Kelly D. Abell
All rights reserved.

ISBN: 978-0692413623

This book contains violence, dark themes, murder, and sexual content.

DEDICATION

This book is dedicated to the victims of violent crimes.
Those that lived to tell about it are not victims, you are survivors.
For those whose lives were needlessly taken and cut short...
You will always be remembered.

Also for the gallant heroes on four legs who solve crimes each day.
Service dogs and K-9 units everywhere, this book belongs to you too!

To my son, who always provides me with inspiration and makes me proud.
You have opened my eyes to so much beauty.

To Artemis Grace, my faithful companion and furbaby, always and forever.

To Hope Elizabeth... this is for you, too, my love.

Contents

ACKNOWLEDGMENTS

This book was shaped over time, and I am grateful for the patience, understanding, and quiet support that made its completion possible.

To those who offered encouragement, space, and steadiness along the way…thank you for staying present while this story found its way to the page.

I am also thankful for the careful revision and refinement that helped bring clarity to the final manuscript. Any remaining imperfections are entirely my own.

Prologue

The forest loomed before her, dense and dark. The uneven ground and treacherous terrain made it impossible to find steady footing. She heard water nearby, a stream or river perhaps.

Blood rushed through her veins, adrenaline propelling her forward. Her thoughts overwhelmed her, and the agony she felt became impossible to ignore. Branches scraped the bare skin of her legs, warm blood running down them. Her entire body hurt, and her broken wrist throbbed with pain. She did not want to die. Her will to live drove her deeper into the forest.

The sound of the water grew closer. She knew if she could just reach the river, she could swim out of this hell. She felt like such a fool. She trusted him. She knew him. He had been so nice and always so polite.

The rustling came from behind her, but the sound of the water was louder. She was closer. The uneven ground caused her to lose her footing, and she tripped, falling forward. Exhausted from the trauma of the rape and torture, she clawed at the mud, her desire to live pushing her onward. She hoped the river would whisk her away from the danger that lay behind her.

Suddenly her hair pulled taut and her head jerked back. She screamed and kicked, fighting hard against the man who had already taken so much from her. She feared more hours of torture and violation. Then something hard struck the back of her head and everything went black.

When she opened her eyes, the disorientation made her feel sick. There was no light. She was surrounded by total darkness. She moved her fingers against the surface beneath her, struggling to comprehend where she could possibly be. Panic set in as she searched through the darkness.

She raised her hands, but a hard surface stopped her. Only a few inches from her face, she felt a smooth, solid barrier. Again she felt beneath her and finally touched something familiar. It was a cigarette lighter.

She grabbed it tightly and flicked it on. The brief illumination revealed the horror of her reality. It was worse than she could have imagined. Surrounded by dirt and earth, she suddenly understood her fate. Terror gripped her. She screamed, even though she knew no one would ever hear her. The fight to live was for nothing. This was her end. Still, screaming made her feel a little better.

The faces of her parents flashed through her mind as she closed her eyes, tears falling quickly. She realized that all of her plans, her goals and dreams, now lay in waste beneath the surface of the dirt. In one vulnerable moment, he had stolen everything from her.

Terrified by the inevitability of her situation, she continued to scream until the lighter went out. Once again she was surrounded by darkness.

1

Nicholas Bennette sat at his desk in Washington's FBI headquarters. Paperwork made his job a complete pain in the ass, but as much as he despised doing it, he was known for his meticulous reports. Still, he preferred fieldwork.

A knock on his door drew his eyes up. Special Agent Bill Giles walked in. A talented behavioral analyst for the FBI, William "Wild Bill" Giles was well respected among his peers. With a stocky build, his wavy black hair had turned gray over the years. His style had always been sweaters and polo shirts. He was rather old school in appearance, unlike much of the new blood in the bureau.

With a smile, Nick pushed back from his desk and stood. He walked to Bill with a hand outstretched. Nick's simple good looks added to his professional presence. Always very well put together, he stood at six foot two with short, dark auburn hair. The years he had spent in the military had turned him against buzz cuts, but he still preferred a short, management-style cut.

Always clean-shaven, he took pride in his appearance. He wore suits and ties with some sort of crazy design on them. Bill had always accused Nick of choosing such things as a means of engaging in quiet rebellion.

After the cordial greeting, Nick and Bill sat on the large leather couch in the center of the room. Bill made small talk at first, but then quickly focused on the point of his visit. "We have a problem, Bennette," he said.

"I figured you weren't here to talk about fishing," Nick said as he pursed his lips.

"We received information through VICAP today about three murdered women, two in Ohio and one in Virginia."

"I see."

"The girls were buried alive, Nick. There's evidence of sexual assault and torture. The MO matches across the victims. We believe we are looking at a single offender here. And because the crimes cross jurisdictional lines, the FBI officially became involved in the case today. It seems we have a serial killer on our hands."

Nick sighed. "How can I help?"

"You're the top guy in violent crimes. You're like a bloodhound. If you're on the case, then I know you'll find this guy. What's even better is that the Ohio State Police has offered the services of one of their best forensic psychologists. They want you to work with her to solve this. Two heads will definitely be better than one here. We're afraid the body count will rise steadily."

A confused grimace flashed across Nick's face. "Why don't you want to be on this case, Bill? And what about your team? I mean, this is the kind of shit they live for. And why is an outsider coming into this when the FBI has its own behavioral people who live, eat, and breathe this stuff?"

"Because we need help with this one, Nick. My team is running on fumes right now. We're really stretched thin. The forensic psychologist recommended by the State of Ohio has solved hundreds of cold cases."

He sighed heavily as he lowered his gaze. "So what's the plan?" Nick begrudgingly asked.

"You're going to go to Virginia first. When you get there, Dr. Lauren Harris, the psychologist, will be waiting for you at the local police department. She has been debriefed and knows the FBI is sending an agent, so she'll be expecting you. The State's forensics team and crime labs have already provided her with crime scene photos and sample analysis reports. I've put everything in this folder for you to review." Bill handed Nick the thick file. "If you have questions, please let me know."

Bill paused and ran his fingers through his hair. Then he continued. "At first the police thought they were dealing with a single murder. Luckily, Dr. Harris did some digging and found the crime in Virginia. The unsub is fast too, Nick. He's committed a murder each month since April. Officials are starting to panic."

"So I need to get packed for Virginia first? Then to Ohio?" he asked with a heavy exhale.

"The third body is near the Shenandoah River. The crime scene is fresh. The body was just found this morning. When I spoke to Dr. Harris on the phone earlier, she explained she always visits the crime scenes, even if the case is cold. In this case, however, it's not."

Bill paused for a heartbeat. Nick knew there was more. Bill hesitated still.

"There's something else, right?" Nick asked.

With a half-hearted smile, Bill nodded. "Well, there is one more thing I needed to talk to you about, Nick. The Dayton field office needs a new director."

"But you're the director there."

"I'm retiring," he replied.

Shock colored Nick's face. "Bill, you're kidding."

"Nope. I've done my time, son. I've had enough of this to last me a dozen lifetimes. So Deputy Director Trenton and I discussed it, and we think you would be great for the job. You are reliable, you're seasoned, you're well trained, and you've been loyal to your country. The government always has a way of honoring exemplary service like yours. Besides that, you're one of the best agents I've ever worked with."

A little embarrassed by the compliment, his face turned slightly pink. He met Bill's gaze. "So you're promoting me?"

"Yes." He paused for a moment. "Of course, the position comes with a raise and"

Before Bill could finish, Nick interrupted. "You're asking me to relocate, aren't you? That's why you're hesitating."

Guilt covered Bill's expression like a shroud. Nick jumped up and walked to the window. He looked out at the D.C. skyline. It had been his home for some time. He'd settled there after serving in the army. He'd built a life for himself. "I knew it," he bit out. "Every government promotion comes with a sacrifice, doesn't it?"

"The FBI will pay for your moving expenses, and they'll help you find an apartment."

"But what about" Nick trailed off.

"I know what you're thinking, and I know you'll work something out. You're resourceful." Bill pursed his lips into a straight line and went on. "This is an opportunity I wouldn't suggest passing up, Nick."

"Why don't you hire Dr. Harris for the director's job? She's already in Ohio, and it sounds to me like she'd be good at it. Is she qualified?" Nick asked, his tone pleading with a hint of anger.

"She is highly qualified, but she will only consider being a consultant for the FBI. Nothing more than that."

"Well, I guess if I want that raise, I'd better start packing, huh?" Mixed emotions caused frustration. Excitement, anticipation, and extreme stress were a bad combination. Still looking out at the city, he sighed. "Damn it, Bill." He shoved his hands into his pants pockets. "I just got my life back together, you know?"

"I know, Nick, but this promotion is a big deal, son. I know you've been working your entire career for an opportunity like this. The reality is that if you want to be the director of the Dayton field office, you have to move."

2

Lauren Harris had been raised in a small town just outside of Dayton. She had returned there when she started working on her doctorate at Wright State University. She had always been a workaholic.

As a consultant for the State of Ohio, she worked in Columbus a great deal. Still, she always found time to assist local law enforcement as well as local prosecutors. Aside from her consulting duties, she worked as a therapist at the Ellis Institute in Dayton and taught classes at Wright State. Her work was nationally recognized, and she often booked speaking engagements as well.

As she sat in the attic going through boxes for the upcoming garage sale, her best friend, Selina Derek, and her cousin, Chelsey Harris, rummaged through moth-eaten boxes of clothing. They did not want Lauren to go through the boxes by herself. It was not healthy.

Selina had been Lauren's dearest friend since high school. Their personal interests had changed over the years, but they had managed to stay in touch and worked hard to remain close. Selina's path had led her in the direction of art and criminal justice. She was a forensic artist who worked for the Ohio State Police. BCI also contracted with her to complete facial reconstructions when needed. Much like Lauren, Selina had worked extensively with local law enforcement. Currently, her home office was at the Homeland Security branch just off Interstate 70, about twenty minutes from the Indiana border.

With a lighthearted personality, Selina stood five feet eight inches tall and had beautiful fair skin and straight black hair. With big brown eyes and a perfect smile, men often swooned. However, with the grueling schedule she kept, she did not date.

More sisters than cousins, Chelsey Harris had always been Lauren's rock. She was a natural socialite, which made Lauren a bit envious at times.

Petite in stature with delicate features, Chelsey exuded a natural beauty. She had long, shiny brown hair and tawny brown eyes. Her humor was one of her most endearing qualities. Her overall sweet disposition was accentuated by her free-spiritedness. Because of this, she had always kept her parents on their toes. Her older brother had been the complete opposite. Dependable, with trackable and achievable goals, he often gave Chelsey the role of the black sheep.

Lauren Harris, a sullen but stunning thirty-five-year-old, had always been cursed with wisdom beyond her years. A perfectionist to the last, she had a tendency to be terribly arrogant. Many times, she rubbed people the wrong way with her air of superiority.

Lauren stood at a slender five foot seven inches with glossy, shoulder-length, light chestnut-colored hair. No matter how much chaos surrounded her, her calm blue eyes always conveyed a sense of control.

Despite being incredibly socially awkward, she was very empathic. She could also be very persuasive. Law enforcement officers had watched in awe as she pulled the deepest, darkest confessions from hardened criminals. Colleagues had watched as she comforted victims. Fellow therapists had commended her on her innate ability to move patients forward toward major milestones.

Lauren had avoided going through the boxes in the attic for a very long time. It helped that her cousin and best friend were there to support her. She stood and walked to the far side of the attic. She bent down and rummaged through yet another cardboard box. She pulled out a photograph and, with a gentle touch, brushed off the dust. She held the framed photo in her hands as she choked back emotion.

Chelsey watched as Lauren stared at the picture in her hand. She sat down beside her. She knew exactly which picture Lauren had found. "We all miss them," Chelsey said in a soft voice.

Not taking her eyes from the photograph, Lauren nodded. Her thumb traced a face. Dust gathered in the creases of her fingerprint.

"You haven't gone through any of this stuff since you came back to Ohio, have you?" Chelsey asked.

"No." Lauren shook her head. The lump of emotion in her throat made it difficult to speak. "I still can't believe they're gone," she whispered.

"None of us can," Selina added.

"I miss them all the time," Lauren confessed. "Every minute of every day."

"I know," Chelsey said as she put her arm around Lauren's shoulder in an effort to provide comfort.

3

After an emotionally trying day, Lauren sat on the couch with her feet up, her legs swaddled in a warm fleece blanket. She carefully studied the details of the two murders. She wanted to be well prepared to visit the third crime scene. She planned to catch a flight to Virginia the next morning. She had already seen the other two scenes and gathered quite a bit of information from them.

Lauren already had a pretty good idea about the type of offender they were dealing with. More answers would come once she saw the third scene. Her eyes grew heavier as she thumbed through the folders. She finally decided to stack the files and place them on the coffee table before she snuggled under the blanket and fell asleep.

At five in the morning, with her eyes barely open, she hurried through the airport terminal. The brief flight ended with an escort to the Warren County Sheriff's Office.

Shoulders squared, she walked in and immediately saw Chris Shilling. He was a brilliant forensic entomologist, a friend, and a colleague. Next to him stood Lisa Wright, a forensic pathologist Lauren was not very familiar with. She had only met her a few times at crime scenes. Lisa was a new permanent addition to Lauren's team.

A quirky but good-hearted guy, Chris never let his intelligence turn him into a cocky jerk. He was not a man who could be easily offended, but when people called him the "bug guy," all bets were off. He tolerated the nickname from Lisa and Lauren, but no one else.

He stood only five foot six inches tall, with curly blond hair and a neatly trimmed beard. He was a bit of a nerd and very kind. As an openly gay man, he often appeared guarded, but not to Lauren. She had met his partner on several occasions and was very supportive of his lifestyle.

The long list of academic successes he had achieved at only thirty-one years old could be intimidating to some. He had contributed to groundbreaking research in forensic entomology and dabbled in botany. He held multiple doctorates and had a photographic memory. He was undoubtedly an asset to the team.

Lisa, a thirty-nine-year-old sophisticate, had transferred from New Jersey. She had worked there and in New York as a coroner. She was a tall, beautiful African American woman standing at five foot six inches, with a thin build, dark brown hair, and dark brown eyes.

It had never been hard for Lisa to make friends quickly, especially with men. Lauren had been present for many of Dr. Wright's lectures and presentations and had noticed how easily she grabbed the attention of the males in the room. She seemed to possess a power over them that Lauren did not entirely understand, but she was clearly adept at it. Male-female interactions were not something Lauren was particularly interested in anyway.

Lauren had spent much of her time working with the Columbus and Dayton police departments. When she ventured into rural areas, the size of the precincts always took her by surprise. Still, the smaller divisions seemed close-knit. Officers and detectives greeted her with bright smiles and respectful handshakes. When she walked into the Warren County office, it looked like a rat race, with people scattering everywhere, chattering about the case and trying to make Chris and Lisa feel welcome.

As was typical when preparing to visit a fresh crime scene, Lauren, Chris, and Dr. Wright wore jeans, hiking boots, T-shirts, and jackets with the State of Ohio's seal on the back. Experience had taught Lauren that a day in the woods involved plenty of mud and dirt. Mobility and practicality were key.

Detective Don Mullins, an easygoing man with a receding hairline and deep-set brown eyes, greeted the team and invited them into the conference room. A man sat at the end of the large, shiny table with a file open, studying it closely. He wore a suit, which led Lauren to believe he might be new to the job or simply too dense to understand they would be out in the woods all day. She assumed he must be a rookie. Her respect for him instantly plummeted.

Rookies, especially ones wearing fancy suits, often came with an unbecoming attitude. They wanted everyone to believe they knew everything about investigations and police work. They typically did not listen to their veteran counterparts and frequently made Lauren's work much harder.

Bill Giles sat beside the man in the suit and tie. He was conversing with another officer until he noticed Lauren and the others enter the room. He immediately stood and made his way toward her. With a friendly smile and a respectful handshake, he said, "Dr. Harris."

She nodded with a confident grin. "Director Giles."

"Please, call me Bill," he said, his hands still in hers.

Once he let go, he shifted his attention to Lisa with a courteous handshake and flashed a crooked smile. "It's been a while. How are you?"

"Wild Bill," she said lightly. "I'm good. Always great to see you. You look well. I hear you're finally retiring."

"Yes. It's time," he answered. "Did you arrive this morning?"

"No, we came last night," she replied, gesturing in Chris's direction. "We stayed at a very nice hotel in town."

Bill shook Chris's hand. "You must be the bug guy."

Chris's face turned a bright shade of red as he pursed his lips. He nodded without saying a word. Lauren looked on with amusement.

Detective Mullins entered the room. "If everyone could please take a seat," he said authoritatively.

Uniformed and plainclothes officers settled around the table while Bill began the introductions. He gestured toward the man in the suit first. "This is Special Agent Nicholas Bennette with the FBI. He'll be working on this case. He's in training for the directorship at the Dayton Field Office."

Nick smiled and waved casually. Lauren picked up on an unspoken intensity between Lisa and the agent. She wondered if they had a history.

Bill continued, "This is Dr. Lauren Harris, Dr. Chris Shilling, and Dr. Lisa Wright, all with the Ohio State Police. Finally, Detective Don Mullins from the Warren County Sheriff's Office." He paused briefly, then went on. "As most of you know, I'm Bill Giles, retiring director of the Dayton Field Office, and I also head up the behavioral unit for the FBI. I'm going to let Detective Mullins take it from here."

The detective stood as Bill sat down. He looked at Lauren. "Dr. Harris, I'm told this sort of thing is your forte. Based on your experience and expertise, can you tell us what you've found by studying the first two victims?"

"I'm happy to share my findings, but I'd like to visit the crime scene first," Lauren said. "I know Dr. Shilling and Dr. Wright have already been working it, but I really need to see it myself before providing a detailed profile and analysis."

"Absolutely," Mullins said with a nod. "I think we can arrange that."

Everyone stood. As Nick pushed away from the table, Lauren took note of his build. He was muscular, with broad shoulders and a trim waist. It was easy to see that he worked out. Admittedly, he was attractive. Despite his inappropriate choice of attire for a crime scene, Lauren felt an instant chemistry. Immediately, she raised her guard.

She met his gaze. "Did you bring a change of clothing?" she asked curtly.

His light brown eyes filled with confusion. "No. Why?"

Chris interrupted. "Because you probably should have. It's muddy out there."

4

Lauren watched as Nick dodged limbs and fallen trees as they made their way into the state forest. After a fifteen-minute hike, they arrived at the scene.

The dirt was still soft from the rain. Crime scene tape still cordoned off the area. Forensics had placed markers on the ground to indicate important aspects of the scene. The thick canopy of trees darkened the area, so forensics had also installed floodlights to illuminate the site for processing.

As they stood outside the perimeter, Mullins looked at Lauren. "Federal forensics already collected samples. The medical examiner wanted to wait until you arrived before doing anything with the body. He consulted with Dr. Wright, who agreed the body shouldn't be disturbed. She said you do your best work at the scenes."

Lauren nodded. "She's right. I do. Thank you for listening to her advice." She lifted the crime scene tape and walked toward the hole in the earth. She stood over it. Scanning the forest floor, she saw that forensics had found no signs of tracks or boot prints. That was disappointing.

"How could someone dig this and not use heavy equipment?" she muttered. "The offender had to have planned this carefully, likely months in advance. He might have even buried this long before he began abducting his victims. This could have been years in the making."

Nick leaned over to Chris as he observed Lauren. "Does she do this all the time? Talking to herself?" he asked.

"Yep," Chris whispered.

Inside the hole lay a clear box. From what Lauren remembered from studying the previous crime scenes, the box was made of sturdy, hard plastic. The walls were at least three inches thick. As she looked down at it, it reminded her of a display case in a jewelry store. However, this box appeared far sturdier.

The case summary flashed through her mind. The victim was a Caucasian female with red hair. The other victims didn't fit this profile, but the method of disposal was consistent. "When did she go missing?" Lauren asked.

"Her family said they received the email on the eighteenth. She said she was going on a camping trip and would be out of range," Mullins answered.

Lauren interrupted. "And then on the eighteenth of this month, the family received a text message with coordinates, correct?"

"Yes," Mullins replied. "When we input the information into VICAP, the two other victims popped up. Same MO. How did you figure out that the numbers were coordinates for where the body was buried?"

"Our team is very good at unscrambling puzzles," Lauren answered.

"The family came to us when they got the numbers," Mullins concluded.

Lauren leaned over the lifeless body of the girl. Just like the others, she wore only a bra and panties. The crusted blood beneath her fingernails indicated she had clawed at the box for some time before giving in to her fate. Smears of blood on the plastic lid confirmed Lauren's suspicions. As with the other scenes, a cigarette lighter lay beside the victim's hand.

The coffin had been undisturbed, still sealed and airtight. As

Lauren continued her visual assessment, she noticed ligature marks around the girl's wrists. Bruising covered her body. There was evidence of torture, just like the other two victims. She was fairly certain the cause of death would be suffocation.

Lauren's team had worked hard to solve the mystery of air supply for the other two victims. After many grueling hours, they discovered there had been only twenty-four hours of oxygen in the box. There was no reason to assume the calculations would be different with this victim.

As she knelt beside the box, she gazed into the milky eyes of the dead girl. "It never ceases to amaze me how much torment the human body can endure," Lauren whispered.

She stood and walked the crime scene perimeter. She waited patiently for what she knew would come next.

Lauren had been born with a profound gift. It had helped her solve hundreds of cold cases. She could see the spirits of victims, and they often revealed crucial details of the crime. Although she was clearly a medium, Lauren could communicate only with victims of violent crimes. Her visions never revealed the perpetrators.

Lauren had learned to use her education in conjunction with her gift to piece together a victim's final moments. Armed with knowledge, training, and revelations shared by the dead, she sought justice for them. While she didn't fully understand her gift, she had learned to embrace it. She knew it had led her to her soul's mission and divine calling: helping people.

Only three people knew what she could do. Her mother and father, who were already dead, and her paternal grandmother, Annie Harris. That was exactly how Lauren intended to keep it. She feared ridicule and discrediting. She had worked too hard and too long to build her reputation to jeopardize it now.

Finding a peaceful spot near the trail, Lauren closed her eyes. She drowned out the surrounding stimuli and focused on her auditory senses. A quiet atmosphere helped, but a quiet mind was essential. The victims communicated telepathically.

She opened her eyes and scanned the area for the apparition. Suddenly, she saw the girl hiding behind a tree not far from the scene. Lauren walked toward the tree and made eye contact with her.

Lauren closed her eyes once more. The sensation of running overtook her body. She felt sticks, dirt, and leaves beneath bare feet. Hunger. Fatigue. Pain. Breathless fear. Then the terror of waking up inside the box. Trapped forever. Lauren quickly opened her eyes, assuring herself she was still above ground. She heard the soft whisper of the victim. "I knew better."

Nick walked up behind her. "You okay?" he asked.

She startled slightly and turned back toward the others. "Yes," she said sharply. "I just needed time to think. It helps me piece things together."

"Oh. Okay. You just seemed kind of out of it."

She refused to offer more information and walked away.

Once the top of the plastic coffin was opened, Chris collected samples from the body. Lisa coordinated the autopsy with the local coroner. Lauren's expertise would be used for the offender and victim profile. Everyone had a role to play. Still, Lauren wondered why Nick's presence was necessary. He wasn't a behaviorist.

"What's her name, Detective?" Lauren asked as she stared at the body.

The detective sighed. "Patricia Zimmerman, age nineteen. She was a student at Virginia Tech."

"Another commonality in victimology," Lauren said. She folded her arms. "The other two victims were also college students. As we've discussed, the families received emails about extended camping trips, then GPS coordinates exactly a month later."

Lauren glanced at Nick, who was bent over the body. "What a shame," he whispered. "Makes me sick," he added, his voice trailing off.

"When it stops making you sick, Nick," Bill said, "that's when you know it's time for a career change."

5

Back at the station, everyone gathered around the conference room table, the worry and anxiety reaching a fever pitch. "So what are we dealing with here, Dr. Harris?" Mullins asked.

"Before I get into this particular case, let me summarize the findings with the other two victims," she replied. "Although I'm confident the medical examiner's report will confirm the connection between the cases, I don't like to assume."

"Is this a serial or not?" Nick asked impatiently.

"Yes," Lauren said as she shot a disapproving glance at Nick. "I believe it is. It matches the profile of a serial killer, three or more murders with a distinct cooling-off period."

Pausing, Lauren grabbed her laptop and opened it. She stood and looked at the projector near the front of the room. Taking the cords in her hands, she made eye contact with Mullins. "May I?"

"Absolutely," he replied as he stood to offer assistance.

Once the laptop was connected, the image of a beautiful young woman flashed onto the projector screen. Lauren took a deep breath. "This is Heidi Musack. She was a twenty-year-old pre-law student in her sophomore year at The Ohio State University. She came from a stable home. She was single, socially well-adjusted, and had no criminal history. She had a solid social circle with several close friends. Heidi's case came to our attention when her mother received a text message with numbers. Those numbers meant nothing to her, of course. Her mother also reported receiving an email from Heidi on April eighteenth, saying she was going hiking. On May eighteenth, her mother received the coordinates. Heidi was found in a grave identical to the one we saw today."

Lauren pressed a key on her laptop and another photograph appeared. "This is Jefferson State Park. There were no heavy equipment tracks, no footprints, no fibers, and no other evidence that could help us identify a perpetrator."

Photographs of the body followed as she continued through the presentation. "Heidi, like the current victim, was discovered wearing only her underwear." She clicked to a morgue photo. "The medical examiner and Dr. Wright determined that Heidi had been raped repeatedly. There was perimortem and postmortem bruising across her body, along with evidence of defensive wounds. Her fingertips were bloody because she tried to claw her way out of the coffin. Oddly, her face was one of the only areas that showed no signs of trauma. In fact, it had been cleaned meticulously. She also had a broken wrist, which Dr. Wright believes was caused by a fall."

Lauren advanced to another photograph, this one of a blonde woman. "This is Julie Parks. She was a twenty-four-year-old graduate student in education at Ohio University in Athens. She also came from a stable home and had no criminal record. She sent an email to her sister on May eighteenth indicating she would be going on a trip and would be out of range. Around June twentieth, Julie's sister received a text message with numbers that meant nothing to her. At that point, our team and the forensics unit decided the information from both victims needed to be entered into VICAP."

Lauren clicked again, and images of the second crime scene appeared. "Julie was found in a plastic coffin with evidence of torture and sexual assault. She was single and lived alone. Her body was recovered in Wayne National Forest. After the second victim, the team determined that the numbers sent to the families were GPS coordinates."

Chris interjected. "Each victim's cell phone was found on the ground beside the grave. That helped us determine the numbers were directions to the site. Our cyber team wasn't able to pull anything useful from the phones."

"So we're dealing with a sex-crazed serial killer again? Another Bundy?" Nick said presumptuously.

Lauren ignored Nick and continued. "The burial sites are identical. The method of death is the same. Based on these consistencies, it is safe to say we are dealing with the same killer."

Chris chimed in again. "Another interesting detail is that both victims were missing a piece of jewelry."

"I believe the unsub is directly associated with the universities in some way," Lauren continued. "That may be how he is selecting his victims. On the other hand, he could be transient, possibly a truck driver. I have no doubt that he is geographically mobile."

"And what about victimology?" Bill asked.

"I'm still working on that," Lauren replied, "but in my experience, an offender has a type. Some prefer blondes. Bundy preferred brunettes. They acted as surrogates for a co-ed who rejected him. The strongest commonality among these women is that they all appear to have strong personalities, stable homes, and no criminal history. They are all students. I believe the offender is attracted to the strength and success these women represent."

"Listen, um…" Nick began.

"Dr. Harris," she corrected.

"Dr. Harris," he said tightly, "you're throwing a lot of information at us. I feel like I'm trying to catch for Major League Baseball. You're pitching too fast."

"I apologize if you can't keep up, Agent Bennette. Perhaps you should take notes."

The tension in the room caused several people to glance at one another. Lauren glared at Nick but continued. "Another commonality is that each young woman contacted a family member on the exact same date each month. Always on the eighteenth. I refuse to believe that's a coincidence."

Mullins spoke up. "Our latest victim, Patricia, was also a student. The dates match as well. I agree that we're dealing with the same killer."

"So what now?" Nick asked, disdain creeping into his tone. "We just sit around and wait for him to kill someone else?"

Lauren's cheeks flushed as frustration rose inside her. "My job, Agent Bennette, is to provide a profile. The goal is for law enforcement to narrow the suspect pool. If I can identify commonalities among the victims and crime scenes, I can construct an accurate picture of the offender. One of my objectives is to arm law enforcement with knowledge."

"Are you psychic?" he asked patronizingly.

Caught off guard, she furrowed her brow and scowled at him, then quickly recovered. "No, I'm not. However, I close cases efficiently. I have solved investigations that sat on shelves for decades. I bring peace to families. I've resolved countless active cases. The results speak for themselves. Statistically."

Hoping to ease the tension, Chris spoke up. "I've taken samples from the scenes and the victims," he said. "Unfortunately, there's nothing yet that points us in a specific direction. I was hoping for more, something to link the scenes. I took as many samples as possible. Once I'm back at the lab, maybe our luck will change."

"I think we need to remember that this offender is extremely careful not to leave evidence behind," Dr. Wright added. "It's possible he's ex-military or former law enforcement. He covers his tracks too well."

Chris spoke again. "On a positive note, once suspects are narrowed down, I can compare soil samples to residue found on a suspect's shoes. That's the hope, anyway. Assuming he hasn't ditched them. If he's as calculated as we think, he's probably buying new shoes and clothing for each kill, then destroying them afterward. That suggests he lives somewhere isolated, where large fires wouldn't draw attention."

"So what do we do now?" Mullins asked.

Lauren's expression softened. "I'm going to ask that you satellite-link me to the Franklin County Sheriff's Office, Columbus Police, and Athens Police. I want to present a preliminary profile so the suspect pool can be narrowed."

Mullins nodded. "We'll make it happen."

6

It took two hours for the uplinks to be established and for the Warren County Sheriff's Office to get organized. Lauren sat in the conference room typing on her laptop. Nick stepped into the room and sat in a chair across from her.

"So you don't think we've seen the last of him, huh?" he asked.

"He's just getting started, Agent Bennette. He's just getting started."

"But how do you know that? It feels like you've pulled all of this out of thin air. It sounds like conjecture. I've never understood how you behavior people do what you do, how you come up with some of this shit."

Lauren was offended. "So you're another know-it-all agent, I see. Because of agents like you, I only consult for the FBI. You couldn't pay me enough to work full-time for the feds. You're a flock of arrogant asses," she said sharply.

Before he could defend himself, Lauren continued. "Agent Bennette, I don't use conjecture to do my job. I work with factual information to formulate possibilities. It's a rare method, but I use statistical profiling to compile information about the offender. Many of my predecessors relied on intuition-based profiling. And while much of profiling does involve intuition, I prefer a more scientifically proven method."

"Hey, listen, Doc, don't get mad," he said, looking down at her. She stood to even the playing field, but Nick wasn't finished. "And we're not all asses." He put his hands in his pockets and relaxed his posture. "As far as your 'methods,'" he continued, using air quotes,

"I just think crimes are solved by good old-fashioned police work, not this mumbo jumbo you behavioralists come up with."

"I really don't have time to debate this with you," she said curtly. "If you'll excuse me, I have a profile to present." She stormed out of the room and entered the area where the webcam was set up.

Mullins and six other officers sat at long tables with notepads and pencils. Nick walked into the room and stood in the back. Lisa and Chris followed him in.

Chris found an empty seat in the middle of the room behind one of the tables. Lisa, on the other hand, walked to the back and stood beside Nick.

As Lauren prepared for her presentation, she observed the interaction between Lisa and Nick. Clearly, they had history. Lisa leaned over and whispered something, turning Nick's cheeks red.

Trying to be subtle, Lauren walked to the back of the room where the projector was set up. She adjusted various settings while eavesdropping.

She heard Nick ask, "What can you tell me about Dr. Harris? She seems sort of uptight."

"She's very professional and extremely well respected," Lisa replied. "She knows her stuff, Nick. Always prepared. Nothing takes her by surprise. She's socially awkward, but once you get to know her, she's pretty endearing."

"A psychologist, huh?"

"One of the best. Like I said, she struggles socially sometimes, but she's really come a long way."

"So she was worse than she is now?" he asked, astonishment

coloring his tone.

"Nick, that's not fair. You don't even know her," Lisa rebuked. "She's a good person. Yes, she's a little odd, but her heart is always in the right place."

Nick nodded, looking unconvinced.

Still occupied with the projector and electronics at the back of the room, Lauren continued adjusting knobs and settings.

She heard Lisa say, "Not to change the subject, Nick, but how long has it been since we've seen each other? Seven or eight years?"

In her periphery, Lauren studied their interaction. Instead of answering, Nick shrugged, his hands still in his pockets.

"That was some night, huh?" Lisa said as she nudged him with her elbow.

Lauren had heard enough and walked to the front of the room. The equipment appeared to be online and functioning correctly. She cleared her throat and made eye contact with everyone before shifting her attention to the webcam. Holding the presentation clicker, she began.

"My name is Dr. Lauren Harris, and I'm a consultant with the Ohio State Police and the FBI."

She discussed the victimology first, then transitioned to the offender profile.

"The unsub will be a white male in his mid-twenties to early thirties. He will be socially adept. He may have a steady girlfriend, be married, or even have children. He most likely lives in an isolated area. This would allow him to commit the murders without risk of discovery. The isolation would also aid in the construction of the coffin and evidence disposal. He is probably physically fit, based on the victims he's chosen. He will be free of physical deformities and likely pleasing to the eye. He is geographically transient, which suggests a job that requires travel, possibly a truck driver, salesman, or technician of some sort.

"The victims show evidence of sexual assault and rape. This is an act of power, not desire. His victims are bright young women. They are physically fit. The torture and burial are about power, or rather, taking theirs.

"The text messages to family members and the GPS coordinates are significant because they indicate he wants to be seen. He wants credit for the abductions and murders. Again, this aligns with the theme of power and control. He requires no ransom and seeks no monetary gain.

"The unsub may have a military or law enforcement background. He is organized and highly intelligent. An offender like this is known as a hedonistic or power-control killer."

Lauren paused, then continued, "I believe the dates are significant to him. The eighteenth of every month must mean something. I think the thirty-day waiting period simply ensures the women are dead. Based on our research, it's unnecessary, since the victims would assuredly die within twenty-four hours of burial."

She paused again. "I should also mention that the emails sent to the families are meant to deter suspicion. They ensure the families won't immediately search for the victims or go public. Based on what my team has found, the unsub doesn't appear to keep the victims long, but I believe the MO is still evolving."

An officer raised his hand. Lauren acknowledged him.

"Are we dealing with a serial killer?"

She nodded. "Yes. He fits the profile. Three victims and a clear cooling-off period. We haven't seen the last of him. He's just beginning. The body count will rise. He wants recognition and public acknowledgment."

"So," Nick said, "we wait for him to take another life?"

Lauren sighed, looking down at the clicker. "I don't like this any more than you do, but this is what I have. I can't tell you what he looks like beyond the fact that he is Caucasian."

"How do you know he's white?" someone asked.

Lauren's tone lightened. "Because the victims are white. Serial killers typically do not cross racial lines. Another possibility, though remote, is that the unsub could be Black and killing white women as a hate crime."

Turning back to the webcam, she concluded, "That's all I have, ladies and gentlemen. Thank you for your attention, and good luck."

Mullins stood and approached her. He pursed his lips. "Thanks for coming to our little town, Dr. Harris," he said. "I hope we can figure this out quickly. The last thing we need is more dead girls."

7

Nick stood in the airport terminal. He glanced up at the departure schedule and then knelt in front of his four-year-old son. Tommy Bennette was the most important person in Nick's life. Tommy simply didn't understand why his daddy was leaving.

Sunlight streamed through the floor-to-ceiling windows, catching in the strands of Tommy's auburn hair. Freckles peppered his face as he frowned and glanced out at the plane sitting on the tarmac.

"You'll have to come see me in Ohio, sport," Nick said as he smiled and touched Tommy's spiky hair.

"When can I come, Daddy?" Tommy asked.

Nick looked up at Jillian. At one time, they had planned to get married. Now she was simply Tommy's mother.

She smiled down at Nick, but only half-heartedly.

"As soon as I get settled in," Nick continued, "I'll make sure you get to come see me."

"It won't be like now, though. I won't get to see you every day," Tommy said as he pursed his lips.

They embraced. Nick's heart felt like it might break inside his chest.

"I'll miss you, Daddy," Tommy said, his voice muffled against Nick's shoulder.

The back of Tommy's small hand fit perfectly in Nick's as he held the boy close. "I'll miss you too, little man." Nick stood and scooped Tommy into his arms. "You be good for your mom." He choked back his emotions as he heard the boarding call.

For the past four years, Nick had been actively involved in Tommy's life. He couldn't imagine being away from him. The reality of the situation made him feel nauseous.

"I'll be good, Daddy. I promise," Tommy replied.

Setting him down gently, Nick grabbed his carry-on bag and brushed tears from his cheeks. "I'll call when I land," he said as he turned to Jillian.

She nodded. "This is a great opportunity for you, Nick. This is what you've been waiting for."

"I know, but at what cost?"

"Listen, as soon as I can, I'll start researching some firms there. If everything works out, maybe we'll move," she shrugged. "I don't have any family here. I know you and I haven't always seen eye to eye, but you're the only family I have. There's no reason for me to stay in D.C."

"Not seeing him…" Nick trailed off as his eyes stung with tears.

"I know. You deserve this, Nick. You've worked really hard."

Jillian picked Tommy up and rested him on her hip. "Bye, Daddy," Tommy said with a wave.

Nick pressed his lips into a straight line and lifted his hand. "Bye, buddy." He slung his duffel bag over his shoulder and walked toward the check-in counter. After handing his ticket to the clerk, he continued down the jetway and onto the plane.

As he crossed the threshold, Nick realized he was leaving everything he had known behind. As promising as the promotion was, it felt as though his soul were being torn from his body. Being offered the director's job was the FBI's way of rewarding his hard work and military service, but it came with too many sacrifices.

Once he arrived in Dayton, Nick settled into his new apartment quickly. It was located in a desirable part of Montgomery County. The streets were quiet, with plenty of metro parks and open spaces where his son could play.

Nick took some time off to get settled. After unpacking a few boxes, he poured himself a glass of bourbon and sat on the couch. With his feet on the coffee table, he picked up the file labeled *Lauren Harris* lying on top. He would have to tolerate her, so understanding her might make that easier.

As he read through the file, he scanned the list of her accomplishments. She had majored in psychology at The Ohio State University. She held two master's degrees, one from Harvard's School of Psychology and another from the University of Nebraska in criminology. Her doctorate was from Wright State University, followed by licensure. He hated to admit it, but her education was impressive.

He had broken in partners before. He didn't look forward to working with Lauren. Because she was so accomplished, he worried she might be overly competitive. He was impressed by her résumé, that much he couldn't deny. Still, he suspected he would have to prove himself, and he wasn't sure he had the patience for that.

8

His work with the Dayton field office began within three weeks of settling in. Nick sat in the high-rise government building, looking out over the Dayton skyline. It was starkly different from D.C.'s. There were no government monuments to color the background of his work. It saddened him.

Nick unpacked more boxes and hung his prized baseball bat on the wall. He mounted the awards he had earned during his time in the Army, along with other pieces of baseball memorabilia.

As he unwrapped yet another knickknack, the phone on his desk buzzed to life. He picked up the receiver and brought it to his ear. The frantic voice on the other end of the line was not what he expected. A local detective relayed more bad news. Nick hung up, knowing the next step was to contact Lauren Harris.

He tried her office phone first, but there was no answer. Then her cell. Still nothing. Finally, he reached her receptionist at the Ellis Institute, who told him Lauren was booked for an all-day lecture at Wright State.

Nick grabbed his jacket, walked out of his office, stepped into the elevator, and waited as the doors closed on the way down to the parking garage.

9

Lauren walked back and forth across the stage as she gave her presentation. The Aztec-printed skirt she wore swished against her legs, the soles of her boots clunking against the stage as she paced.

She pressed the button on the presentation clicker and continued. "Ladies and gentlemen, the important thing to remember when trying to understand the mind of a criminal is to consider any historical information available to you. Current behavior is demonstrative of past behavior. Also, beware of malingering. Criminals are notorious for faking illness. I could cite countless examples of offenders who have attempted this, but Kenneth Bianchi is a prime example. He's known as one of the Hillside Stranglers. In an attempt to escape justice, he pretended to have multiple personality disorder."

"Dr. Harris," a voice echoed from the back of the auditorium.

She immediately recognized it and scanned the crowd. Nick stood near the rear with his arms folded. "Agent Bennette, as you can see, I'm in the middle of a lecture."

"We gotta go," he said gruffly.

Her expression told him everything he needed to know. She was annoyed and more than a little embarrassed.

"Agent Bennette," she said, her voice edged with anger.

"What is today, Doc?" he asked.

She froze for a moment, her thoughts racing. Then the pieces fell into place. "Ladies and gentlemen," she said, "I sincerely apologize, but I need to cut this short. You can pick up the handouts on the back table. If you have questions, my email address is included." She walked to her leather bag and began packing up her notes. "Classes begin in about three weeks, and I teach a course that covers this subject matter in depth. Thank you for coming."

Nick walked toward the front as the audience shuffled out of the auditorium. Lauren continued dismantling her presentation equipment.

She glanced at him. He wore dark bootcut jeans, hiking boots, and a white polo shirt. "I wish you would've been a little more polite instead of barging in," she said sternly.

"I'm just following orders. I was told to retrieve you ASAP. We're heading to Coopers Rock State Forest. It's a long drive."

"Another girl?" she asked, already knowing the answer.

"A local detective said she was found in a plastic box, and he had the good sense to check VICAP. Your presentation was linked. After he watched it, he called me."

"And just so we're clear," Lauren added, "you can call me Dr. Harris, Lauren, anything but Doc. That isn't my name." Before he could respond, she continued. "When was she found?"

"This morning, around seven. The detective said the victim's brother received a text message with the GPS coordinates. The crime scene is still fresh. They specifically requested you. Since you're a consultant being paid with federal dollars and you're the expert, I'm required to escort you."

Without another word, she slung her laptop case over her shoulder and grabbed her other belongings. Nearly sprinting up the aisle, she pushed through the double doors, with Nick close behind.

"Where are you going?" he asked.

"To my office. I need to change clothes and grab an overnight bag."

10

Lauren remained quiet on the drive south as she typed on her laptop. Tension hung heavy in the air, and the lack of cordial conversation only made it worse.

Nick finally broke the silence. "Doesn't that give you a headache?" he asked, nodding toward her hands.

"What?" she replied with a scowl.

"Typing while we're moving."

She shrugged. "Not really. I'm used to it."

Silence settled again, but only briefly.

"So, are you from Ohio originally?" he asked, even though he already knew the answer.

"Yes," she said shortly, continuing to type.

"I'm from North Carolina."

"I should have recognized the Southern drawl," she said.

"You've got a bit of a drawl yourself, you know."

"A little, I guess. I tried to lose it. I always thought it made me sound unintelligent."

"So you think I sound stupid?"

Caught off guard by his defensiveness, she replied, "No. I meant that cultures differ based on geography. I'm from Appalachia. Despite the assumption that people from Appalachia are less intelligent, I'm clearly the exception. You're from the Deep South.

Your culture is different from mine. I meant no offense, Agent Bennette."

"You know, Doc," he said sharply, "you're exactly what I expected when Bill told me about you. You're too smart for your own good."

She stopped typing and turned toward him, studying his hard-set jaw and the way his hands gripped the steering wheel. "Stop calling me Doc. And what are you talking about? I'm lost."

"You? Lost? I don't believe it."

"Do you think sarcasm makes you sound intelligent?" Lauren asked. Anger flared. She disliked his insinuations, his tone, and most of all, the way he made her feel vulnerable. "Before you continue insulting me, let me set you straight. I didn't say anything negative about you or your culture."

"And what makes you the expert?" he asked, briefly taking his eyes off the road.

Her pulse spiked. "I minored in cultural anthropology. Culture is essential in understanding human behavior, especially criminal behavior. An offender's culture plays a role in belief systems and, sometimes, in why crimes are committed."

Silence followed. Lauren returned to her typing as the car engine droned.

Nick softened slightly as he considered her explanation. "So you work for the Ohio State Police, but why as a consultant? Why not full time?" he asked. "You've made it pretty clear why you don't want anything to do with the FBI."

"Because the State Police can't afford me full time."

The answer rubbed him the wrong way. Just as he suspected, she came across as conceited. He couldn't resist. "I did my research on you, Dr. Harris. You went to Harvard. Impressive," he said curtly.

She glanced up from the screen, unsure where this was headed.

"You're a brainiac from some wealthy family in the suburbs," he continued.

Now she was furious. He knew nothing about her family or her losses. Yes, they came from a small town outside Dayton and were prominent, but that said nothing about who she was. "Yes, Agent Bennette, I am what one might call a brainiac. I'm also a damned hard worker. As for my family, you know nothing about them. You don't know where I come from. You don't know me. Who do you think you are to speak to me that way?" Tears stung her eyes as emotion surged.

He refused to relent. "I've always said too much education can make a person stupid. No offense, but most people I've met with all those degrees are idiots. They lack basic logic," he said, glancing at her. "They don't know how to use common sense or instincts."

Lauren's calm was being tested. She took a slow breath, closed her eyes, and tried to steady herself. Her cheeks flushed as emotion rose.

When she spoke again, her voice was measured. "No offense," she said flatly. "The instincts you think I lack kept me alive during graduate school. I conducted research inside a state penitentiary. A riot broke out during one visit. My instincts kept me alive. Every time I work a case, my instincts take over." She shifted in her seat and glared at him. "I've taught women's self-defense classes for years. I've led groups for sexual assault survivors and victims of violent crimes. My instincts have helped people through the darkest moments of their lives. I believe carrying a firearm is one of the best means of personal safety. I'm a card-carrying member of the NRA and encourage responsible gun ownership. If you're worried I'm not physically capable, I can probably run faster than you. And I could probably kick your ass."

She took another breath and continued. "As for your educated-idiot theory, you're judging me without knowing me. That tells me you're narrow-minded. You assume I can't handle fieldwork, and I don't know why. Read the article I published about the prison riot. That research earned me a scholarship to continue my studies. My work has won awards. I'm a recognized authority in forensic psychology. The FBI sought me out. After you've read my work, then you can question my abilities, education, and experience. I've wanted to do this work since I was a child."

She faced forward and resumed typing as her anger cooled.

Of course, he had to speak. "Well, good," he said. After a pause, his tone softened. "Listen, I didn't mean—"

"You meant every word and every implication," Lauren cut in. "You think that because I studied and earned my degrees, I don't understand the real world. You don't know who I am. Until you do, keep your opinions to yourself."

He shook his head. Reluctantly, he felt a flicker of respect. "You're a fiery one," he said. "I'm not sure this is going to work."

"We don't have a choice," she replied. "We're stuck with each other. We might as well make the best of it, Agent Bennette."

11

They arrived at the hotel in town and checked in. Lauren changed into a pair of jeans, hiking boots, and a pink scoop-neck cotton tee. She pulled on her FBI vest, gathered her hair into a neat ponytail, and secured her shoulder holster before checking her firearm.

She opened her door, stepped into the hallway, and shut it behind her. In the parking lot, she spotted Nick pacing beside the Suburban with his phone pressed to his ear. His bicep flexed as he spoke.

Lauren might have been guarded, but she wasn't blind. He was handsome. Casual clothes made him even more appealing. Still, his blatant disrespect canceled out any attraction she might have felt.

When he noticed her waiting by the vehicle, he ended his call. "You ready?" he asked sharply.

"Yes," she replied, bending down to double-check her laces.

"We're meeting with the local detective and a state police investigator first," he said as he opened the driver's door. "Then we'll talk to the girl's family and friends."

"You have inferiority issues, don't you?" she asked.

He stopped short. Confusion creased his face. "What?"

"Inferiority issues. It's when someone feels inferior to a counterpart. It can happen when a person feels weak, incompetent, or even impotent."

"I am not impotent," he muttered. "What the hell?"

She smirked. Getting under his skin felt satisfying. "You're thinking of impotency in a sexual sense," she clarified. "That's not what I meant. When someone barks orders like that, it's often compensation for insecurity."

"Don't analyze me, Doc," he snapped as he climbed into the Suburban.

"I'm not analyzing you. I stated a fact," she replied. "And stop calling me Doc."

Nick grinned. The irritation in her voice was music to his ears.

Once Lauren was inside, he started the engine and pulled onto the county road. They drove to the local police department and parked.

Inside, they met with the local investigator and a state police detective. The victim, Madeline Abbott, was a twenty-year-old graduate student at West Virginia University. Like the others, she came from a stable, well-respected family.

Lauren studied the photograph clipped inside the manila folder. Madeline had black hair and bright brown eyes. She had been found in the same manner as the others. A text message containing GPS coordinates had been sent. An email about a camping trip had gone to Madeline's mother and brother. She had been missing since June eighteenth.

Madeline was single and a biology major completing an internship at a local hospital. Unlike the other victims, she was also a mother. She left behind a ten-year-old son.

At fifteen, Madeline had become pregnant and leaned heavily on her family for support. The detective described her as a devoted mother who took excellent care of her child.

After the briefing, Nick and Lauren followed local authorities to the crime scene. Portable lights illuminated the area as forensic teams worked methodically, collecting samples and evidence.

Lauren navigated the terrain, dodging branches and rocks. In her periphery, she caught sight of a tall, slender, dark-haired woman peering from behind a tree.

She pushed deeper into the forest, resisting the sensations the victim tried to show her. She wanted to examine the scene first.

Standing at the edge of the grave, Lauren peered down. The victim had been badly beaten, yet her face showed no visible trauma.

Lauren knelt briefly, then shook her head and stood. She moved away from the activity and focused on finding Madeline again. The apparition appeared behind another tree.

Lauren met her gaze.

Suddenly, she felt herself running. Her head jerked back as hands tore at her hair. A necklace was ripped from her neck. Fear closed in, suffocating, until everything went dark.

Nick's voice startled her. "Doc, you all right?"

She nodded. "I'm fine. I'm trying to process everything," she said quietly. "And for God's sake, don't call me Doc."

Confusion crossed his face. "What do you want to do here, Doc?" he asked.

She wondered how many times she would have to correct him. The nickname irritated her, but there were more pressing concerns. "Madeline can be taken to autopsy."

A wave of dizziness hit her. Nick reached out instinctively to steady her. Each interaction with a victim left her drained. It was a side effect she still hadn't learned to manage.

"You okay?" Nick asked, genuine concern in his voice.

She nodded. "I'll be fine."

12

Nick and Lauren sat at Jack and Linda Abbott's kitchen table. Madeline's little boy played video games with his cousins in the front room while Madeline's brother, Jackson, poured a cup of coffee and walked to the table to take a seat.

Linda Abbott was a beautiful woman with long black hair, olive skin, and deep brown eyes. She spoke with a thick Arabic accent. She tried to be sociable, but her grief was impossible to hide.

Jack Abbott looked much older than Linda. Deep-set crow's feet and worry lines across his forehead told a story of stress and responsibility. His skin was tanned from time spent outdoors. A golf bag in the corner suggested he engaged in an affluent man's sport, and the furnishings throughout the home reflected a comfortable, well-established lifestyle.

Lauren began as she set her coffee cup down. "First, I want to say how truly sorry we are for your loss, Mr. and Mrs. Abbott."

Both of the Abbotts nodded.

"She is so special," Linda said sorrowfully. "I mean—was special." Tears streamed down her face. "I came into her life when she was twelve," she added.

"My business took me away from home a lot," Jack clarified.

"I was a flight attendant," Linda continued. "Maddie was just the sweetest thing. She was so kind."

"My first wife—Maddie's mother—died of cancer when the kids were very small," Jack said. "I thought my life was over, but Maddie and Jackson were so resilient. I learned so much from them.

Maddie was such a good girl. When she got pregnant at fifteen, I knew something had happened. That just wasn't like her. She was so… so modest."

Lauren nodded as Jack continued.

"She was raped," Jackson blurted out, leaning against the counter. "I took her to some damned party. It was my fault."

"Son, it wasn't your fault," Jack said quietly. "We've talked about this."

Jackson wasn't deterred. In a hushed tone, he explained everything. Someone he had gone to high school with had developed a crush on Maddie. Instead of asking her out, the boy raped her at a party. Despite the assault, Maddie refused to press charges.

They arrived at the hotel in town and checked in. Lauren changed into a pair of jeans, hiking boots, and a pink scoop-neck cotton tee. She pulled on her FBI vest, gathered her hair into a neat ponytail, and secured her shoulder holster before checking her firearm.

The realization that Maddie had already endured such a violation—only to lose her life to a serial killer—made Lauren feel nauseous.

"How was her relationship with her son?" Nick asked.

"She always said it was meant to be," Linda replied. "She never complained. She never cried. From the moment she found out she was pregnant, she loved him. She quit high school and later earned her GED. She was so bright," Linda said, choking back emotion.

"Mr. and Mrs. Abbott," Nick asked gently, "was there anyone special in Madeline's life? Anyone she brought around or talked about?"

"No one," Jackson answered.

"After she was raped, Maddie didn't date," Linda added.

The television in the living room went silent. The adults in the kitchen stopped talking. Everyone took a sip of their drinks. Then Howard walked through the doorway toward Linda.

He was a beautiful little boy. With bright blue eyes and dark hair, he seemed blissfully unaware of the weight surrounding him, which was exactly as it should be. Linda wrapped her arms around him. His soulful eyes met Lauren's.

"You're here about my mom?" he asked.

Lauren nodded. "Yes. I'm Lauren, and this is Nick."

"I miss her," he said, lowering his gaze.

"I know," Lauren replied softly.

In her periphery, Lauren spotted Maddie standing in the living room. The sight reminded her that the dead are never far from the people they love.

Over the years, Lauren had learned how to navigate the emotional residue victims left behind. They often felt unfinished, incomplete. At times, those feelings overwhelmed her. She had learned to retreat inward when necessary, mastering the ability to remain composed as waves of emotion washed over her. It had taken years of practice.

"My mom is a good lady," Howard added.

His voice brought Lauren back to the present.

"We're real sorry about your mom, Howard," Nick said kindly. "Was there anyone your mom was dating? Anyone she might have liked?"

Lauren locked eyes with Maddie, who still stood in the living room. Her lips moved, but Lauren couldn't hear what she was saying. She was muted.

"She played games online with some guy," Howard answered.

"Did you ever meet him?" Lauren asked, shifting her attention back to Howard.

"No. Mom said he was just a friend she liked chatting with."

"Did she ever tell you his name?" Nick inquired.

"No," he replied.

"Mr. Abbott," Lauren asked, "did Madeline live here with you?"

"No," Jack replied.

"Maddie and Howard lived with me," Jackson interjected.

"And she never mentioned anyone?" Nick asked.

"No," Jackson said, shaking his head.

"We'll need her computer," Lauren said.

"I'll bring it to the station if that's okay," Jackson agreed.

"That's perfect," Nick confirmed.

13

A couple of hours passed. As Lauren and Nick sat at the local police station typing up their reports, Jackson dropped off the computer. Lauren drop-shipped it to the BCI lab. Deep down, she knew technology would reveal answers, because the unsub was clearly contacting the women online. It might also explain the level of trust the victims had placed in him. Social networking could very well be the missing piece.

It was late when Lauren finally made it back to the hotel. After showering, she fell asleep with the image of Maddie's body burned into her mind. She dreamt of Maddie's family and everything that had been left unresolved.

The next morning, Lauren and Nick went to the morgue. Even after all these years, Lauren hated the sights and sounds of the place. The chemicals and decomposition assaulted her senses. Mostly, she felt out of her element. Dr. Wright was far more adept at the technical processes. Still, Lauren understood how critical the autopsy findings were in accurately constructing victimology.

The local medical examiner handed Lauren a large envelope. "Preliminary findings," the doctor said.

Lauren nodded. "Thank you."

Nick and Lauren left the building and stepped outside. Lauren tore open the envelope and skimmed the report. Every injury was consistent with the other victims. They were, without question, dealing with a single offender.

Nick raised a brow as he watched her. "Don't you want to go back in and see the body?"

"No need," she replied, holding up the report. "I have enough right here."

"I figured you would want—" He trailed off as she cut him off.

"No," she said more firmly. "That's Dr. Wright's area of expertise. I don't view bodies unless they're still at the crime scene. Autopsy photographs are sufficient."

"Oh," Nick said, smirking.

"What?" Lauren asked, confused by his reaction.

"Make you a little green around the gills?"

"Certainly not," she replied. "It's just not my strong suit." She shifted the subject. "We should head back to Ohio. There's no reason to stay here. We've learned everything we can."

"You don't think you can help?" Nick asked, confusion creeping into his voice.

"No more than I already have. There are no eyewitnesses. This guy is a phantom. He leaves nothing behind. It's almost as if he was never here. Unfortunately, the only way to navigate crimes like this is patience. He'll make a mistake."

Nick's tone hardened. "He'll just keep killing, Doc. You said that yourself. You act like you don't care. Where's your empathy?"

The accusation caught her off guard. "I do care," she said sharply. "But right now, I'm powerless. We have nothing to work with. Hopefully BCI can recover something from her computer. We need warrants for all of the victims' devices. That could be extremely helpful."

"I'm not ready to leave yet," Nick said. "I think there's more here."

"You're in charge," she replied as she walked toward the car. "I'm along for the ride."

14

Lauren's head ached as she sat in the hotel room studying the crime scene photographs. She hoped something would jump out at her, something she had overlooked, but she kept hitting the proverbial brick wall.

She removed her glasses and squeezed the bridge of her nose. She had been staring at the photographs for hours. Her eyes were tired, and her body longed for sleep, but it was far too early to turn in for the night.

She thought of Nick and understood his frustration with the case. She wished the reality were different. Unfortunately, the unsub seemed to be one step ahead of them.

Although Lauren empathized deeply with the families and understood the victims' final moments, she had learned long ago that patience often won the day. She trusted the process. Still, the body count would rise. She did not know how to prevent that yet. She certainly did not want it to be true, but for now, she and her team had nothing tangible to work with.

She stood and stretched, working out the kinks in her back. Shifting gears, she turned her attention to her personal responsibilities. She had been working on a novel for the past year, and her publisher's deadline was fast approaching.

She opened her laptop, and the screen flickered to life. She wrote for a couple of hours before hunger finally crept in. Rather than call a cab or ask Nick for a ride, she decided to go downstairs to the hotel's bar and grill. She wanted to avoid him if possible. However, when the elevator doors opened, she spotted him sitting at the bar.

With a heavy sigh, she realized that avoiding him now would make her appear antisocial. Steeling herself, she took the empty stool beside him. Her desire to make an effort outweighed her desire for solitude.

She opened her laptop again and resumed writing. The bartender quickly took her order and returned with a glass of sparkling white wine.

In her periphery, she saw Nick's lip curl in mild disapproval before his expression softened. "You know, Doc," he began as he swallowed a bite of steak, "I have to admit your high priced education must have paid off. If you can come up with an accurate profile and solid victimology, you must have had some intense training."

"Here we go again," she muttered under her breath. Turning to him, her expression weary, she said, "I am a forensic psychologist, Bennette. Psychology began as a soft science, yes, but behaviorism introduced the scientific method. That reclassified it as a hard science. I evaluate evidence and develop working hypotheses. What exactly do you think a forensic psychologist does?"

He took a drink of beer, wiped his mouth with his napkin, and replied, "You pick people's brains."

"No," she said evenly. "I actively listen. That is a skill you seem to lack."

As she watched his cheeks flush, Lauren realized that if things did not improve, alternative arrangements might be necessary. His ongoing disrespect was undermining any chance of building a functional working relationship. She cared about the case, not personal rapport, but cooperation was essential if they were going to stop the man responsible.

"What is that supposed to mean?" he snapped. "I listen."

"I meant no disrespect," Lauren clarified, her tone softening. "You are a man of action. You served in the Army. That speaks volumes about your character. You are decisive, driven, and committed. Those are strengths, not flaws."

He was silent for a moment before asking quietly, "What do you know about that?"

Lauren took a sip of wine. "I have done my research, Agent Bennette. You were a sniper, one of the best. You served in the Gulf War, Somalia, and Bosnia. You enlisted the moment you turned eighteen. That suggests either deep loyalty to your country or an urge to escape a difficult home life."

"You do not know who I am," he snapped, pointing his fork at her.

"It does not feel good to have assumptions made about you, does it?" she replied calmly. "You do not know me either."

"I did my duty," he said stiffly. "I was a soldier. That is all."

His gaze lingered on her. She shifted uncomfortably and glanced at the menu. "What?"

He shrugged. "In spite of being a huge pain in my ass, you are stunning, especially when you are angry."

She stared at him, trying to interpret the comment. "I cannot tell if you are patronizing me or making a terrible attempt at flirting."

"No," he said more sincerely. "You really are something else."

Unsure how to respond, she flagged the bartender and ordered food. Turning back to her laptop, she began picking at her cuticles as her thoughts raced. Writer's block had plagued her lately, and the stress of the case and her deadline weighed heavily.

"You should stop doing that," he said, pointing at her fingers.

She glanced down at her damaged nail beds, sighed, and nodded.

"So beneath all that logic, you are a bundle of nerves," he observed.

She chose not to respond.

"What are you working on, Doc?" he asked, leaning closer.

She closed the laptop. "Nothing," she said sharply. "And I have asked you repeatedly, please stop calling me that."

"Nothing?" he pressed, ignoring her request. "You have been on that laptop nonstop."

With a sigh, she removed her glasses and set them on the computer. "I am writing a novel. The deadline is less than two weeks away."

"A book?"

"Yes."

"Published?"

"Yes."

"You are awfully young to be publishing a bestseller, are you not?"

"Writing is about creativity, not age," she replied.

"So the publisher offered you a contract?"

"Yes."

"Is there anything you cannot do?"

"I am Wonder Woman," she said dryly. "Although my lasso seems broken. I cannot get people to tell the truth." She smirked at her own wit.

"So you do have a sense of humor," he said, the tension easing. "It is nice to see you smile."

She blushed slightly. "Of course I do. What is life without laughter?"

"I agree. Boring people are no fun."

The bartender set a bowl of salad in front of Lauren. She unwrapped her silverware and poured ranch dressing over the greens.

"You have been pretty serious, and a little boring, until now," Nick added.

"You were rude to me," she reminded him. "I do smile. I do laugh. You are not as enchanting as you think, Nicholas Bennette."

He cleared his throat. "You are right. I have been an ass."

"That is an understatement," she said, stabbing a piece of lettuce.

"What do you say? Truce?" he asked, extending his hand.

She set her fork down and shook it. "Truce."

15

Lauren settled into a routine as the semester got underway. She taught classes on Monday and Wednesday evenings. She saw her therapy and group clients on Tuesdays and Thursdays, starting at 8 a.m. and ending her day at 6:30 p.m. Fridays were reserved for consultation work. She traveled to various precincts to assist with investigations. Sometimes she testified in court. Other times, she prepared witnesses or assisted with jury selection. On Tuesdays at 8 p.m., she taught a self-defense class at the local YMCA. In between it all, she worked on her novel while continuing to search for a way to stop the Phantom serial murders.

When Lauren's parents died, she remained in their home within the private lake community. The inheritance money she received went toward maintaining and updating the property. It was a beautiful Cape Cod, distinguished by a large weeping willow tree. The tree had been one of the reasons her mother fell in love with the house.

The front yard was flat, but the backyard sloped downward toward a pier and Lauren's boathouse. A long line of wooden steps led down the grade. When her parents first purchased the home, the steps were in disrepair, but that never discouraged them.

The covered front porch featured white spindles that stood out against the gray vinyl siding. Inside, the living room boasted a stone fireplace and original hardwood floors. Exposed wooden ceiling rafters, matching window casings, and floorboards gave the space a rustic feel. Wooden blinds hung in the windows, accented by long beige ruffled curtains.

Lauren kept her parents' burgundy checkered sofa and had the ottoman reupholstered to match. A flat-screen television sat in the corner on a large wooden entertainment stand.

She decorated the house with primitives, charming baskets, and a distinctive Americana style. Carefully placed antiques enhanced the warm and inviting atmosphere, creating a cozy, nostalgic space. Every corner told a story, making the home feel like the perfect backdrop for a Country Sampler photo shoot and a true reflection of rustic country living.

Upstairs, the house featured three bedrooms, a guest bathroom, and a master bath with a garden tub. Lauren kept the queen bed that once belonged to her parents, paired with a polished cherry wood dresser and nightstand. The bed was covered with a handmade wedding ring quilt in shades of tan and peach.

The guest bathroom carried a nautical theme, while a staircase at the end of the hallway led to a finished attic and an additional bedroom. Lauren's favorite room, however, was the study connected to the master bedroom. She preserved her father's large mahogany desk and left the built-in wall shelves untouched, allowing the scent of old books to linger in the air, something she cherished. Her father's brown leather chair and matching ottoman completed the room, making it a timeless and comforting space.

The home also included a partial basement, a feature her parents had valued given the area's tendency for severe spring storms and tornado activity. The basement housed old remnants of carpet, along with the hot water tank, heating and cooling systems, and water softener.

The house had always been Lauren's sanctuary. Growing up there, she learned to ride her bike along the street, climbed trees in the yard, and fished with her father from the dock. She cherished the time spent gardening with her mother. Those memories were sacred, and living in her childhood home felt like the most meaningful way to honor her parents and keep their spirit alive.

16

The slivers of sunlight danced across the walls of Lauren's bedroom as she lay in Simon's arms. He had been a fixture in her life since college. They met when she was twenty, while she was vacationing in Florida with her aunt and uncle. Originally from Australia, Simon had relocated with his mother after his parents divorced.

Although he was shorter than Lauren typically preferred, his deep blue eyes and curly blond hair more than compensated for any perceived imperfections. With a winning personality and a sharp sense of humor, Simon easily captured her attention.

Lauren and Simon maintained a no-strings-attached arrangement. They had always been sexual partners, but neither of them was interested in a commitment beyond that.

Simon now traveled all over the world as an author for the same publishing house that had contracted Lauren. His focus was nonfiction, specifically writing about wars and historically significant events tied to Australia. Still, he had assisted Lauren with some of her fictional short stories and encouraged her to pursue a larger project, particularly a novel.

Simon sighed and kissed Lauren's forehead. "I've missed you," he said in his thick Australian accent.

Lauren exhaled. "Where are you headed next?" she asked.

"I'm booked in London and then Tokyo. I'll be traveling for the next several months, but I'm looking forward to it." He paused, studying her blue eyes. "How are things going with the novel?"

"I'm trying not to pull my hair out by the roots. Writer's block has been awful, but I think I'm almost finished. Rhonda has the first set of chapters," she replied.

"Rhonda is a sweetheart," he said.

Lauren snickered. "I know you're sleeping with Rhonda."

"That's old news, my dear. You've known that for quite a while," he replied. "But enough about me. How are things going with the FBI agent? When I read your email venting about it, I sensed a hint of competitiveness. Maybe even a bit of romantic interest?" His tone was playful.

"He is an ass," Lauren replied flatly.

"Oh, come on," Simon said, a hint of reproach in his voice. "Have you even given him a chance? He might be a decent guy. Maybe you're just being stubborn."

"I'm not being stubborn."

He laughed. "You're one of the most strong-willed women I've ever met. You don't even realize it, do you, love?" Simon studied her intently. "Deep down, I think you like this bloke. He gives you something you need. I'm not sure what it is, but you won't admit it to yourself yet. Give it time."

Lauren was finished with the conversation. She sat up abruptly and walked into the master bathroom. She grabbed her robe, slipped her arms through the sleeves, tied the belt, and sat on the edge of the bed.

"He's a complete idiot," she said sharply. "Vile and disrespectful."

"Well, look how long it took me to earn even a fraction of your respect," Simon replied. "You're not the easiest person in the world to contend with."

She turned and gave him a playful slap on the stomach. "Keep it up and the next time you visit, things won't be so friendly."

"I wouldn't want that," he said, leaning in and brushing her hair away from her face. The soft strands slid through his fingers like silk. The intensity between them deepened, and he sensed it was time to satisfy their shared desire once more.

17

Chelsey and Selina sat on the deck, waiting for Lauren to bring out their drinks. The sun was beginning to set over the water, casting a warm glow across the lake. The gentle sounds of the shoreline created a calming atmosphere as the noise of boat engines and jet skis faded into the distance.

Lauren slid the patio door open and handed Selina her drink first, then passed one to Chelsey. She stepped outside wearing gray Capri sweats and a black bikini top. Citronella candles flickered on the tables, keeping the mosquitoes at bay.

As soon as she sat down at the glass-top table, her cell phone buzzed. "What now?" she muttered to herself. Seeing Nick's name on the screen, she rolled her eyes and answered. "Hello."

"I'm really sorry to bother you at home," he began, trailing off.

"But," Lauren said with a sigh.

"I got the final autopsy report for Maddie. An object was inserted into her vaginal cavity."

Lauren stopped breathing for a moment as the words registered. "What?"

"You heard me," Nick replied.

"He's escalating," she said. "What was the object?"

"A rock."

"Just like the Green River Killer," Lauren said quietly.

"Who?" Nick asked.

"The Green River Killer. Washington State was terrorized by a serial killer for over twenty years. With some of his victims, he inserted rocks or other objects into their vaginal cavities."

Selina and Chelsey exchanged a look.

"Christ," Chelsey whispered.

Nick exhaled sharply on the other end of the line. "For fuck's sake," he muttered. "Is this worse than you thought?" Concern weighed heavily in his voice.

"It's certainly not good," Lauren replied. "It confirms he's a sadist, but that isn't unexpected. Most hedonistic offenders with power and control issues are deeply sadistic. That fuels their need for domination."

"Well, that doesn't make our job any easier," Nick said, his tone defeated.

"You're not wrong, Agent Bennette," Lauren said quietly. "You're not wrong."

18

Labor Day weekend finally arrived, marking the end of summer. Lauren had always looked forward to the extra time off so she could spend it with her family. Each year Lauren's aunt and uncle hosted a Labor Day cookout at their house across the lake. Lauren had typically driven her boat to their dock and sometimes stayed the night.

As Lauren lay on the dock with Selina and Chelsey, the slight breeze provided soothing relief for the sweat that had begun beading on her skin. Lauren wasn't exactly a fan of the heat. She preferred the cool, crisp season of fall.

In the distance were squeals of laughter as her nieces and nephews played in the water and along the beach. The voices of her aunt and grandmother carried on the breeze. Her uncles, cousins, and grandfather left at dawn for their fishing adventure on the pontoon and returned exhausted and empty-handed. They'd been napping for several hours.

Lauren's Aunt Ingrid and Uncle Jim Harris had owned their home on the lake as long as she could remember. The fact that they had purchased their house in the lake community encouraged her own parents to buy there. Ingrid and Jim had raised their three children there, Chelsey being their youngest. Joshua was the eldest son and Lucas landed in the middle.

Truddy and Doug Peterson, Lauren's other aunt and uncle, had really pitched in to help when Lauren's parents passed away. They had always wanted children but were never able to conceive. So, they had gladly helped Ingrid and Jim with Lauren.

Morgan Harris was the patriarch of the family. He was a retired judge and a pillar of the community. He had paved the way for his children to become successful attorneys and local leaders. The entire family was wealthy and served members of the local community with care and generosity.

The matriarch of the Harris clan was Annie. She'd married Morgan when he'd returned from serving overseas as a pilot for the Army. Annie had embraced Lauren's gift. She had even encouraged her to use it to help others. Whenever Lauren had exhibited feeling uncomfortable with her abilities, Annie had assured her to square her shoulders and be proud.

Lauren's father, Jason, and her Uncle Jim had become very affluent lawyers. They both worked for Morgan's firm. Lucas and Josh had decided to follow in the family footsteps by becoming attorneys. Doug, on the other hand, was a blue-collar man, a contractor by trade. He and Truddy had met while she toured a corporate job site with Morgan. Sparks flew, and they were married quickly.

Beth Warnock, Lauren's mother, had been best friends with Ingrid. They had both taught at the local elementary school. They had grown close over the years, and Ingrid introduced Beth to Jason Harris, the tall, handsome, successful lawyer in town. The rest was history. They had fallen in love quickly, got married, and had Lauren within three years of marrying.

Lauren sat up and looked out at the water. The beach towel underneath didn't provide much cushion against the worn wooden slats of the pier.

Chelsey glanced over. "So, tell us more about this mysterious FBI agent," she encouraged.

"There's really nothing to tell," Lauren answered, still watching the boats on the lake. Even thinking about him made her feel a little on edge. Despite their truce, she kept her guard up. His initial interactions with her still weighed heavy on her mind.

Chelsey supported herself on her elbows and moved her sunglasses to the tip of her nose. Batting her eyes, she said, "My dear cousin, how long has it been since you have been with a man?"

Both women anticipated an answer, Selina following suit and sitting up.

"I don't believe this is an appropriate conversation," Lauren said disagreeably.

"You're such a prude," Chelsey said.

"Why isn't this appropriate?" Selina asked with air quotes.

"Because I don't feel that I should discuss sex with you two. You'll just make fun of me," Lauren replied. "And both of you know that I see Simon. We are very active sexually."

Selina scoffed. "Honey, Simon isn't very available to you. Honestly, I think he's been married this entire time."

"He is not married," Lauren argued. "I would know if he were. He is a highly respected writer. He has helped me find an agent, and if it weren't for him, I may not be looking at a book deal. And I know he sleeps with other women. It doesn't bother me."

Chelsey shook her head. She was aggravated by the conversation. "You're unreal."

"Simon and I have known each other for a very long time. I like what we have. It's simple," Lauren explained.

"Let's talk about what you have in common," Chelsey said with spirit. "Sex. That's it."

Lauren's cheeks warmed. "I like the fact that there isn't any pressure. We don't have the stress of maintaining a relationship."

"He is definitely an Australian hottie. I'd have sex with him," Selina said with a shrug.

Lauren nodded. "He is very handsome. He performs very, very well. Excellent stamina."

Selina and Chelsey smirked. "Your relationship with Simon is safe," Chelsey said.

"What?" Lauren asked, a twinge of shock in her tone.

"You can't commit," Chelsey said confrontationally. "You're so afraid of loss that you are too terrified to even take a chance on anything that might last. Something meaningful. For all you know, Simon might be madly in love with you. And what if he is? What would you do then?"

They waited for an answer, but Lauren sat in silence.

Chelsey answered for her. "You'd run."

"Maybe she thinks she's too good for a relationship," Selina interjected.

Lauren's fuse was quickly growing shorter. Still, she didn't offer a rebuttal or counterargument.

Chelsey took off her sunglasses. Her mouth agape, she put her finger up in the air as if she'd just solved string theory. "You think you're too good for the FBI agent. Please tell us you haven't been mean to him."

Her face dropped. She stammered as she tried to answer.

"Oh, you have been mean to him," Selina said as she fell back onto her towel and put her hands on her head.

"Well, he was mean to me first," she protested. "He was very cruel. You are assuming that I think I'm superior to him. I mean, intellectually, I am far more superior. Otherwise, we're equals. At least, I think we are."

"And you called him an ass," Selina snipped.

"Does he know you see him as less?" Chelsey asked.

She didn't answer. Chelsey and Selina's expressions told Lauren that they were completely appalled by her behavior.

Selina sat up again. "You're oblivious."

Chelsey shook her head in disbelief. "If the FBI agent believes that you see yourself as better than him, you'll never have a true partnership." Angrily, she stood and looked down at Lauren. "You always do this. You've always pushed people away. I don't think you fail to recognize social cues. I think you refuse to. You wear a mask, Lauren. Just because you have two master's degrees and a doctorate, along with countless certifications, doesn't make you smarter than anyone else. It just means that you know how to study."

"Why are you so angry?" Lauren asked as she stood to her feet.

"Because you hide behind a brick wall. You push away any shred of happiness that might come your way."

"I don't."

"You do!" Chelsey argued.

Knowing that Chelsey was growing more upset, Lauren quickly made an effort to deescalate the situation. "I'm sorry I've upset you. I didn't mean to."

"All any of us want is for you to be happy. You deserve it. If the FBI agent knew that you felt this way, it would hurt his feelings. And I know that you don't intentionally hurt people, Lauren. You have too much empathy for that. So, why would you allow yourself to have such a distorted thought pattern?"

Instead of continuing with the disagreement, Lauren just wanted a resolution. She didn't like upsetting Chelsey or Selina. Still, she felt like she needed to provide some clarification. "As I said, he was very mean to me. I defended myself. I don't believe I've come off as superior to him."

"You're not really that great at hiding how you feel when it comes to that kind of stuff," Selina added.

Before the conversation went further, Lauren's cell phone buzzed, causing the wood on the pier to vibrate. A text message from Nick flashed up on the screen. It read, "Travis from BCI faxed results. Where are you?"

Already frustrated from the conversation, she furrowed her brow and typed, "With my family."

He replied, "Can I come share the results with you?"

Flipping the phone open, she dialed his number. When he answered, she didn't give him time to say anything. "It's Saturday. It's Labor Day weekend. Can't this wait?"

"Doc, I wouldn't be bothering you if it could wait. I have my son this holiday, so do you honestly think I'd be working if it wasn't something super important?"

Guilt washed over her. She didn't know he was a father. In fact, she couldn't imagine him as a dad. Obviously, someone found enough interest in him to sleep with him and get pregnant. Still, it was hard for her to comprehend. He seemed to detest women, especially women who were intelligent.

"If you want to come and share the report, I can give you directions to my aunt and uncle's house. Bring your son. There are children here. I'm sure he would enjoy playing." She paused. "I'm surprised Travis with BCI didn't reach out to me directly."

"He just faxed the results to the FBI and the after-hours worker called me. Travis probably knew you wouldn't be bothered with work on Labor Day weekend."

"Probably," she agreed. "I have very clear boundaries. Work-life balance matters to me."

After giving Nick directions, she hung up. Chelsey and Selina stood patiently waiting. "So, he's coming here?" Chelsey asked.

Lauren nodded. "And he has a son, which is rather shocking."

"We'll get to meet him and decide what we think of him. Good!" Chelsey exclaimed.

Selina held up her hand, gesturing Lauren to stop. "Wait a second. Why would you be surprised that he has a kid?"

"He just doesn't seem like a father to me. I can't believe anyone would have sex with him. He is so incredibly abrasive. I would be willing to bet he is quite selfish in bed," Lauren answered.

Selina rolled her eyes and started toward the house. Chelsey followed behind. Reluctantly, Lauren grabbed the beach towels and then made her way up the hill..

19

The social interaction continued on the deck. The family conversed, laughter and chatter filling the air. As Lauren stood next to Ingrid, she heard tires on gravel. She peered around the side of the house to see the driveway. Nick opened the door of his SUV and then shut it. He opened the passenger side door on the driver's side, but before Lauren could observe anything else, she was asked to help put bibs on children and prepare them for the meal.

As Jim finished things up on the grill, Ingrid and Truddy made trips in and out of the kitchen carrying bowls of potato salad and other delicious dishes. Others continued sunbathing. Chelsey and Selina helped with the youngsters, too. Lauren saw both of them stop as if they were frozen in time. Their mouths slightly open, Lauren turned to see Nick standing beside the deck with a tall redhead and a small child.

Chelsey walked over to Lauren first. "And you can't imagine why anyone would have sex with him?"

Selina followed up with, "Can I check your pulse, because I think you might be dead."

"Someone's here!" one of the children shouted.

Lauren finished tying a bib on one of the babies and called out, "It's for me. It's work."

She walked down the wooden steps and toward Nick. She had slipped on a purple cover-up for modesty's sake. She didn't want to be walking around in her bikini. Her hair was a mess from the entire day in the sun.

As she got closer, Lauren's eyes locked with Nick. He wore a pair of blue swim trunks, a white tank top, and a pair of flip-flops. His aviators sat on the top of his head. The little boy clung to the red-headed woman's hand. He was similarly dressed to his father. The woman wore a white sundress with matching flip-flops.

With a casual wave, Nick threw up his hand. "Hey, Doc," he started. "This is my son Tommy, and his mom, Jillian."

Nodding at Lauren, Jillian said, "Call me Jill."

Lauren smiled. "I'm Lauren Harris."

"It's a pleasure," she said. "I've heard so much about you from Nick."

Lauren masked her surprise. She moved her focus to the child. "I'm so sorry you had to interrupt your holiday for this," she said compassionately. "I'm sure it could have waited."

Jillian interrupted with a subtle headshake. She gestured between her and Nick. "Oh, we're not together. I just came with Tommy so he could visit Nick."

"I see. I just know how important family is. Work-life balance is a priority. So, I just hate that your day was impacted."

Nick was done with the pleasantries. "Can we go inside?" he asked as he darted his eyes. His tone was hushed, as if he didn't want anyone to hear him.

Before they could move toward the front door, Ingrid called out. "Lauren, don't be rude. Come introduce your friends."

Lauren pursed her lips and shrugged. "Well, I guess you're meeting my family."

Ingrid stood on the deck beaming. Her slender build came from years of training for 5Ks. She had black hair in a bob style cut. Her tanned skin showed slight signs of aging. She wore her sunglasses on top of her head and squinted to shield her brown eyes from the late afternoon sun.

Throwing up a hand, she waved. With a sing-songy tone, she said, "I'm Lauren's Aunt Ingrid. So good to meet you all."

"This isn't a social call," Lauren protested.

With a friendly nudge, Ingrid gave Lauren a disapproving glance. "Good Lord, don't be rude." As she motioned for the group to settle down, Lauren rolled her eyes. The buzz of conversation didn't diminish, so Ingrid resorted to a high-pitched whistle. The silence fell. Still beaming, Ingrid began. "Everyone, these are Lauren's friends…" she trailed off, leaving it to Lauren to explain.

Clearing her throat, Lauren smiled. "This is my partner, Nick Bennette, his son Tommy, and his girlfriend Jillian."

With grins and waves, everyone greeted them warmly while Nick leaned in to whisper in Lauren's ear. "She's not my girlfriend."

Lauren nodded and tried to speak above the commotion. "Not his girlfriend, sorry."

Missy, Josh's oldest child, got up from the picnic table. Her strawberry blonde pigtails damp from swimming in the lake, she had new freckles popping out across her nose and cheeks from spending the day in the sun. She smiled sweetly as she held out her hand to Tommy. "You want a hot dog? You can sit with us."

Tommy peered up at Jill and Nick for approval.

"Go on, buddy," Nick said with a nod.

Hand in hand, Missy and Tommy crossed the deck to the grill.

Truddy was on her feet by that time and moving toward Jill. She looped her arm through Jill's and introduced herself. "Come, Jillian. Let me get you something to eat," she offered as she encouraged Jillian to move toward the table filled with food.

With her family entertaining Jill and Tommy, Lauren led Nick into the house through the sliding glass door. They walked through the kitchen and to her uncle's study. She hadn't noticed that Nick was holding a thick envelope the entire time. He handed it over and she pulled the papers out. Quickly, she read over the report. "I was right," she murmured. "The unsub was communicating through the internet."

"This is good, right?" Nick asked. "It's a break in the case."

Lauren continued reading through the documents. "I don't believe it's a break, but it's very positive. Travis couldn't trace the IP address. Everything is encrypted, so the unsub definitely has knowledge of computer systems and information technology. Still, this is odd."

"What's odd?"

"Well, Travis is a hacker. This is what he does." She paced. "If anyone can crack this, Travis should have been able to."

"So what's that mean for us?" Nick asked.

"As I said, we're looking for someone who has a solid understanding of computer systems and might be a hacker, too. He's covering his tracks extremely well," Lauren said with a hint of defeat in her tone.

"So...?" Nick asked.

"So, now we know he is sadistic and smart. He is luring his victims through the internet." She scanned the report again. "And Travis says here that each victim was in contact with him for several months. He groomed them that way. Again, everything is encrypted, but we can at least see a timeline."

"What now?"

"We keep waiting. If he's as intelligent as I think he is, he knows we're onto him."

Nick folded his arms and peered out the window at the festivities. "I hate waiting." He shook his head. "I'm sorry I messed up your holiday for this."

"It's okay," Lauren replied. "I'm just sorry you had to take time away from your family."

Still standing with a defensive posture, Nick turned to face Lauren. Their eyes locked. "Jill and I aren't together either."

"You've said that. Why is it so important that I know that?"

With a shrug, his cheeks turned slightly pink. "Well, I guess it's not important that you know that, I guess. I wanted to marry her. We were engaged. She wouldn't, though, but we got Tommy out of the deal."

"Okay," Lauren said expectantly. "Well, you have a beautiful son together, so as long as you work well together, that's all that matters."

Their eyes still locked, his gaze softened as did Lauren's. "You don't have to explain your personal life to me, Bennette." Her tone was kind and thoughtful.

Jim popped his head in the door. "Hey, you two want something to eat? There's plenty left."

"I don't want to impose," Nick insisted as he shook his head.

Lauren's empathy toward Nick finally broke through. She realized he had taken away from his day with his family to deliver the BCI report from Travis. "You aren't imposing at all. Spend the day with us."

An expert in pushing people away, she tried to do the same with Nick. Although he had been very unpleasant to her, she wondered if he too tried to protect himself. Based on their conversation at the hotel bar, he was remorseful and wanted to try to make the partnership work.

"Come on," she encouraged. "Let's grab some food."

Turning the corner in their acquaintanceship, Nick and his family spent hours with the Harris clan. The uneasiness that Lauren and Nick felt began to melt away as they conversed and laughed. The apprehension replaced by growing respect still brought up terrifying emotions in Lauren. She wondered if Nick felt the same way.

20

For the rest of the evening, the family dispersed into smaller groups. The men fished off the dock. The children played in the water and on the beach. The ladies busied themselves by tidying the kitchen and relaxing on the deck, discussing upcoming events and reminiscing over days long passed.

At dusk, Jim started the annual Harris s'mores roast. With the help of the other gentlemen, he started a fire and arranged the chairs and blankets while the women prepared the chocolate and marshmallows.

Standing on the deck, Lauren watched the bustle in the lower half of the yard. She saw Nick and Josh sitting together, laughing hysterically at something. She wasn't surprised that they gravitated toward one another. Josh had also served in the armed forces. She knew that would be a common interest for he and Nick.

Jillian settled in nicely, too. Cora, Josh's wife, and Holly, Lucas's wife, welcomed her warmly with conversation about hobbies and interests. Tommy played with the other children and enjoyed roasting s'mores.

Chelsey stood beside Lauren. She shook her head. Lauren glanced at her. "What?" she asked curiously.

"He is a very nice guy, Lauren. How could you not be attracted to him?" she remarked.

With a guilty nod, Lauren folded her arms. "I've been hateful to him. And I never said he wasn't attractive. His attitude's off-putting."

"That's like the pot calling the kettle black," Selina smarted off as she walked past them carrying an enormous bowl of popcorn.

"So Jill told me that Nick left his life in D.C. for the job in Dayton. The separation from his son has been really hard."

"That explains his level of anger and agitation," Lauren said as the light bulb finally popped on.

"You're a therapist. You know what separation from loved ones can do to a person. You counsel military vets every single day. College students who've never been away from home. Children who've been put in foster care. You of all people should be able to understand how he's been feeling." Chelsey spoke bluntly, but Lauren appreciated the candor. As she pursed her lips and then smiled, Chelsey gently touched Lauren on the shoulder. "I think you could have been too hard on him."

"I think you're right," Lauren gladly admitted. "He didn't tell me about the sacrifices he'd made to take the director's job. I wish he would have."

"Maybe it takes a while for him to trust. You should understand that, too."

"He caught me off guard," she admitted.

Shocked by the statement, Chelsey raised her eyebrows in disbelief. "Now that's a feat. Nothing catches you off guard."

They observed the crowd in the yard. The sun sat low on the lake as beautiful hues of purple, red, and orange painted the dusky sky. The laughter of the family made Lauren a little tearful. Chelsey felt it and snaked her arm around Lauren's shoulders. "He seems like a really nice guy. Everyone's just welcomed him right in. It's like he's always been here. Maybe it's time to lower your defenses. He might do the same."

"I'm so sorry," Lauren said softly.

"I don't think it's me you need to apologize to," Chelsey said.

The sky darkened further as the cool air began to settle in. Smoke from the fire billowed upward. As she watched Chelsey make her way down the incline toward the others, Lauren contemplated the realizations. Her family and friends meant everything to her. They were her world. The loss of her parents had left a tremendous void. Sometimes the emptiness consumed her. Nothing had ever tempered the grief. She often wondered if anything would ever fill it. She tried to be hopeful and found solace in her career.

Lauren noticed Nick walking up the wooden steps toward the house. She observed him, the bitterness falling away, now replaced by understanding. She couldn't deny that he was quite attractive. When he did smile, he lit up the room. The sound of his laughter, although often fleeting, was somehow comforting.

As he approached, her arms folded in an attempt to stay warm, she smiled. "Do you want to go out in my boat?" she asked.

"Are you sure you're up to braving the lake after that wipeout on the skis today?" he joked. "As I recall, that was a pretty big spinout."

"How could I forget," she said with an eye roll.

"If you're brave enough, though..." Nick trailed off with a wink.

"I think I can handle it. I'll get my fishing pole and change clothes. It's getting a little too chilly for a cover-up."

She turned and walked inside. After grabbing her duffel bag, she changed into a pair of black yoga pants and tennis shoes. She kept her bikini top on and just put a sweatshirt over it.

Grabbing the boat keys, she walked out of the kitchen and back onto the deck. She offered Nick a change of clothing. Jim always kept extra clothes lying around. Nick agreed to a pair of jeans and a T-shirt with a flannel.

They walked down the hill to the dock. As they passed the group, Ingrid asked, "Where are you two going?"

"Fishing," Lauren answered as she glanced over at Selina and Chelsey.

She untied her twenty-foot Bayliner and jumped in as Nick followed her lead. After starting the engine, she skimmed the water and drove into a nearby cove. The fishing had always been good there. It was the perfect spot to admire the full moon.

With her line in the water and the fishing pole in her hands, she gazed at the calm surface. The sounds of the jet skis had stopped hours ago. The quiet whisper of the leaves and the sound of the water sloshing against the hull made Lauren appreciate the moment. Still, memories of her parents flooded her mind. The sadness was overwhelming, but she held it together. Before she knew it, she said, "My mother and father took me out here a lot." She couldn't believe she'd let the words come out.

Nick listened attentively.

"My mother loved the water. My dad used to call her a mermaid," Lauren said with a sad smile.

"What were their names?" Nick asked.

"Beth and Jason." With a slight chuckle, she continued. "My mom used to jump off the side of this very boat. She'd call to me. I was so afraid, but the sound of her voice…" she trailed off. "She gave me faith."

Her eyes burned with tears as the lump in her throat grew. "I didn't think those days would end," she admitted, her voice quivering with emotion. She didn't even understand why she felt the need to talk to Nick about these things.

"So how old were you when they died?" he inquired as he reeled the line back in and cast it out again.

"I was twelve. My Aunt Ingrid and Uncle Jim raised me after my parents died. Well, my entire family helped raise me. My grandparents. My Aunt Trudy and Uncle Doug. My cousins became more like my siblings," she replied. A heartbeat of silence passed. "Sometimes I feel incredibly alone, though. Almost like an orphan," Lauren admitted.

"From what I saw today, you are far from alone," Nick quietly disagreed.

With a nod, she brushed a tear away and pushed everything into her core. Thinking about these things and sharing those vulnerabilities with Nick was difficult.

"I know you already know this. You're a therapist. You probably talk about grief with your clients all the time. But you know that you and your family keep your parents alive. Every time you talk about them, just like you're talking about them to me right now, or when you have your cookouts and celebrate the holidays, you keep them present in your life," Nick stated.

As she struggled to keep her composure, she nodded and sighed. "I know you're right."

The rhythmic lapping of water against the hull intensified as a boat glided by in the distance. "I'm really grateful you could join us today," Lauren admitted, her voice warm with sincerity.

"Really?" Nick said with surprise.

"Absolutely. In fact, I owe you an apology. I've been terrible to you and shamefully unfair. It's extremely difficult for me to get close to people."

"Listen, I pulled out the gloves first. I was rude and downright cruel." He cleared his throat. "When I think about the way I talked to you during the car ride… I am so sorry, Doc. It was really unfair of me."

"I didn't realize you had to relocate for the job in Dayton. That you'd left behind a son. I know that must have been incredibly difficult."

He nodded. "I just knew that talking about it wouldn't change anything. You're not the only one who has trouble letting people in."

She smirked. They were much more alike than she'd wanted to admit.

He went on. "I had a pretty terrible childhood, so my instincts tell me to wall off."

She frowned as pity washed over her. Her professional instincts made her want to say, "Tell me about that." The personal part of her knew to simply listen.

Nick continued. "My dad was a raging alcoholic," he started as he focused on some distant point across the lake. "He was pretty terrible to my mom, so she took off when my brother and I were little. My grandma and grandpa eventually took custody of us, but that wasn't before my dad took to wailing on me. I tried to protect my brother. He was smaller than me, and I was the big brother, you know?"

"I'm an only child, but I can certainly relate to the hierarchy within a family unit." She turned and gently touched Nick's arm. "I'm so sorry, Bennette."

He looked down at her hand, surprised by such a bold gesture. Still, he seemed to appreciate it and nodded. "Eh... nothing to be sorry about. I turned out okay, right? I served my country. I have a great job. A beautiful son." He looked up at the night sky. "I still worry about my brother, though. He's still trying to find himself. He just hasn't settled down."

"He sounds like Chelsey," Lauren remarked. "She has such a wild spirit. She goes wherever the wind takes her."

Nick chuckled. "She's different," he agreed.

The sounds of the night filled the silence. "You know, Doc," Nick continued, "no matter what, it's how we've turned out that counts. Those things that hurt us have taught us lessons we need for today, you know?"

She wholeheartedly agreed. His positive outlook was refreshing. "Well said... and thank you."

"For what?"

"Just listening. I don't really talk to anyone about the death of my folks."

"Maybe you should learn to lean on people a little more. And I'm a great listener," he said as he turned to look at her. "I need to take my own advice, too." He laughed.

21

Nick drove Jillian and Tommy back to Kettering. His eyes drifted to the rearview mirror. Tommy lay sleeping in his car seat. Nick's lips curled into a smile. For the first time since he'd moved, he felt hope.

Jillian noticed that his disposition was changing, finally for the better. He had been sullen and somber when they'd talked on the phone since the move. When she and Tommy arrived a few days ago, his attitude seemed a little more positive. Still, there was a sadness in his eyes. He seemed lost. Spending time with the Harris family seemed to have helped Nick turn a corner. Jillian couldn't stay quiet about it either. "Today was great, huh? What an awesome bunch!" she remarked.

He nodded. "Yeah. I'm glad Tommy had fun, too."

"And, my God, she's gorgeous," Jillian continued.

Nick scowled with confusion. "Who?"

"Dr. Harris."

Because of the tension in their interactions, Nick hadn't given much thought to Lauren's appearance. During dinner at the hotel, he'd commented on her beauty, but beyond that, he hadn't really noticed. His bitterness had gotten in the way and tainted his vision. "Yeah, I guess," he said with a casual shrug.

"She's smart. She has a big family. I mean, that's something you've always wanted… a big family."

"What are you talking about?" he deflected.

"Oh, come on, Nick. I've known you too long."

"We're just colleagues," he reminded himself as he said the words aloud. He knew he couldn't let his thoughts drift any further. Sure, they had made progress in their partnership today, but he didn't want to get ahead of himself. Self-preservation was key.

"Well, since you're obviously in complete denial, I'll change the subject," she said with a smile. "So, Josh and Lucas have a law firm in town. I guess they inherited it. Anyway, I talked to them about how I'd been thinking of relocating here to accommodate your relationship with Tommy. They invited me to visit the firm and consider a job there."

"That was generous of them," he observed.

"I know, right? Ingrid even offered to provide childcare. She also told me if I was uncomfortable with that, because, you know, we don't exactly know these people, she could give me a list of daycare centers in the area."

"I think the Harrises are genuinely good people, Jill," Nick said as he glanced over at her.

"I completely agree. I don't know if I've ever felt so welcome at a family gathering before."

"So, you're really thinking about moving here?"

She nodded. "Yeah. It's been a difficult adjustment for Tommy. He's started acting out a little. I know he misses you. I told you I would always support you as a father. We might not be together, but co-parenting has been a breeze with you, Nick."

Hearing this filled him with pride. However, he was very disappointed that Tommy had been having such a hard time since the move. "Why haven't you said anything about Tommy acting out?"

"I knew you were trying to settle in here. I just didn't want to worry you."

"Is he hitting and stuff?"

"Biting. He's been biting kids at daycare."

"Well, biting is normal, but it's still not okay."

"I've talked to him," Jill assured him. "He's been better, but he cries a lot. He just misses you."

"Moving has been tough for me, Jill. This wasn't an easy decision."

"I know. But it was the right one. I knew that. That's why I didn't fight you on it," she admitted.

"Well, maybe things are lookin' up. I mean, the Harris family seems to be willing to open their home to us. I never dreamed that we would end up crashing their Labor Day cookout."

"They didn't mind, though. They welcomed us with open arms. It was nice to celebrate the holiday with them," Jill concluded with a sincere smile.

Nick's struggle with relocation seemed to be resolving itself. He hoped that Jill would decide to move. Having Tommy close by would certainly fill the void in his life. He missed spending time with him. Jill was right, though. The sacrifice had been necessary.

22

Lauren sat at her desk catching up on notes. She glanced at the clock. It was a little after two. She'd dismissed group early today. Everyone seemed to do really well in session, so she felt like they deserved a reward.

As she typed in the electronic chart, the phone buzzed, startling her. Nick's face appeared on the LCD screen of her flip phone. She picked up the device and opened it. "What's up?" she asked expectantly.

"Hey, Doc, I have some bad news," Nick blurted out.

"Another body?"

"Yep," Nick replied.

"Where?"

"Shawnee State Forest. It's somewhere in the southern part of the state."

"That's only about three hours from here. My family used to go camping there. It's really beautiful this time of year."

"Well, we need to hit the road," he added.

"Let me finish up some things here. I'll reschedule my appointments for this week and see if someone can cover for my group. I also need to reach out to Selina to see if she can teach the self-defense class." She wedged the phone between her ear and shoulder. "Tell me about the crime scene."

"The crime scene was just discovered about an hour ago, so it is completely fresh. The FBI forensics team is already headed down there."

"Okay. I'll meet you at your office in about an hour. Fifth floor, right?"

"Yes. Fifth floor of the federal building."

"I'm assuming we're staying in a hotel."

"I'm not sure yet. I'd suggest bringing an overnight bag," he concluded.

After hanging up, Lauren finished her notes and made a few phone calls. Once that was finished, she grabbed a change of clothes from the closet in her office. She slipped into a pair of jeans and put on a gray sweater. She pulled on her hiking boots and secured the laces.

As she drove through Dayton, she eventually reached the parking garage for the federal building. Her security clearance gave her full access, so she didn't have to deal with the guards as she drove in.

She found an empty space, parked, and turned off the engine. After hopping out, she grabbed her overnight bag and jacket from the backseat. Walking toward the elevator, the distant hum of the interstate reminded her of the drive still ahead.

When the large metal elevator doors slid open, Lauren stepped inside. She rode up to the fifth floor, where the receptionist looked up and smiled. Offices lined the walls, and cubicles filled the room. The area buzzed with chatter, ringing phones, and the constant hum of printers, adding to the busy office atmosphere.

"I'm here for Special Agent Nicholas Bennette," Lauren said politely.

"Is he expecting you?"

"Yes. I'm Dr. Lauren Harris."

"Oh my, you're Dr. Harris!" The surprise in her voice caught Lauren completely off guard. "I've read your work. Your case studies are so intriguing."

"Thank you," she said with a gracious smile.

"Go right in. He's the first door to your right."

Lauren heard his voice before she located his office. He was talking on the phone. She loitered in the doorway, trying to be polite and not interrupt him. He saw her and motioned for her to come in. He threw up a finger, signaling that he just needed a few more minutes. She sat down on the couch and patiently waited.

"We will be there in about three hours," she overheard him say. "For Christ's sake, I'm begging you, have your people entered the information into VICAP. We need to try to keep track of this guy. And you said that the GPS text was received this morning? By who? We'll make sure we touch base with them. And you guys have Dr. Harris's profile? Okay. We'll call when we're about a half hour out and meet you at the scene." He nodded and then said, "Sounds good. Bye."

"Busy day?" she asked.

"It's about to be," he answered as he grabbed his suit jacket off the back of the chair.

"Please tell me you have clothing to change into. You have got to stop wearing suits to crime scenes." The humor in her voice was laced with seriousness.

"Well, I…"

"Bennette, that is FBI 101. Always be prepared," she scolded.

He winked and smirked. "I have a pair of jeans and a shirt in the car. Since I met you, I've kept an overnight bag in my trunk."

"Good. At least you're learning something."

"Let's go. We need to get down there before the forensic team tears the scene to pieces."

23

The drive started peacefully. The rapport Lauren and Nick built over Labor Day weekend made their working relationship so much better. Relieved, Lauren didn't feel like she had to walk on eggshells.

With her laptop open, Lauren typed diligently. She still had deadlines to meet. Although the first set of chapters had already been sent to her publisher, there were more changes to make with the second half of the book. She also needed to catch up on more therapy notes. She was typically great at time management, but lately she'd struggled.

"You know, Doc," Nick began, "I read your paper about the prison riot."

With a momentary pause, she looked over at Nick. "I'm surprised."

"You must have been scared half to death."

"Not really," she shrugged as she drew her attention back to the laptop screen. "I bonded with many of the inmates early on. I had been interviewing many of them about their impulse control issues related to their crimes. Luckily, I had already gained their respect."

"So, in your article, you said that it was a religious disagreement that started the riot."

"Yes. There's a very distinct pecking order in prisons, especially when it comes to religion. When religious groups disagree, it often results in violence. A lot of the incidents aren't even reported, mostly because the guards don't want to be bothered with the paperwork and because it's an everyday occurrence."

"Really?"

"Oh yes," she replied with a nod.

"The stuff you said in the article reminded me of turf wars with gangs."

"It is very much a turf war. Gangs exist within the prison system as well. Many of the same factors come into play."

"But they didn't make you an official hostage. That's what surprised me."

"The world outside of the prison considered me to be a hostage."

"In your article, you disagreed with that."

"I didn't consider myself to be a hostage, and neither did the prisoners. I was never worried about being harmed. Many of them wanted me to go to the negotiating table for them. They wanted me to mediate a settlement between the two religious groups. There were four men who kept me safe throughout the entire ordeal."

"I remember reading that."

"Miles Camden was the one I worked with the most. He was a lifer. He had been there long enough to understand the internal politics and daily operations. I had been interviewing him for over a year. He murdered his wife and later killed people at a gas station."

"Your report said that Prisoner M had killed twelve people at a local store."

"That's correct."

"I believe that Miles Camden had been rehabilitated. He had become very active in the Catholic religion. There's very little factual truth to many aspects of the Catholic faith, but it has anthropological significance."

He glanced at her and then focused on the road. "I'm Catholic."

"Well, then you know what I mean. It's very structured. Very ritualistic. Miles benefited from the legalism and structure the Catholic religion provided. He felt that he could atone for his sins and lead a better life. He met with a priest each week. He participated in Mass. He was devoted in every sense of the word."

She grinned slightly. She didn't consider her work courageous. It was her job to understand the criminal mind. That meant interviews with violent offenders and time spent in state and federal prisons.

Since Nick had taken an interest in the topic, she continued the conversation. "How long did you serve in the military, Bennette?" she asked.

He cleared his throat, visibly uncomfortable with the direction the discussion was taking. Lauren felt the tension rise immediately. "I'm sorry. I can see that this subject affects you," she said.

"No, no. Don't apologize. It's just that when it comes up, my head immediately goes back there. It's hard to manage sometimes."

"That's a very normal response. I'm sure you have some PTSD from serving, especially as a sniper."

"You want to know the saddest part about all of it?"

She waited.

"Being a sniper means one thing. I was good at killing people. The guilt nearly ate me alive. I leaned on a priest during those times. I don't know what I would have done without my faith," he admitted.

"I understand. We don't have to talk about it."

"It's okay, Doc," he continued. "It's just a part of my life I'd rather forget. I enlisted to escape my past. I didn't realize it would come with such a high price."

As an attempt to lighten the mood, Lauren changed the subject. She discussed her classes for the semester and then her book. Nick listened and reciprocated. He shared some of his own interests along with a few recent successes at work.

After an hour and a half of conversation, a quiet settled in the car. The drive down U.S. 23 South stirred memories for Lauren. The Harris clan had spent a lot of time in Shawnee State Forest. Two weeks every July had been dedicated to family reunions, camping trips, fishing, and hiking there. Lauren knew the trails like the back of her hand. She had made friends with many of the locals during those vacations.

The silence made Nick a little uncomfortable, and he noticed the crease between Lauren's brows. She was deep in thought. "What are you thinking about?" he asked.

She snapped back into the moment. "I have a personal history with this part of the state," she replied as she looked out the window. The trees passed quickly as the memories surfaced. "Growing up, my family and I spent a lot of time here. It makes me sad to be coming back for such an awful reason."

"I'm sorry. I could have gotten someone else to cover for you," he said as guilt washed over him. "You have to talk to me about this. Don't leave me in the dark."

"I didn't need anyone to cover for me. I'm the assigned consultant on this case. I won't let emotional memories interfere with my work," she assured him.

He nodded as Lauren continued her quiet battle with the past.

24

Nick pulled into the parking area. The lot was filled with government vehicles. BCI. FBI. The local sheriff's department.

Once Nick found an open spot, he killed the engine. Lauren opened the door and stepped out. In the distance, she saw a young girl standing at the edge of the woods. She wore only underwear and waited patiently. She was tall, with a slender build and long blonde hair. Her transparency signaled to Lauren that she was staring at the latest victim of The Phantom.

I'm here to help you, Lauren called telepathically.

Why has this happened to me? The confusion in her tone was heartbreaking.

That's what I'm here to find out, Lauren replied.

Quickly collecting herself, Lauren walked toward the horde of police officers. Despite her social awkwardness, she spotted a familiar face and walked to him. With a handshake, she smiled. "Detective Frank Collins, correct?"

"Dr. Harris. You remembered me," Collins replied cheerfully.

"Of course I do. How have you been?"

"Pretty good. They transferred me here a couple of summers ago. It's real different down here," he said as he squinted against the late-day sun.

"Well, you're at the foothills of the Appalachian Mountains now. The culture is very different than that of northern Ohio." She looked around at the other officials gathered at the edge of the forest.

"Who's the lead on this?" she asked.

"That'd be Detty," Collins replied. "He's in there working the scene right now. Dr. Shilling and Dr. Wright are here, too."

"Great." She remembered her manners. "By the way, this is Special Agent Nicholas Bennette with the FBI," she said, nodding in his direction.

Nick and Collins shook hands cordially. Meanwhile, Lauren was distracted by the apparition barreling through the trunks of the trees.

"Shall we?" Lauren said, intent on following the ghost of the victim.

With a nod, the three of them started up the trail. As they closed in on the scene, Lauren saw Chris crawling around on the ground with his kit beside him. Dr. Wright stood with the local coroner, discussing something. Teams were scattered around the scene collecting evidence and taking photographs. Local law enforcement had already taped off the area and kept a watchful eye on the perimeter.

The closer they got to the scene, the sicker Lauren felt. The victim stood just outside the crime scene tape. People passed through her as they came and went.

Finally reaching the hole in the earth, Lauren knelt and looked inside. The body of a lifeless blonde woman lay inside a clear plastic coffin. Ligature marks were visible on the wrists. However, there was another mark Lauren hadn't seen on the other victims.

"Burn marks?" The words escaped her before she could stop them. She looked up at Dr. Wright.

With a furrowed brow, Dr. Wright walked over and knelt beside her. She then crawled into the hole next to the coffin. Carefully, she examined the body. "On the wrists," Dr. Wright confirmed. "Yes, those are burn marks."

"This is new," Lauren said as the nausea worsened. She stood to regain her bearings. Walking away from the scene, she lifted the tape above her head and moved deeper into the forest. Once she was a safe distance away, she closed her eyes, using her hand to steady herself as she leaned against a tree trunk.

The victim's scream tore through her, and electricity shot through her body.

Through the victim's eyes, Lauren examined the surroundings. She felt the material beneath her fingertips. It was a mattress. Her hands were above her head when the electricity surged again. It felt like fire running through her body. She felt herself jerking uncontrollably, teeth gnashing and eyes rolling back into her head. The smell of sweat assaulted her senses. Then suddenly, she caught a whiff of men's cologne. It was sweet, but unfamiliar.

Lauren felt someone cleaning her face with a sponge. The harsh smell of bleach blistered her nostrils.

The scene changed instantly.

She stood in the dark woods. Above her, stars danced against the black velvet sky.

Run, bitch. Run.

The voice was unusually calm.

The instinct to sprint took over, and she felt herself moving forward as branches scraped her flesh. Then a fall, tumbling down an incline. The horror this victim imparted to Lauren was gut-wrenching.

Lauren opened her eyes quickly, realizing her breaths were labored. During the vision, she must have bent over because she was now kneeling on the forest floor, her hands steadying her on the soft ground.

"Doc," Nick called frantically.

Then his touch. He knelt beside her, his hand firm on her back. "Doc, you okay?"

She cleared her throat and stood. "Yes. I'm fine. I'm okay."

He stood as well. "You don't look so good." His eyes scanned her, assessing whether she might need medical attention.

"I'm fine," she promised.

"Do you need some water? You're flushed."

"I'm fine. Really."

"Do you want me to get some water for you?"

"No. No. I'm fine," she insisted.

Abruptly, she turned and walked back toward the crime scene tape. Nick followed closely behind.

"Did you see the burn marks?" she asked as she glanced over her shoulder at him.

He scowled. "Burn marks?"

Lauren led him back to the hole and jumped in, Nick following. She pointed to the victim's wrists. "She's been burned with something."

Dr. Wright interrupted as she stood above them. "I'm going to go back with the coroner."

Lauren made eye contact with Dr. Wright, then with Nick. "This victim was tortured more than the others, I think. Either he is finding more pleasure in causing pain, or she fought him harder than the others. To exert control, he had to take things up a notch. One thing is clear, though." She pointed to the abrasions on the body and the scratches on the victim's feet. "He is hunting these girls."

The others struggled to understand how she had reached that conclusion, so she continued. "Look at her feet. The scrapes. The bruising all over her body. Some of these injuries aren't consistent with torture. They are injuries you'd get from running through the woods. What if the unsub is capturing them, torturing them in another location, then bringing them out here to offer hope? By taking away their hope, he is exercising the highest level of control. He is hunting them for sport."

A collective hush fell over the scene.

"It makes sense," Lauren said as all eyes rested on her. "It fits."

She looked toward the apparition. Lauren knew she had pieced the puzzle together correctly when she saw the victim nod.

I wasn't done yet. I wasn't done living.

Meeting this victim provided more answers than Lauren had anticipated. Still, she was grateful. It felt as though the unsub had spent more time with this victim, which may have been why Lauren was able to collect so much information from her.

One thing was clear. He was escalating, and the puzzle was coming together to form a very clear picture.

25

Lauren and Nick stood in the conference room of the local police station. They sipped on cups of coffee as they waited. Finally, Liam Detty walked in. He held out his hand.

"Dr. Harris, it's good to see you again," he said.

Lauren smiled. She quickly took note of his appearance. He hadn't changed much since the last time she'd seen him. With jet black hair and crystal blue eyes, he could easily pass as an Elvis impersonator. He was lean with chiseled features and a brilliant smile. He wore a pair of army green cargo pants and a button-up collared shirt with his name on the left pocket.

Nick stepped in. He held out his hand, and Detty took it. "I'm Special Agent Bennette with the FBI."

Lauren jumped back in. "How did you get assigned this far south, Detective? I think I met you just outside of Cleveland on another case. It's been at least four years."

"I guess I'm just lucky. I just go wherever they want me," he said with a chuckle.

"I understand that," Nick said with a nod. "I was transferred from D.C."

"I bet this is a culture shock," Detty remarked.

"Eh... not too much. I'm originally from the Carolinas, so I'm used to some of this. I will say that things feel different in this part of Ohio though, at least compared to the western half," Nick admitted.

Impressed that Nick seemed familiar with the regional differences, Lauren flushed a little pink.

"I'm familiar with Dr. Harris's work," Detty said. "And how's Selina?"

Lauren knew that Detty had always had a mad crush on Selina. She wasn't quite sure why Selina had rejected his interest, but that wasn't really any of her concern. "She's well. Working hard as usual."

Although she was happy to catch up, it was time to get down to business.
"So, who do we have, Detective Detty?"

"Betsy Mullins, age twenty-two," he said, referring to a file in his hand. He opened it and continued reading. "Student at Morehead State. She was home on break when she went missing."

Nick held up his hand to pause the conversation. "Wait. So, she was actually reported missing?"

Detty kept reading. "Yes. Her mother told the hotline that she had left the house on the eighteenth for a camping trip. She was supposed to meet some friends from the local college here. They were supposed to be here through the Labor Day holiday. When they didn't hear from her, they got worried and reported her missing. The local sheriff's office says her mom received a text from Betsy's phone."

"With a series of numbers, correct?" Lauren asked.

"That's what it says. The deputy logged it into VICAP, and then BCI took jurisdiction immediately."

"Have the parents been notified that she was found?" Lauren asked.

"Not yet. We wanted to wait until you arrived."

Lauren nodded, caught in a swirl of emotions. Part of her felt a familiar weight settle in, knowing what would come next.

Dr. Wright walked in the door, surprising Lauren. "I wanted to stop by and see if you all might want to join us at the morgue. Dr. Shilling is doing the autopsy today."

As much as Lauren wanted to decline, she knew she couldn't. She nodded instead.

As they piled into Detective Detty's van, Lauren sat in the front passenger seat while Dr. Wright and Nick sat in the back. While making small talk with Detty, she tried to ignore the conversation behind her.

In a hushed tone, she heard Dr. Wright say, "So, Nick, how do you like Dayton?"

"It's okay," she heard him answer. "I just miss Tommy."

"Well, you know where to find me if you ever get lonely. Columbus isn't too far of a drive," Dr. Wright said pointedly.

Lauren didn't hear a reply. She continued her conversation with Detty until they pulled into the parking lot at the morgue.

They didn't make it through the glass double doors.

Ben and Tina Mullins, Betsy's parents, stood waiting. They had been called in to identify their daughter.

26

Nick and Lauren opted out of the autopsy. After contacting Collins to bring Nick's vehicle to the medical examiner's office, he and Nick drove to Ben and Tina's house.

Their beautiful two-story farmhouse was situated on several acres of land. They lived on the edge of the county and owned a horse farm. They were several hired hands who also lived on the property. Lauren knew all of them would have to be interviewed.

As Ben and Tina sat with Lauren and Nick on the enclosed back porch, the cool breeze blew through the screens heralding the season of Autumn. Lauren quickly learned that Betsy was an only child. She was a pre-med student with excellent grades and a healthy social circle.

"I'm so sorry for your loss," Lauren began as she pressed her hands against the warm cup of tea. "I know this is a very difficult time. I wondered if you wouldn't mind answering just a few questions for us. It might help."

Ben and Tina shot looks at one another. Then they both nodded.

"We believe that Betsy was the latest victim of a serial killer. "Had anyone new come into her life recently?"

The parents eyed one another again. Then Tina shook her head, but Ben spoke. "No," he replied. "We knew all of her friends."

"Can we take her computer? We believe that the perpetrator has been contacting his victims online."

"Sure," Tina answered. "She left it here when she went camping. I'll go get it."

"Wait," Lauren said before she got up. "Can we see her room?"

"Of course," Tina replied.

Ben stood. "Follow me," he said as he pulled open the screen door and walked into the mudroom. He led Lauren and Nick upstairs. At the first room on the right, he stepped aside allowing Nick and Lauren to go in first. Ben followed behind and went to her desk. He unplugged her laptop and handed it to Nick.

The sudden rush of burning sensations caused Lauren to close her eyes. Then the smell of cologne became stronger. In her mind's eye, she was surrounded by gray walls, gray ceilings, and gray flooring. The pain became unbearable until finally Lauren snapped back into the present. As her eyes flew open, she said, "We'll have the computer back to you as soon as we can, Mr. Mullins."

"Keep it as long as you need it. We'll do anything to help," Ben said.

"You keep it as long as you need. I want this solved, Dr. Harris. Whatever we can do to help, you let us know."

27

By the time they arrived at the Holiday Inn, it was well past dinnertime. As Lauren and Nick walked to the front counter, the smell of chlorine from the indoor pool drifted through the air. Splashing and laughing came from the area, and Lauren was taken back to another time. Once again, she was reminded of her younger years. She'd been at the hotel before with her family. She'd also been there to attend a conference at the local college.

Nick's voice startled her as she realized she was in a daze, watching the children playing in the water.

"Hey," he called to her, "they have a suite with a king bed and a pull-out couch. That's all they have available."

"That's it?" Lauren asked as she turned and walked to the counter.

"Yep."

Lauren shrugged. "I guess we'll take it."

Riding the elevator to the eighth floor, they stepped out and found their room. After going inside and settling in, Lauren sat at the desk typing up the preliminary report. She also recorded her visions. She wanted to be able to refer back to them, hoping that eventually she could make sense of what they meant.

The room felt emptier without Nick's presence. He had stepped out to fetch some Chinese food, leaving behind a stillness that seemed to linger. The balcony door stood wide open, and a gentle breeze flowed in, causing the sheer curtains to dance and billow dramatically.

An email alert popped up on Lauren's computer. She clicked the icon. The correspondence was from her friend, Joann Smith. She and Joann had met during a case. Joann had worked for the Ohio State Police Department. Eventually, she left to explore greener pastures. She had decided to follow through on her dream of becoming a doctor. Now she taught at Ohio State University and worked in the medical center.

Lauren and Jo, as she was called, had a special bond. Lauren had helped Jo through a few failed relationships. She had a soft heart, worn on her sleeve and easily broken. Still, Jo didn't give up. She hadn't allowed the hurt to taint her faith in a happy ending.

Bringing up the email, Lauren began to read it:

Hey Lauren. It's been a while since we've talked. I hope you are doing well. I miss seeing you. We should catch up for lunch someday soon.

I saw your newest article today in a journal lying in the doctor's lounge. I guess that's why I decided to touch base with you. I also wanted to share some happy news with you. I've met someone.

His name is Skylar Collins. I met him years ago when he worked for the state police. He was in IT. Well, since then, he signed on with an IT firm in Akron. He is so wonderful. He is respectful and smart. He treats me well.

I really want you to meet him. Please let me know when you're free to get together. You've always been so good at reading people. I would rather you met him sooner rather than later. Email me to let me know what your schedule looks like.

Be seeing you,

Jo

A happy smile found its way to Lauren's lips, but a pit formed in her stomach, making her feel uneasy and even anxious. However, she brushed off the anxiety, assuming it was probably because of Jo's poor track record.

The door opened, and Lauren looked up from the laptop. Nick walked in with plastic bags filled with food hanging from his arms. She stood and rushed to help him.

They set the bags on the island in the middle of the kitchen area. Pulling food out, they divided up the portions. Lauren walked to the table and sat down. She stared off, getting lost in thought as she contemplated Jo's email.

"Hey, Doc," Nick said. "Wake up."

Lauren swallowed her food. "I'm sorry. What were you saying?"

An eyebrow raised, he smirked. "Where were you just now?"

Lauren told Nick about the email. She also expressed some concern based on Jo's history with men.

"Do you know the guy?" he asked.

"No. I'm not familiar with him at all. I've never met him or even heard of him."

"Well, there has to be a reason why it doesn't feel right to you," Nick reasoned.

"Jo hasn't always been the best judge of character, so that's probably it."

Lauren stirred her food around and then made eye contact with Nick again. She found herself trailing off in yet another direction. She considered the chemistry between Dr. Wright and Nick.

"Bennette," she began, "tell me how you know Lisa Wright."

"Lisa?"

"I want to know."

Clearly, he was embarrassed. His cheeks turned bright red. "Well, um…" he began as he cleared his throat and shifted his weight in the chair. "Um, Lisa and I know each other… we, um… we grew up in the same neighborhood. We got back in touch a few years back. That's all there is to tell."

Lauren shook her head as she looked up from her plate of food.

"What?" Nick protested.

"I think you've had an intimate relationship with her," Lauren said bluntly as she picked up another piece of sushi with her chopsticks.

"Excuse me?" Nick nearly choked.

"You and Lisa have clearly had sex. It's easy to see. There's obviously attraction there. Chemistry. It's perfectly normal and completely acceptable," Lauren answered.

Nick still couldn't speak. He shoved his own eating utensils into the box of food. His contorted grimace told Lauren she was onto something. His body shifted defensively. "What?" he asked.

Lauren met Nick's gaze. "She's an attractive single woman. You're an attractive single man. There's no judgment here."

He smiled wryly. "So, you think I'm attractive."

Now it was Lauren's turn to feel uncomfortable. She picked up the chopsticks and grabbed another piece of sushi, being careful not to make eye contact. She steeled herself and said, "The point is that it's obvious that you two have been involved somehow. I'm just curious, is all."

"How do you know that we've been involved at all?"

"Bennette, I'm a psychologist. Reading people is what I do. You get very nervous around her. She becomes unusually confident around you. It's easy for even the untrained eye to recognize."

"Listen, I don't want you to think…" he started, but was quickly interrupted.

"Like I said, it's perfectly normal," she shrugged. "I don't judge."

"I'm not… I mean, I was, but I'm not…" Realizing he was tongue-tied, he closed his eyes and took a deep breath. As he exhaled, he leaned in to meet Lauren's gaze. "Listen, Doc, Lisa was my first, okay? I lost my virginity to her. Then when I came back from serving in 1995, she was visiting her family. We hooked up again… and again… and another time."

Lauren snickered.

"But we haven't since… well, it's been a few years, I think."

"So you have had sex with her."

Nick stammered.

"Why are you so shy about this?" Lauren asked. "It's okay."

"Well, it doesn't sound okay."

"Really, Bennette, it's perfectly natural to engage in sexual contact with someone that you have a past with," she said, shifting to a clinical tone. "It's even more common for people to engage in sex without emotional attachment or commitment."

"No. No. I'm not like that," he said, shaking his hands and pointing at her with his chopstick.

"You don't have to be so modest," she kept assuring him. "Many men and women just come together for intercourse with no attachments. Most ancient cultures did not exercise monogamy. In fact, most societies felt that it was unrealistic. Our modern society, however, has pushed it, so now it's the norm. Realistically, it isn't the way human beings are made. Men are hardwired to want to plant their seed in as many gardens as they can. It ensures the survival of humans, and evolutionary theory teaches us that survival is what drives every single species on this planet. Procreation is a tremendous motivator."

"That's not me, Doc," Nick disagreed. "And will you stop talking like a psychologist or anthropologist or... whatever. I openly admit that I've explored, but I thrive in a monogamous relationship. I can't sleep with someone that I don't have an emotional connection to. It's just not my style. It's unfulfilling."

"Some would disagree," Lauren said as she focused on the last piece of sushi.

He stopped and leaned even further onto the table. Their eyes met once again, intensity forming between them. "Do you disagree?" he asked in a softer tone.

She quieted, realizing she was clearly on the spot. Still, she found courage and answered. "I engage in sexual encounters where there are no emotional attachments or commitments." She thought of Simon. "I have a long-term partner that sex is the only thing between us."

"So you're in a relationship?"

"No. Not at all. We only have sex. That's it," she explained. "I have never been in a serious, long-term, committed relationship with anyone."

His mouth fell open in shock, and surprise lit up his eyes. "You've never been in a relationship? How is that even possible? You're in your thirties."

"I don't need to have an emotional connection to experience intimacy. Besides that, emotional connection and a long-term relationship have never appealed to me. It has little value."

"Doc, there are animals who mate for life. Wolves. Eagles. Penguins. They find the one, and they're all in. They are committed to each other for life." He paused. "So you don't believe that there is someone out there for everyone? Someone meant to love only you for the rest of his life?"

"What if there's a woman made especially for me?" she deflected.

"Are you a lesbian?"

"Well, no."

"You're avoiding the question, Doc."

"I'm not," she lied. "I just believe there's love beyond gender."

"Just answer me," he pushed.

"I... I..." she stuttered. "I think the idea of two people being bound together by a piece of paper and some words is old-fashioned and unrealistic. And the examples that you gave... those are all members of the animal kingdom. They are incapable of complex cognition. They mate for life for survival, just as I pointed out earlier. Apples to oranges."

With a serious look in his eyes, Nick kept going. "Lauren, what about your family? Look at them. Your family has how many happy, successful marriages?"

"They obviously believe in monogamy. I have found that no strings attached works best for me. It's a personal choice, I suppose."

"You know what I think it is," he continued. "I don't think you've met the right person. You're the kind of woman who needs someone to sweep you off your feet. You need someone to impress you and challenge you." He leaned across the table and tapped her temple with his index finger. "You need someone to get around that big brain of yours and grab your heart."

He took back his hand and shifted his focus back to the food in the box. "I also think you're afraid," he said as he secured more noodles with the chopsticks. "You're scared to death that someone will break your heart. You're afraid of loss."

Rebelliously, she shook her head in disagreement. "I'm not scared." Tears stung her eyes as emotion swelled in her throat.

Nick looked up again, their gaze locked. "I can see it in your eyes. You want exactly what your parents had. You've just lost hope."

"No... I am just being logical."

Nick disagreed again. "You're not being logical at all. You're being cautious."

28

Running became tiring. She felt like she had run for hours. The adrenaline coursed through her veins. She trembled as she looked up at the full moon, feeling the damp earth beneath her feet. The cold wind blew against her bare skin as she tried to catch her breath. The chase and fear kept her from taking in a lot of air.

Suddenly, she felt someone grab her around the waist. Her feet lifted off the ground, and she screamed. No one came to help her. She fought hard, scratching and kicking. She couldn't see his face as she tried to claw at him.

She landed with a thud as he threw her to the ground. The impact knocked the wind completely out of her. Then she felt him hovering over her, his grip tightening on her wrists. He held both of them with one hand as he inched her underpants off. She knew what would happen next and shut her eyes tightly, anticipating him.

She dissociated to avoid the pain of more violation. The cologne lingered in her nostrils. She continued to fight against him. She'd scratched him so many times already. She'd hoped that enough of his DNA lay under her nails.

After he finished, he yanked her up by the hair and slammed her against a tree. He beat the back of her head against the trunk. She tasted blood and felt it running down her thighs.

Falling to the forest floor, she struggled to stay awake. She knew she had to keep her heart beating. She lost the battle as she slipped into unconsciousness.

She jerked awake, surrounded by darkness. She remembered cave diving in college. It was the only comparison she had to the darkness she faced now.

Trying to orient herself, she felt around. The surface was smooth and cold. There would be a light somewhere beside her. She needed that. Finally finding it, she flicked it, and the flame lit up the small space. Her worst fears were realized; he'd buried her just like the others. Panic gripped her, and she screamed. She tried not to hyperventilate, knowing it would deplete the precious oxygen in the coffin. Still, screaming made her feel better somehow. It confirmed she was still alive.

She heard her name in the distance. Hope rose up. Someone was nearby, and they heard her. She screamed again, and they answered back, calling her name.

She sat up and opened her eyes, her hair matted to her neck and cheeks by her sweat. Nick sat on the side of the bed, holding her by her shoulders. "Lauren, you were having a nightmare. Are you okay?"

Unable to stop shaking, she could only nod. Her hands trembled in her lap. She looked down at them to make sure they were clean. No blood or flesh under her fingernails.

Nick looked at her with grave concern.

"I'm… I'm fine. I'm sorry I woke you," she said as she pushed the hair away from her face.

"It's fine. It's almost six." Her hands still in her lap, he put his on top of them in an effort to calm her. "Do you want to tell me about the nightmare?"

"The murders. I was a victim… I think."

"I'll get you some water," he offered as he started to get up.

"No," she said, clutching tightly to his hands. "Don't leave me." The words came out before she could stop them.

He nodded and gently brushed some damp strands of hair from her cheeks. "I'm not going anywhere, Doc." Despite his reassurance, tears continued to flow uncontrollably. She felt his warm touch as he wiped away her tears, and with his gentle care, she began to calm down.

"You hungry?" he asked.

She smiled half-heartedly and nodded. "Yes."

"I can order room service," he said softly.

"Am I bleeding?" she asked as she looked down at her arms and felt the back of her head.

"No, Doc. You're right here with me. You're safe."

Lauren was missing something. The look on his face told her as much. "What is it, Bennette?" she asked.

"I got a text from Lisa after you fell asleep. Dr. Shilling confirmed burns on the wrists. There were also severe vaginal tears, indicating that she was tortured for an extended period of time. There was also evidence of anal penetration."

Tears welled in Lauren's eyes again. "He took his time with her," she said as her lips quivered.

"Forensics wasn't able to find prints. Chris didn't find anything. This guy truly just vanishes somehow."

"He really is a phantom," Lauren concluded.

29

Lauren's book hit the shelves in October. *Dread* climbed quickly through the bestseller rankings. Lauren was interviewed by local media as well as national news outlets. The publicist scheduled signings and public appearances all over the country. Weeks blurred together in hotels and airplane terminals, which put a damper on Lauren's commitment to work. Still, she saw clients through telehealth, and she taught her classes online. She was truly burning the candle at both ends.

October 18th came and went. With no new victims, Lauren hoped that the situation had run its course. She caught herself wondering if he might be like the Zodiac. He killed for years and then just stopped one day.

As Lauren sat in yet another hotel room, waiting to be picked up for another television interview, she received an email from the state police regarding Betsy. Her parents had reported that Betsy always wore an antique engagement ring, which had not been recovered at the crime scene. Lauren opened the attachment and saw a picture of the ring. It was truly magnificent, a single diamond set in gold, with emerald chips adorning the sides. The ring had belonged to Betsy's paternal great grandmother.

During her travels, Lauren remained in touch with Nick almost daily. She asked him to go back through the crime scene reports to see if the victims were missing any jewelry. Lauren had a hunch that the unsub was collecting trophies.

Nick kept her apprised of personal matters as well as work related ones. During one phone conversation, he told her that Jillian had flown back to the area for an interview with Josh and Lucas. They had offered her a job at the firm. She had found an apartment near the lake community and agreed to ask Ingrid to provide childcare. Nick told Lauren that Tommy had started calling Ingrid and Jim Nana and Papaw.

As for the Harris family, they kept in touch with Lauren during her time away. Trick or Treat planning and pee wee football games preoccupied them. Fall also meant indoor soccer and basketball at the YMCA for her nieces and nephews. Jillian was quick to involve Tommy, too. Next year he would be starting kindergarten, so the exposure to team sports would definitely help him with much needed social skills.

Lauren managed to talk her publicists into allowing for a break at Halloween. She promised she would return right after and work up until the Thanksgiving holiday. She put her foot down, however, and explained that once Thanksgiving came around, Lauren would be taking time off to spend with her family and catch up with work.

Preparing for a costume party, Lauren sat at the kitchen table with Selina and Chelsey. They talked about costumes and decorations. Of course, the menu was a topic of conversation as well. However, things shifted in a completely different direction rather quickly when Lauren mentioned Liam Detty.

"I've invited him," she blurted out.

"Lauren, why?" Selina protested.

"Because he really likes you. I think he will have fun, too."

"Since when did you become Cupid?" Selina bit out. She folded her arms angrily. "I cannot believe you've done this to me."

"He is a very respectable man, Selina. Kind. Sincere. Pleasing to the eye."

"You've been around Nick too much. He's got a very

sentimental side. I can tell," Chelsey said with a confident nod. "He's changing you," she added.

"I enjoy his company. We have a great deal in common," Lauren admitted.

"Well, I'm glad," Chelsey said.

"Just because you've reached the outskirts of bliss doesn't mean you have to push it onto those of us who are less willing," Selina protested.

"Liam Detty is a good man."

"You don't even believe in relationships. Why are you forcing me to possibly be in one?" Selina asked.

"Just because it doesn't work for me doesn't mean it won't work for others," Lauren replied.

"You should give him a chance," Chelsey agreed.

"I don't really have much of a choice, do I?" Selina concluded as she stood and walked out of the room.

"Who else is on the guest list?" Chelsey asked curiously as she glanced over at the handwritten notes Lauren was keeping.

"Family mostly. Josh, Lucas, and their wives. Chris is bringing his husband, Jenson. Jo and her new boyfriend are coming. Nick, of course. Lisa Wright also indicated she may come. Nick is also bringing his brother, Brandon."

"So, is Lisa Wright coming as Nick's official plus one?" Chelsey asked smartly.

A twinge of jealousy shot through Lauren. "I don't know. That's really none of my business," she concluded as she also stood and walked out of the room.

30

After hours of cleaning and preparation, Lauren went upstairs to put on her costume. She chose the Princess Leia slave costume from *Return of the Jedi*. She put her hair up and secured the wig with bobby pins. She stood in the mirror and looked at herself.

The costume was not something she would have normally chosen. Nick and Chelsey had convinced her to go big, so she did. She had the figure for it, so why not?

When Lauren walked downstairs, Selina and Chelsey were standing in the kitchen preparing hors d'oeuvres. Chelsey chose to dress up like a flower child. The costume suited her personality perfectly. Selina, on the other hand, decided to dress as the opposite of her character. She chose a devil costume.

The doorbell rang. "I'll get it!" Chelsey shouted.

Lauren peeked around the corner to see Chelsey flinging the door open to two men standing on the porch. She didn't recognize either of them. One wore a Zorro costume complete with mask and sword. The little fake black mustache made the costume even more believable. The other man wore a pirate costume with an eye patch. Chelsey must have looked baffled, because Lauren heard Nick's voice come from Zorro, saying, "Chelsey, it's Nick."

"Oh my God, I'm so sorry!" she exclaimed as she put her hands to her cheeks. "I didn't even know who you were!"

She laughed and invited them in.

Nick politely introduced his brother. "This is Brandon."

"Hi there," he said with a nod.

Still looking on, Lauren watched as the sparks flew between Chelsey and Brandon. Even with the costume Brandon wore, Lauren could see the resemblance between him and Nick.

Nick and Brandon walked into the kitchen, where Lauren stood still preparing food. Nick's mouth dropped open, and he curled his lips into a smile. Their eyes met, and Lauren felt herself blushing. She was scantily dressed, and she wasn't used to being this open. She wasn't sure how Nick would react.

"Very sexy, Doc," he said with a wink. "And bold!"

She smiled in response. "Zorro?" she commented. "You look good in black."

She hadn't seen Nick since September, so they embraced. They lingered for a moment until Nick pulled away slightly. "Glad you made it back in one piece," he said softly, their noses almost touching.

"It's good to be home," she replied softly.

Nick broke away and drew his sword from its sheath, pointing it gallantly. In a playful Mexican accent, he exclaimed, "Ah ha!"

"I think Chelsey likes your brother," Lauren said as she glanced back into the living room.

Nick looked, too, but then turned his attention back to Lauren. "Need any help with anything?" he asked.

"Can you finish this fruit tray?" she asked.

"Sure," he answered, stowing his plastic weapon.

Chelsey walked into the kitchen on Brandon's arm. "This is Nick's brother, Brandon," she said, batting her eyes.

"I heard," Lauren replied. "It's a pleasure to finally meet you," she added.

Selina also smiled in his direction.

Lisa and Chris came together dressed as Raggedy Ann and Andy. Jenson was unable to attend due to work. Liam arrived dressed as Elvis, of course. Then Jo and Skylar arrived dressed as Helen of Troy and Achilles. Lucas and Holly were Dracula and a witch, while Josh and Cora came as the King and Queen of Hearts.

Once the playlist was selected, the music played throughout the house on the state-of-the-art sound system. Josh and Lucas focused on the barbecue. Their wives mingled with the other guests.

Lauren made her way around to the guests gradually. She tried to balance hosting with food prep. Then she found her way to the margaritas that Chelsey was making. She grabbed one for herself and another for Jo and made her way out to the living room. Jo stood by the fireplace talking to Lisa.

Handing the drink over, Lauren smiled. "I'm so glad you were able to come."

She sipped the drink. "It is so incredibly wonderful to see you," Jo said. "It's been too long."

Jo's stunning green eyes were accentuated by her long, naturally curly dark hair and fair skin. She had once been short with a heavier build. She had lost sixty pounds over the last year. Now she looked athletic and fit.

She turned to the tall, muscular man standing beside her. Lauren hadn't been able to focus on meeting him with all of the chaos of the other guests arriving, so she wanted to show him special attention now.

His inviting smile and smooth tone of voice took Lauren a little by surprise. "I'm Skylar," he said with a friendly nod. "Good to meet you."

"It's so wonderful to finally meet you," Lauren said.

"Jo talks about you all of the time. She's been bragging about your new book."

"She's biased, I'm afraid," Lauren said casually. "Jo is wonderful," she added as she gently touched Jo's arm.

"Yes, she is," he agreed as he put his arm around her and kissed her forehead.

Once everyone ate, the group settled in for games and more conversation. As the night grew older, Chelsey and Brandon paired off and went outside. Liam and Selina sat on the porch swing engaged in conversation. Lisa and Chris left rather early. Lucas, Holly, Josh, and Cora left earlier than expected. Ingrid texted, saying that the kids were sick.

With the thinned-out crowd, that left Jo, Skylar, Nick, and Lauren sitting in the living room. As they talked, Lauren assessed Skylar carefully. He seemed very personable and madly in love with Jo. As they sat on the couch together, he just couldn't keep his hands off of her. It was rather endearing, and Lauren was incredibly happy that she had finally found someone worthy of her.

As Lauren sat in the chair, Nick sat on the matching ottoman in front of her. She held a mudslide in her hand. Her head felt swimmy as the alcohol took hold of her. Nick stuck with beer.

"So what do you do, Skylar?" Nick asked curiously.

"Well, I once worked for the Ohio State Police. I was in the forensics department. I was their lead IT guy. Then I got an offer from a private company and became a contractor. I work with universities and colleges to get them online and running. I also have private business clients, hospitals, insurance companies. You name it. If someone needs to go online, I can help them."

"How long have you been doing it?" Nick asked.

"Oh, wow. I think I started that about five or six years ago. That's how I met Jo," he answered as he smiled at her.

"Oh," Lauren said with a smile.

"I was teaching," Jo started.

"And I was called to the university because Jo's computer had stopped recognizing the system's access codes," Skylar said with a smile.

"And so he fixed it and boldly asked me out," Jo concluded.

"I bet you make really good money now. Private IT work has to pay better than government work," Nick remarked.

"That is definitely the truth."

Lauren took a drink and continued. "You said you service private businesses and universities. So which universities do you service?" she asked curiously.

Skylar thought for a moment. "Well, my regulars include Wright State, which I believe is your alma mater," he answered with a grin.

She nodded in acknowledgment.

He started counting on his fingers. "I also service the University of Dayton, Columbus State, Southern State, Ohio State, Ohio University, West Virginia University, Virginia Tech, Shawnee

State, Morehead State, Indiana University, Michigan, Michigan State. That list goes on and on. That's just a few of the schools."

"A few?" Nick asked as he took another sip of his beer.

Skylar threw back a shot of whiskey. "I go wherever they need me."

"And you repair computer systems and bring new systems online?" Lauren asked curiously. "That's your main role?"

"Yep. Hardware and software. I can do both."

"Wow. Impressive," Nick interjected.

"He is brilliant," Jo added as she snaked her arm into his. "He's even been sent to Washington, D.C., to set up systems for the feds. Everyone wants him. The government offered him an exclusive contract, but he turned them down."

Skylar changed the subject. "So, Jo tells me that you're a profiler?" he asked, focusing on Lauren.

"I suppose that is essentially what I do."

"How?" he asked curiously. "I mean, how do you really know someone you've never met?"

"It's complex, I suppose. It's like solving a jigsaw puzzle. Profiling isn't all I do, though. I teach and am a therapist."

"She also teaches women to kick people's asses," Nick added with a smile.

Jo and Skylar looked confused.

"She teaches self-defense classes," Nick clarified.

They nodded.

Skylar continued. "I think you'd have to be pretty gifted to correctly profile anyone. From what I remember from working in the police department, you take little bits of information and figure things out from there. It's sort of like building a computer from scratch."

"I definitely don't think I could build a computer, that's for certain," Lauren laughed. After taking a drink, she continued. "Profiling isn't terribly complicated. In reality, most people are very predictable. For example, I can assume that tonight Chelsey will sleep with your brother," she said bluntly as she looked at Nick.

Nick laughed. "He's not like that."

"Oh, but she is. And I can also assume that Selina will finally say yes to Liam's repeated pleas for her to go out with him."

"What makes you say that?" Jo asked curiously.

"Because Selina's general personality is the type that requires people to go the extra mile. She expects perfection to a point, but once she has been convinced, it's hard for her to say no, and Liam has been interested in her for years."

"Really?" Nick said with surprise. "Hmm."

"Selina isn't the brick wall she proclaims to be. And you don't have the back story on Liam and Selina either," Lauren added.

"Well, that's not really profiling if you have the back story, is it?" Skylar said a little snidely.

"The back story of any situation helps. For example, most serial killers experienced some sort of abuse or neglect as children. That's their back story. For instance, Aileen Wuornos had a terribly tragic childhood, as did Ted Bundy and Gary Ridgeway."

Intrigued, Nick listened intently. "So you think that our Phantom was mistreated as a child?"

"Most likely, but not always. There is always an exception to the rule, Nick. There are some individuals who develop strength and resilience. They rise above. Just like a child who grows up at the hands of an abusive, alcoholic father can turn out to be a well-respected, kind, honorable man with a career based on service to others." She winked.

He beamed. The compliment meant a lot to him.

"Don't misunderstand," Lauren continued. "There are also many situations where the killer grows up in a healthy environment and is still drawn to killing."

"See what I mean, Skylar?" Jo said as she nodded in Lauren's direction. "Isn't she brilliant?"

"Quite," Skylar agreed. "So, now I'm curious. What are your thoughts on the Phantom?"

Nick stepped in before she could answer. "We're not really allowed to talk about an active investigation."

Lauren totally ignored Nick's lead. "I think he is highly intelligent. He's careful. Calculating."

"Doc," Nick chided.

"Oh, Bennette, I'm not going to say anything that would get us in trouble," she assured him as she started to slur.

"Do you think you're smarter than he is, Lauren?" Skylar asked in a gruff tone.

The room quieted. Lauren temporarily sobered at the odd question.

"Let me rephrase," Skylar continued. "You're clearly intelligent. Jo has told me that you can read just about anyone. So, I wonder how this guy has managed to outsmart you."

Lauren thought hard for a moment. "I definitely think he has a knack for killing. I can assure you, however, that we will catch him. That's the advantage of working as a team. What I don't think of, Nick does." Again, she looked at Nick.

"Well, I sure hope you catch him. I know he has the college campuses on edge," Jo added.

"We will get him," Nick said confidently. "It's just a matter of time. They always make a mistake."

31

Everyone settled into their respective rooms a few minutes before three in the morning. Chelsey and Brandon headed downstairs to the futon in the basement. Liam and Selina left together, presumably to go to her house for the night. Because Jo and Skylar were too drunk to leave Lauren's house, they slept in the guest bedroom.

Nick and Lauren were left alone on the couch. She'd changed into a pair of sweatpants and a T-shirt. The wig was long gone, replaced by a messy bun.

Nick's costume lay in a pile on the floor in the downstairs bathroom. He put on a pair of gray sweats and a black long-sleeved cotton shirt.

As they sat quietly watching the flames in the fireplace, Lauren rested her head on the back of the couch. "I'm quite drunk," she said. She giggled giddily and then turned her head to smile at him.

He smirked and then got up to rearrange the wood in the fireplace. Looking over his shoulder, he said softly, "Go to bed, Doc."

"I don't think I can walk up the stairs," she said with a laugh.

"I can carry you."

"I will just sleep here. You can take my bed upstairs."

"You're not sleeping on your couch. Not when you have a perfectly good bed upstairs," he argued.

Nick stepped forward and scooped Lauren into his arms. With

her head nestled against his chest, he carried her up the stairs to her room. He placed her on the bed and grabbed a fleece blanket from the rocking chair. Spreading it over her, he sat down on the bed.

She stirred slightly and opened her eyes. She propped herself up on her elbow. For a moment, they were lost in the moment. She leaned up and kissed Nick gently on the mouth. He kissed her right back, then quickly came to his senses, pulling away.

With a scowl, confusion flashed in her blue eyes.

"I can't do this," he whispered as he put his palm against her cheek.

"But I want you to," she whispered, still nearly touching his lips with hers.

"No, you don't. You're drunk, Doc."

"This is true. I am quite drunk. But I want this. I want you," she slurred.

"I won't take you like this. You need to get some sleep. You won't remember this when you wake up."

"I need you now, Nick," she said, brushing her nose against his. "Please don't make me beg."

He kissed her forehead, her face still in his hand. "It's getting more difficult to tell you no. You're so beautiful. And you drive me fucking crazy most of the time. Those eyes. I've seen them a thousand times in my dreams," he admitted as her scent caused him to struggle.

He finally mustered enough self-control to break away from her and stand.

More than anything, he wanted to be with her. He wanted to

touch her, to be close to her. But this wasn't how he'd imagined it. He respected her too much to have sex with her while she was drunk. More than that, he respected his friendship with her tremendously. Her true, sober consent meant everything to him.

By the time he finally talked himself out of being open to her advances, she lay on the bed, sound asleep. He tiptoed out of the room and down the stairs to the living room. He took the blanket off the back of the chair and snuggled onto the couch.

Sleep didn't come easily. Hearing Brandon and Chelsey having sex annoyed him. He finally got fed up, grabbed a throw pillow from the chair, put it over his head, and drifted off to sleep.

32

The next evening arrived sooner than Lauren expected. After a late night and very little sleep, dinner felt less like a plan and more like momentum, she didn't bother resisting.

Nick, Lauren, Jo, and Skylar sat at the dinner table looking at their menus. The club was busy with patrons drinking and conversing. The dance floor was crowded, too.

Lauren ordered an old fashion but promised herself that she wouldn't allow things to get out of hand. Nick abstained from alcohol. Jo had a couple of whiskey shots and was gradually becoming intoxicated. Skylar was the designated driver, so he too avoided alcohol.

A slower song came on, and after a moment, Skylar leaned over to Lauren. "Care to dance?" he asked.

Lauren glanced at Jo. She nodded with approval. "Go for it," she said. "I'm too drunk to even stand."

They walked to the dance floor and casually embraced. They swayed for a few beats before he spoke. "You know, I haven't been able to stop thinking about your profession. It just fascinates me," Skylar said as they moved to the music.

"Really? Why do you think that is?" Lauren asked curiously.

"Well, you're so incredibly brilliant, yet The Phantom is one step ahead of you. He evades you. He must be rather good, don't you think?"

"Sometimes it's simply a game of patience," Lauren replied. "As someone who works in IT, I'm sure you've dealt with situations that seemed impossible."

"Oh yes," he agreed. Then his expression changed slightly. "But the point is that I solve the problem no matter what it takes."

They continued to sway as the music filled the space between them.

"Well, so do I," she said. "The issue is that human behavior tends to be very complex. It comes with complex situations that aren't always easily resolved. I would assume technological problems are different."

As they continued dancing, he smiled wryly. "I do wish you the best of luck in catching him before he hurts anyone else."

"Thank you," she said with a nod.

They danced quietly for a few moments. Then Lauren broke the silence. "Jo is a wonderful woman. I hope you know that."

He beamed. "I do. She is fantastic. I am going to ask her to marry me."

Lauren's face lit up. "Really?"

"Please don't say anything to her."

"I promise I won't."

"I am going to ask her around Christmas time."

"Well, congratulations in advance. I wish you all of the happiness in the world," Lauren said with a smile.

"I am sure she'll want you to be in the wedding. She always talks about how much you mean to her."

"She means a lot to me, too."

"She is more than I could have ever hoped for. A guy like me doesn't deserve a woman like her," he concluded.

33

The television appearances and book signings continued through the month of November. Telehealth and online teaching on top of everything else were proving to be a challenge. By the time Thanksgiving finally rolled around, Lauren was exhausted. She looked forward to some family time and some much-needed rest.

Jill, Nick, and Tommy were included in the Thanksgiving festivities. From the annual parade on Thanksgiving night to putting up the Christmas tree on Black Friday, the weekend was filled with fun and family.

December roared in with snow and ice. As Christmas approached, Lauren dreaded it. Of all the holidays, Christmas was her least favorite. It marked her parents' wedding anniversary. Each year she drove to the cemetery to visit her parents. Sometimes Selina went with her. At other times, she went alone. This year, she wanted Nick to come with her.

Since the Halloween party, Lauren felt more vulnerable around him. Instead of fighting it, however, she embraced it. She allowed herself to draw closer to him. She let herself be more vulnerable. They were becoming best friends.

Selina was building a new life for herself. She and Liam were a couple. So, more and more of her time was spent with him and his family. Lauren knew that this was exactly how things should be, but because of Selina's absence, she spent more and more time with Nick. She often found herself at his apartment after her days at Ellis.

After a long day of teaching, Lauren sat at her desk in the study. Her cordless phone was wedged between her ear and shoulder as she typed while listening to Nick. He went on about a basketball game he was watching on television.

Suddenly, silence fell.

"What's wrong, Doc?" he asked. "I've been blabbing this entire time, and you've hardly said two words. I've lost count of the uh-huhs and yeahs."

She stopped typing. "It's nothing."

"Come on," he insisted. "I know you're not being honest. I can hear it in your voice."

She took a deep breath and closed her eyes. She explained the situation about her parents' anniversary. Then she said, "I want to know if you'll go with me this year to visit them."

Immediately, he replied, "Of course I'll go with you."

"I just don't want you to miss Christmas morning with Jill and Tommy. Are you sure?"

"I'll go, Doc. Don't worry."

"Listen, Bennette…"

"Stop it," he interrupted. "Really, it's no problem. The way I see it, Jillian, Tommy, and me will end up at your family's place anyway. They've sort of adopted us."

The thought made her smile. "I think it's wonderful."

"It's great for Tommy," he agreed, then paused. "And for me."

"My family loves you. My aunt and uncle are just doting on Tommy like he's their own grandson."

It was quiet for another moment. "I can't thank you guys enough for taking us in. It's really made a difference in my life.

Asking Jill to come here to work... I owe you."

She disagreed. "You don't owe me anything, Bennette."

Lauren stood up and walked downstairs to grab a sparkling water from the fridge. "You never really talk to me about you and Jill."

"That's because there's nothing to talk about. We've always co-parented well. Everything is about Tommy. We fell out of love with one another." A heartbeat passed. "I always worry that it bothers you about... well, about me and Jill."

"Why would it bother me?"

"Because I don't want you to think that I'm still involved with her. Or that I'm carrying a torch for her."

She walked back up to the study. "It's none of my business," she protested.

"It is your business, Doc. I respect your feelings, and if something makes you uncomfortable, then I need to know about it."

"It doesn't make me uncomfortable at all. I think what you have is wonderful. There are countless studies citing positive outcomes in children who have been raised in strength-based co-parenting situations. Tommy is reaping the benefits of your relationship with Jill."

"We don't have a relationship, but I get what you mean."

She sat down behind the desk and stared at the computer screen.

"So, what exactly does your family do for Christmas?" Nick asked.

She rocked in the leather chair, then decided to get up and move to the comfortable chair in the corner of the room. She snuggled into a blanket and admired the bookshelves before answering. "Well, we meet at my aunt and uncle's house around eleven. We eat too much food, and then that evening we go to Middle Village to ice skate. The kids love the sleigh hill there."

As he made a clicking sound with his tongue, Nick said, "See, that's what I mean. You guys value time with one another. I've never had that."

"That makes me feel sad," she said, pulling the blanket up under her chin. "I'm so sorry, Nick."

"Don't be. Never too late, right?"

"Right," she concluded.

Lauren's eyes grew heavy. The silence on the line made her wonder if they'd gotten cut off. "Nick, are you still there?" she asked.

"I'm here. I just don't know how to say this," he said, his voice hesitant.

"Say what?"

"I want you to know that whatever you need, all you have to do is ask. We're partners. We look out for each other. I know we've really come a long way since we met. We've become a big part of each other's lives. I think that's a huge step in any professional partnership. I just want you to know that I won't let you down."

She smiled. "I know."

"Don't be afraid to lean on me, Doc."

"You know that I'm also here for you, too, right?"

"You've proven that."

34

Saturday afternoon at the Dayton Mall was hectic. Selina, Chelsey, and Lauren roamed from store to store looking for Christmas gifts as they fought the crowd.

They took a break at one of the restaurants inside the mall. Lauren's thoughts were far away. She couldn't stop thinking about Nick. Selina was the first to notice the distance in Lauren's eyes.

"What's going on with you, honey?"

Taken by surprise, she answered, "Huh?"

"Tell us what's going on. You've been weird all day."

"I don't know what you mean," Lauren protested.

"Bull shit," Chelsey said bluntly. "Something is going on."

"I don't really know how to talk about this sort of thing."

"For fuck's sake, Lauren, just talk. Sometimes I can't believe you're a therapist," Chelsey bit out.

"Providing therapy is different. Patients talk. I don't usually have to talk back about personal things. I just give them advice and then listen."

"Okay, we get it," Selina interrupted. "What is going on with you?"

"It's Nick," Lauren answered, uncertainty coloring her expression.

"Is he okay?" Chelsey asked.

"Oh, yes. He's fine. I just… I… My God, where do I start?" she said, stumbling over her words.

"You are falling for him," Selina said with a smile and a nod.

Lauren looked at both of them. "I don't know what this is that I'm feeling."

"Oh wow. This is big," Chelsey blurted out.

"I don't know how to weed through all of these emotions. You both know how I feel about relationships."

Selina reached across the table and put her hand on Lauren's. "I am going to give you some truth, okay? You can be pretty cold emotionally. We all know that. In fact, I've wondered if you've ever truly connected with anyone your whole life. I know that your parents' dying played a really big role in the way you protect yourself, but maybe it's time to start thinking outside of the box."

"What's going on, Lauren?" Chelsey asked inquisitively. "Has he come onto you?"

"Not really," Lauren began. She told them about how she made a fool of herself the night of the Halloween party. She explained how gracious he was about everything, but that he indicated he wanted something more from her. She told them that the conversation wasn't really specific, but there were certainly things they needed to talk about. Neither of them had been ready at the time.

Chelsey and Selina grinned at one another.

"Sweetie, he knows how you are," Selina continued. "He knows how distant you can be. He is probably afraid to crowd you or to make you feel trapped. He is keeping his distance because he isn't just afraid to hurt you."

"He's also afraid you'll hurt him," Chelsey added.

"What do I do? I don't know how to do these things," she admitted. The hopelessness in her voice made the two of them frown.

"You do know how. You've just never had any practice," Selina answered.

"And Simon doesn't count, so put that comparison right out of your head," Chelsey demanded.

"Dig deep, honey," Selina went on. "Remember what your parents were like. That's where you'll find your answers."

After the very productive day of shopping, Lauren sat on the couch in the living room, staring into the flames of the fireplace. She followed Selina's advice and concentrated on her parents. Their love affair had been unlike anything Lauren had ever seen. Their love for one another had been timeless. She remembered them always holding hands and smiling. They truly enjoyed each other's company. They'd often get lost in each other. They had stayed up late talking. They had been best friends as well as lovers. It was as if they'd wandered the earth aimlessly until they'd found one another. Their lives hadn't been complete until that moment.

As the flames warmed her skin, Lauren wondered if she could ever find a love like that. Maybe there was value in monogamy. Still, she realized that with a deep connection to another person, the risk of being hurt rose exponentially. She had never allowed herself to get that close to anyone. She'd avoided a situation like that her entire life. She'd never considered relinquishing control until now.

Despite the fear and uncertainty, Nick had opened her eyes to something different. The desire for him took over her rational mind. She was in love with Nicholas Bennette. Now she had to decide whether to confess and risk rejection or remain silent and simply appreciate the friendship they shared.

35

On Christmas morning, Lauren busily prepared for the day. She packed the gifts in large bags and took them out to the garage, stuffing them in the trunk.

The doorbell startled her a little, but then she realized it was time for Nick to arrive. She quickly walked to the door and opened it. He stood on the front porch with snow melting in his hair.

"I'm sorry. I'm running terribly behind," she said as she gestured for him to come in.

"What's wrong?" he asked as he stomped the snow off his boots before coming inside. He took off his black leather jacket and gray wool scarf and hung them on the hook beside the front door. He pulled off his gloves and stuffed them into his jacket pocket.

"I am trying to get all of the gifts ready to take to Jim and Ingrid's."

"Let me help you," he said as he followed her up the stairs.

She walked to her bed and grabbed more gifts, stuffing them into large red velvet bags.

Nick lingered in the doorway to her bedroom. "You look pretty," he complimented.

She looked down at herself. She wore a pair of jeans, a light red cashmere V-neck sweater, and Christmas socks. Her hair lay on her shoulders in soft curls. Smiling at him as he walked toward her, she replied, "Thank you."

She took note of his attire as well. He wore a pair of dark-washed boot-cut jeans, a gray thermal, and a black graphic T-shirt, tightly fitted to his chest.

With Nick's help, they transferred all of the gifts to the Suburban. Lauren made one last trip into the house to grab her black parka and white angora toboggan with matching gloves. She opened the fridge and grabbed the dozen roses that lay wrapped in tissue paper.

Nick waited for her in the car. She hopped in, nervous and a little breathless.

"Ready?" he asked.

She nodded.

"You'll have to tell me which cemetery we're going to," he said as he pulled out of the driveway and onto the snow-covered street. It had snowed overnight, and road crews in town weren't out yet.

Lauren rattled off the directions to the cemetery in town. It took only fifteen minutes. She continued directing him to the correct part of the cemetery until they arrived at their destination. He stopped the car. Lauren pushed the door open and got out. She grabbed the roses and started to shut the door.

"Do you want me to stay in the car or go with you?" he asked.

"You can do whatever you want. It really doesn't matter to me," she answered as she closed the door.

The snow crunched under her boots as she made her way to the large marble marker with the word *Harris* etched on the stone. Two smaller grave markers sat to the right of it. In front of the stones, next to a large pine, was a concrete bench.

Lauren knelt down in front of the first grave marker. She cleared snow off the marble and then focused on clearing snow from the one beside it.

She took a deep breath and pursed her lips. "I'm sorry I haven't been here much," she whispered. "I've been a little busy." She placed the roses on the ground in front of her mother's stone. "I brought your favorite."

She stood and walked to the bench, where she sat down. "I published my book, finally. I dedicated it to the both of you," she added.

She looked down at her long fingers wrapped in the angora gloves. "I really wish you two were here because I need some help," she continued quietly. "My partner, Nick… I respect him so much. He's smart and kind, and he is such a wonderful father. You would love him. The family has really taken to him. I don't know how to feel. I don't know how to let go. I don't know how you two made things work. I just know you did. I don't know how to tell him what I want or how I feel. I'm afraid he will break my heart."

The snow flurries brushed against her skin. The wind made the tears in her eyes sting. "I know what you're thinking. It's the same thing everyone else thinks. *She's a psychologist. She's been taught how to relate to people.* All of the training and education in the world couldn't have prepared me for what I'm feeling right now. I hate being unsure. I don't know what to do. I need you right now."

Lauren closed her eyes, the image of her parents appearing in her mind's eye. "Selina and Chelsey, they've tried to help me. They reminded me about how much you two loved each other and that you both taught me everything I needed to know."

A tear rolled down Lauren's cheek, the wind freezing it before it could fall. She knew she needed to go before it started snowing again, and she would be late if she didn't leave now. She stood and smiled down at the graves. "He brought me to see you today. I think he might be my person."

She knelt one last time, steadying herself with her hand on the cold white marble. "I know there's a life after this. It's a fact I've never been able to ignore. So if either of you can hear me, I am begging you to help me. Help me know what to say and how to open up to him without fear."

She cleared away the newly fallen snow and stood. Sniffling and choking down emotion, she shoved her hands into the pockets of her coat. "Thank you for giving me so much. I miss you both." Weakness took hold as memories flooded her mind. "I have to go, but I'll come back soon. Merry Christmas and happy anniversary to you both," she whispered through tears.

She turned on her heel and saw Nick waiting outside the car. She smiled as she walked toward him.

"You okay?" he asked.

She couldn't speak, so she nodded.

Unexpectedly, he took her into his arms. "I'm so sorry," he whispered.

"Thank you for coming with me," her voice muffled against him.

They drove back to the lake community in silence. When they reached Ingrid and Jim's driveway, Lauren put on a happy face. As they grabbed some of the bags from the car, they heard the sounds of children playing inside. Then the front door flew open. Tommy ran to Nick, who dropped the bags and scooped up his son.

"Hey buddy!" he said, kissing his cheek.

"Daddy!"

Chelsey came through the kitchen and into the large living room. "You guys need any help?" she asked.

Lauren nodded.

After Brandon and Chelsey helped bring in more bags, Lauren went to the guest bedroom to put her coat on the bed with the others.

Chelsey stood beside her. "Did you go see them this morning?"

"Yes."

They embraced. "Mom and Dad said they were going to go later," Chelsey added. She broke the embrace, then placed her hands on Lauren's shoulders. "And Nick went with you?"

"Yes."

"Have you talked to him yet about…?"

"No. I just can't."

"Don't be afraid, Lauren. And don't push things either. If something's going to happen, just let it happen. Let's just try to enjoy today, okay?"

With a nod, they walked arm in arm back into the living room, where everyone was gathered.

Saturday afternoon at the Dayton Mall was hectic. Selina, Chelsey, and Lauren roamed from store to store looking for Christmas gifts as they fought the crowd.

36

Ingrid prepared a wonderful Christmas lunch just as she had every year. Afterward, the adults gathered in the living room to watch the children open their gifts. Scattered on the floor, the children tore open their presents.

As soon as Josh announced that it was snowing again, the children's attention turned immediately to the outdoors. Excited, they bundled up in snowsuits, gloves, hats, and boots, barely able to contain their energy. Moments later, they were outside, eagerly running through the snow. Some began making snowmen and snow angels, while others grabbed sleds and raced toward the hill, sliding down with laughter toward the frozen lake.

The adults finally opened their gifts. Nick and Lauren went last. She knelt beneath the tree and pulled out a small rectangular box. Handing it to Nick, she watched as he opened it. He pulled out a shiny gold watch.

"Oh my God, Lauren. This is too much…" he trailed off as he looked at it with amazement.

She scolded him as she shook her head. "Read the back."

As instructed, he turned it over and read the inscription aloud: "Trust stands the test of time." With misty eyes, he looked at her. "It's beautiful."

She pursed her lips and blushed. "I'm glad you like it."

He pointed to a small square box in the back under the tree. "That one's from me."

She pulled it out and tore the wrapping paper off of it. She flipped it open, and amazement colored her expression. "It's lovely," she murmured.

As those nearby leaned in, curious to see what lay in the box, Nick stood and then sat down beside her on the floor next to the tree. He took the box from her hand and pulled out a gold chain with a circle pendant made of diamonds. He put it around her neck and fastened it.

She touched it gingerly, looking down at it in complete admiration. "Nick, this is…" She choked up for a moment and then steadied herself, breathing through the surge of emotion. "I love it," she said as she looked into his eyes.

"A circle never ends," he said softly.

37

New Year's Eve proved to be chaos for Nick as he paced in the FBI's interrogation room. He had been working on a confession with a suspect for the last three hours. The evidence easily established guilt. The facts were solid. Still, he wanted the suspect to admit to what he'd done.

As he sat at the cold metal table, Nick glared at the object of his anger. His calm demeanor, however, prevailed as he spoke. "Look, buddy, I know that you killed your wife. We have eyewitnesses saying you were leaving the house with something wrapped in a bedspread. Her DNA is all over the trunk of your car. You took her body into Indiana, and you threw her away like trash. You dumped her."

"I didn't do it!" the man shouted.

Frustration built as Nick stood and began to pace, finally slamming the door behind him as he left the room. Out in the hallway, he paused, pinching the bridge of his nose to ease the throbbing in his head.

His thoughts drifted to the interview techniques Lauren had shared with him. He had read her articles and even studied tapes where she'd coaxed confessions from the most hardened offenders.

He went to his office and picked up the phone; calling her was his only option. He requested that she come to the federal building, and luckily, she was nearby at the Ellis Institute and had just finished with a client. She told him she could be there in about fifteen minutes.

When she stepped out of the elevator, he was already waiting for her. As they walked toward the interrogation room, Nick introduced her to a fellow agent, Gene Williard, who had been assisting with the case. Gene had a strong personal stake in the outcome and was eager for a confession.

She shook her head and folded her arms as they stood outside the interrogation room. "I'm confused. Why are you pushing a confession? You have physical evidence tying him directly to the crime," she asked.

"Because if we can get him to confess, we don't have to worry about begging for a conviction," Nick replied.

"Well, I understand that, but…"

He quickly interrupted her. "Please, Doc," he continued. "I need this guy to tell us what he did. We both know he strangled his wife. He took her away from their three kids. He left her parents without a daughter. This guy is scum." He folded his arms and widened his stance, his eyes narrowing to meet hers.

She sighed. "Okay. Let me see what I can do." She shrugged and walked into the room.

Nick observed the situation from behind the two-way mirror. He saw Lauren's confidence rise as she sat down at the table across from the accused.

"Mr. Fenton, I'm Dr. Lauren Harris. I'm a consultant for the FBI," she said calmly.

Fenton sat with his arms crossed in defiance.

"Mr. Fenton, I've been asked to speak with you about the death of your wife."

"I didn't do what they are accusing me of!" he shouted.

"I'm not here to accuse you of anything, Mr. Fenton. I'm here to try to give you closure. To help your children deal with the death of their mother. To help you hear her voice, even though she isn't here."

Their eyes met. His face softened a little. "I loved her."

"I know." She waited a moment before continuing. "So, why don't you tell me what happened from your point of view?"

He sat quietly for a moment, biting his nails. Beads of sweat formed on his forehead. His face flushed. Every single physiological clue told Lauren he was, in fact, guilty. Still, she knew what she had been tasked with. "Mr. Fenton, I know you had a very turbulent relationship with your wife. There are hospital visits that indicate physical altercations. So, what happened that night?"

"I have already told them everything I know!" he exclaimed.

"I respectfully disagree." She paused and placed her hands on top of the table. Her gaze locked with his. "But you will tell me what happened. I know that the argument was over money."

"No, it wasn't," he snapped.

Lauren said nothing.

Silence.

He shifted in his chair. "It was about money."

"It's always money," she said. "You're a gambler. You'd tried to win some money at the race to pay her back, right? You'd used all the money in savings. You had to win the bet. When you didn't, you had to confess to her. And that made her very angry, didn't it?"

Silence.

"She accused you of being lazy and throwing your life away. That made you very angry."

"She always accused me of that! She didn't understand that all it would take was just one win, just one streak of luck for me to get us out," he said as he stabbed the table with his index finger.

"So, what happened after you argued?"

"We didn't stop arguing. She got in my face, just like she always did. Yelling at me. Pushing me. She didn't understand that it would be different. She finally shoved me. I lost my balance."

"What room of the house were you in when you argued?"

"It started in the living room, but I went out to the garage to get some distance, ya know? Separation. That's what the therapist suggested. But here she comes, screaming. The kids were at her mom and dad's, thank God. I didn't want them to see us fighting anymore."

"So you protected them?"

"Always." His tone and appearance softened. "I love my kids. They are the best thing that came out of that marriage."

"Of course you love your children. But she accused you of taking food out of their mouths."

His mouth dropped. "How did you know that?"

Again, silence.

"She just kept pushing me," he continued as he shook his head, his lip protruding in anger. "I pushed her back." Suddenly, tears filled his eyes. He choked down his emotions, his hands trembling as he remembered the incident. "She fell really hard. She hit her hhhh… her head on the car fender. There was sss… so much blood."

"You'd never seen so much blood in your life, had you?" Lauren asked.

"It was awful. I tried to wake her up, but she… she wouldn't wake up… I tried CPR…" Tears rolled down his cheeks. "It was an accident. I didn't mean to hurt her."

"So why didn't you call 911? Get some help?"

"I… I…" he stammered. "I panicked. I didn't want to go to jail. I knew they'd think I did it on purpose because of our history. I didn't, though."

"You just got angry," Lauren interjected.

He nodded.

"So then what happened?"

"Well, I had to do somethin', so I got a comforter from the bedroom. Honestly, I went sort of on autopilot at that point."

Lauren leaned forward and put her hands together as she laced her fingers. "Mr. Fenton, telling me that you went on 'autopilot' doesn't undo what happened." She paused before continuing. "You need to say the words out loud."

"I don't want to leave my children at all," he said sadly.

"You've just confessed to pushing your wife into the fender of a car, Mr. Fenton," Lauren said evenly. "There's no turning back now. You can either tell me the rest of what happened, or I can walk out of here and let the agents arrest you for murder."

He dropped his head as shame covered his countenance. "I wrapped her in the blanket and waited until after dark to put her in the trunk. There was just so much blood. I tried to wrap her head in a towel, too, but the blood kept coming through. I got in the car and drove. I don't even know where I was going. I kept hoping she'd just wake up. I pulled over and threw her down the hill. I thought maybe the animals would get her before anyone could find her. I went back to the house and cleaned up everything."

"Mr. Fenton, why didn't you just tell all of this to the agents? The intent to commit murder clearly wasn't there. Now, the situation after the fact is a different story, but this wasn't premeditated at all. It was a crime of passion."

"They kept yelling at me." He ran his fingers through his hair. "It was an accident. I kept telling them I didn't do it, but I knew if I told them what really happened, they'd never believe me," he replied.

Leaning in further, Lauren continued. "You should know that your wife only wanted what was best. You fought often, sometimes viciously, but sometimes intense passion borders with intense violence. Sometimes it's hard to see the line that separates the two."

He began sobbing uncontrollably, burying his face in his hands.

"I'm sorry, Mr. Fenton. Truly, I am. I believe that you didn't mean to do this."

He shook his head. "I didn't. I never wanted this to happen."

Gene walked into the interrogation room and cuffed the suspect. He stood him up and led him out of the room.

Lauren remained at the table, staring at the corner of the room. Nick walked in and sat down across from her. "We've been at him for hours. You come in here, and in less than fifteen minutes, you got a full confession. What the hell is that about?"

"Are you angry with me?" she asked.

"Not at all. I just want to know how you do it."

"First of all, I don't raise my voice. I don't yell at anyone."

"I didn't yell."

"Yes, you did. I know you, and you yelled at that man."

"He killed his wife!" he exclaimed angrily.

"See, you're yelling at me!" Lauren said as she stood up.

Nick shrugged. "I don't yell…"

"Nick, you must be able to relate to the accused. This man accidentally killed his wife. He didn't premeditate anything."

"Killing is killing, Doc."

"No, it isn't. When you've got someone like this man and compare him to The Phantom, well, honestly, there is no comparison."

Nick paced. "I just keep thinking of the three kids. They're never going to see their mother again."

"I understand how they feel. You can't let that cloud your vision, though."

"I know you understand," he said with a nod.

He collected himself as his breathing returned to normal. Lauren and Nick walked out of the interrogation room and into Nick's office. He knew he had a report to type up. However, he was preoccupied with the New Year's Eve plans.

"We still on for tonight?" he asked.

Lauren leaned against the door facing. "Of course we are. It's

New Year's Eve."

38

Lauren stood in front of the closet. She had no idea what to wear to Selina's New Year's Eve party. With the phone wedged against her ear, Chelsey droned on about how she should choose something elegant yet fun, revealing yet modest, and sexy yet practical.

She hung up, frustrated by the mixed messages. As she gazed into what felt like an abyss, she remembered some advice her mother had once given her. "Simple is best."

Lauren reached in and chose a playful yet glamorous mini cocktail dress in midnight blue with subtle sequins. The off-the-shoulder design with a fitted silhouette accentuated her waist. Lauren also chose a pair of sheer black tights with strappy stilettos. For accessories, she picked small gold hoop earrings and the necklace Nick had given her for Christmas. She wore her hair down in soft waves.

Lauren stood in front of the mirror, gazing at her reflection. She barely recognized the woman looking back at her. She felt exposed in a way that had nothing to do with skin. As her thoughts drifted toward the possibility of intimacy with Nick, she heard the familiar rumble of the Suburban pulling into the driveway.

With a careful breath, she made her way downstairs, through the hallway, and into the kitchen. Hearing a knock, she crossed the front room to answer the door. There was Nick, standing on the porch in a long wool coat, hands tucked into his pockets, and a beige scarf draped around his neck. His slicked-back hair, a richer, darker shade of auburn in the evening light, gave him a polished, almost magnetic look.

The moment he saw her, his expression softened, revealing a

glimmer of surprise and admiration. Lauren froze, a wave of panic washing over her as she glanced down at herself, suddenly self-conscious. "What is it? What's wrong?"

A slow smile spread across his face, his gaze sweeping over her with genuine awe. "There isn't a damn thing wrong, Doc," he murmured, his voice warm and reassuring. "You look… just… stunning," he stammered, almost breathless as he took in every detail. He did not look away.

She felt a blush creeping into her cheeks. "Well, thank you," she replied shyly.

Nick leaned in a little closer, his eyes sparkling. "Are you sure we have to go to this? We could have a party right here…"

Still beaming, she replied, "Although your offer is extremely tempting, I promised Selina we'd come."

He nodded, a hint of playful disappointment in his smile, then held out his hand. She placed hers into his as they walked together toward the car. Her fingers curled tighter around his than necessary.

Selina's family owned a bar across town, which they closed every New Year's Eve for a private party. They usually invited at least a hundred people, but the turnout was typically around fifty.

Lauren led Nick through the back entrance, and the crush of bodies inside overwhelmed her. The music blared, making it difficult to navigate through the crowd.

Across the room, Selina waved, and she and Liam pushed their way through the throng toward Lauren and Nick. Lauren managed a smile, despite feeling like she might scream. She could tell Selina was already intoxicated; the smell of alcohol was strong, her eyes glassy, and her speech slurred.

Liam greeted Nick with a handshake and offered Lauren a friendly hug. "Glad you could come," he said sincerely.

Lauren nodded, wishing she could just go home. The atmosphere felt suffocating. She felt Nick shift closer to her side.

"Glad you invited us!" Nick shouted into Liam's ear.

Selina smirked at Lauren. "This is killing you, isn't it?"

"It's a bit too much," Lauren admitted.

Nick chimed in, "We're going to say our hellos and bounce."

"Hey," Selina interrupted, "Jo and Skylar are here!"

"They are? Where?" Lauren asked, intrigued.

"Probably downstairs in the pool hall," Selina replied. "I bet they're having sex on one of the tables right now. He can't stop touching her," she slurred.

Ignoring Selina's insinuation and her drunken state, Lauren took Nick's hand. "We're going to put our things in the business office," she said, pulling him along.

They navigated to the back of the bar and climbed a set of stairs to the second floor, then to the third. Lauren opened the third door on the right, took off her wrap, and held her arm out for Nick's coat.

As he unbuttoned it and shrugged it off, she admired his solid black, single-breasted suit jacket and matching trousers. His tie, a festive color, coordinated with his eccentric socks.

"Always the agent," Lauren said with a grin.

"You know it," he replied.

Boldly stepping closer, she straightened his tie and whispered,

"You look very handsome."

Nick gazed into her eyes, brushing a strand of hair away from her collarbone. His touch lingered there. He leaned in and kissed her forehead. "You're beautiful, Doc."

The enticing scent of his aftershave made her heart race, and she felt an urge to kiss him passionately right there. But she had promised to mingle for at least an hour, and she wanted to respect Nick's values. He was too old-fashioned to consider anything else. The restraint made it harder, not easier.

It seemed his thoughts were mirroring hers as he leaned in closer and whispered, "I cannot wait to get you back home." His voice dropped, controlled and deliberate.

Her breath hitched at the thought of their first touch. The anticipation was almost unbearable, coiling low in her stomach, but she reluctantly resolved to stay for the allotted time.

As planned, Lauren and Nick stayed for about an hour and then headed back to Lauren's house. When they pulled into the driveway, Nick didn't shut off the engine right away. Lauren had her hand on the door, ready to get out, but when she saw Nick hesitating, she didn't move. Neither of them spoke.

"Something seems off with you," he said bluntly.

"I just don't know how fast to go with you," she admitted.

"Why?"

"Well, I'm trying to respect your boundaries and the fact that you have a Type A personality. You are very alpha male. I'm trying to be submissive to that," she explained. "I don't want to do anything that might push you away."

She shifted in her seat. "Nick," she started. "I'm not running. This is all new to me."

Silence permeated the cabin of the car. He did not rush to fill it. Lauren reached over and took his hand. "You are going to have to teach me what you want from me." Her eyes invited him in. She held his gaze. He understood.

She pulled the latch on the car door and got out, keys in her hand. Behind her, she heard the car's engine stop, the door open, then shut, and the crunch of snow under Nick's feet. She felt his presence before she heard him. After unlocking the front door, she pushed it open and stepped inside. She tossed her keys into the basket on the foyer table and removed her wrap. Then she went to the kitchen and called out, "Do you want anything to drink?"

Nick didn't answer, so she proceeded to the fridge with the intent of getting sparkling water for both of them. When she turned around, Nick stood in front of her, close enough that her breath caught. He leaned in and kissed her lips tenderly. Desire quickly set them ablaze.

He cupped her face in his hands as he kissed her more passionately. He pushed her hair aside and kissed her neck and then her ears. He slowed there, intentionally. "Will you let me make love to you?" he asked breathlessly.

"Yes," she whispered. The word felt like crossing a line she had already chosen.

Lauren didn't care where they ended up. She just wanted him. They kissed and twirled until they ended up in the middle of the living room. Nick turned her around and unzipped the back of her dress. It fell to her feet. She kicked off her shoes and leaned against Nick, his erection pressing against her as he held her breasts in his hands. He held her there, grounding her.

Kissing her neck and shoulders, Lauren hastily turned and pulled his suit jacket off, then loosened his tie. Next, she went to work unbuttoning his shirt while he loosened his belt and unzipped his pants. Their movements were urgent, but careful.

As he kissed her mouth, she felt her tights rip from her body. Then Nick guided her to the couch. He stood beside her, removing the torn tights from her body and slipping her panties past her knees. His erection was close enough to her that she leaned up and put him in her mouth. A groan escaped his lips as he laced his fingers through the hair on the back of her head. He did not guide her. He let her lead. She moved on him in a rhythmic, deliberate motion, but he needed to be inside of her, so he pulled away and positioned her on the couch. He steadied himself as he looked down at her. Their eyes locked, their bodies in desperate need of relief. He waited. She grabbed his forearms as he guided himself into her.

Time stopped as they joined for the first time. The sensations of their shared bond caused their blood to run hot. They moved together, each breath bringing them closer to ecstasy.

Nick leaned down and kissed her neck. "I love the way you feel," he whispered as he moved with her. He teased her, nipping with his tongue, and then met her mouth, kissing her deeply, trying to tame the flames of passion that engulfed them both. They were intoxicated by one another.

He rose, still steadying himself on his knees as the backs of her knees rested in the crook of his arm. He licked his thumb and then pressed it against her clit. Her back arched as he made circles with his thumb. Watching her get closer and closer to the edge gave him more pleasure than she could possibly know. She was right. He was an alpha male, but he also wanted her to find fulfillment first. Her needs mattered more to him. He wanted to be drunk on the satisfaction of bringing her to orgasm.

The signs were there. Her nipples hardened. Her stomach muscles clenched. She closed her eyes as the moans grew more intense. The tightening sensation around him brought him closer, too. "Come for me, Lauren," he encouraged. His words pushed her over the edge of complete bliss. He followed right with her as he reached orgasm and pushed hard into her. His body tensed as he felt the pulsing of his release. He groaned, his chest heaving as he breathed.

As the moment passed, they lay limp in each other's arms. Nick leaned in and kissed Lauren's forehead, her sweat leaving a salty taste on his lips.

There was nothing to say. Words would only taint the shared experience. Instead, Lauren pulled a blanket over them and rested her head on his chest. This time they were together. It wasn't like the night she'd confessed some of her feelings to him. She hadn't been able to pull him in during the night and take him. Now things were different. He was hers, and she was his. The certainty of that settled deep inside her. The bond she felt to him terrified her, but she was prepared now. She'd had a taste of him. She only found herself wanting more.

39

Eventually, Lauren and Nick went up to the master bedroom and snuggled under the covers. They slept for a while and then made love again, repeating the cycle through the night and into the morning.

Around 9:30 a.m., Lauren woke up in Nick's arms. She lay still as she admired his perfect face. She knew she was falling quickly. There was relief in that certainty. She knew he would lead her safely through all the uncertainties.

Her insecurities had always held her back. As accomplished as she was, getting close to people had always been her Achilles' heel. Nick had changed all of that for her. Things felt right with him. Natural.

She didn't realize he had awakened. He stared at her as she remained lost in thought.

"Morning, beautiful," he said quietly as he leaned in and kissed her forehead.

She smiled. "Good morning."

"What are you thinking about?" he asked curiously.

She shook her head and smiled. "You."

"Happy New Year," he added.

She just couldn't stop smiling.

"You still okay? With us, I mean?"

"Yes. Absolutely."

"No doubts?" he asked.

"None at all. I'm sorry it took so long for me to get here. To understand what this means to me."

"No need to apologize," he assured her. "We're here now. That's all that matters."

"There's nowhere I'd rather be, Nick," she said as she kissed his bare chest.

He rolled over as she moved onto her back. "You think you got one more in you?" he asked with a smirk.

40

Winter months had always been hard for Nick. He lacked motivation, but this year things were different. Lauren made things better in his life. For the first time in a long while, he didn't feel like he was bracing himself for the next thing to go wrong.

Jillian and Nick decided to put Tommy in a basketball league at the YMCA. That seemed to be helping with separation anxiety and social skills. Brandon transferred to the University of Dayton to finish his studies. He had moved in with Chelsey just before New Year's. Theirs was a whirlwind romance, but as long as Brandon was settling down, that was all that mattered to Nick. He knew better than to assume things would always stay easy, but he let himself appreciate the moment anyway.

Nick spent most of his downtime at Lauren's. He was rarely at his apartment. He felt like a discussion about moving in wouldn't go well. Still, he loved being with Lauren and playing house, so to speak. She'd even given him a key. He turned it over in his pocket sometimes, as if weighing what it meant.

He rested beside her after a few hours of lovemaking. She slept soundly next to him. He stroked her soft brown hair. She stirred. Slowly, her eyes opened and then met his.

"I didn't mean to wake you," he whispered.

"It's okay. What time is it?"

"It's close to noon," he answered as his fingertips traced designs on her shoulder.

She leaned up, meeting his lips. The phone on the nightstand rudely interrupted their attempts at intimacy. Nick exhaled through his nose, half amused, half disappointed.

Lauren leaned over and grabbed the phone. She raised her eyebrows, a surprised grimace on her face.

"What's wrong?" Nick asked curiously.

"Nothing's wrong. Simon's getting married," she answered as she put the phone back down.

"Who's Simon?" he said as he settled onto his back and put his arms up, his hands behind his head. He stared at the ceiling, already wishing he didn't care.

Lauren explained everything. Nick listened intently. His insecurities got the best of him, though. It was written all over his face. He hated how quickly it crept in.

"There's no one else now, Nick," Lauren assured him.

He nodded. He didn't have the words. He wasn't sure reassurance would ever completely quiet that part of him.

"Nick, I know what you're thinking," she said.

He lied. "I'm not really thinking anything. Everyone has a past, right?" The words sounded casual, even to him.

She sat up and leaned against the headboard. She pulled the covers up under her arms. "Nick, I can see how uncomfortable this has made you. I'm committed to you. I didn't think I would ever find myself in a position like this. Yet, here I am. And I'm perfectly content with it." She didn't rush the silence that followed.

Once he realized how foolish he was being, he nodded. He needed the reassurance, though. "So this Simon guy, what was he like?" The question slipped out before he could stop it.

"Are you asking if he satisfied me?"

Nick couldn't believe how childishly competitive he felt. He rolled his eyes. However, he did want to know how their sex life compared. The impulse embarrassed him.

"You are really concerned about this, aren't you?"

"I wouldn't say that I'm concerned," he protested, even though he knew that wasn't entirely true.

"Nicholas Bennette, you are the most wonderfully passionate, sensual man I've ever met." She melted beside him and turned onto her side. "The way you touch me, the way your hands feel on me... There's nothing like it. You can disarm me with one glance." She rested her hand against his chest, grounding the words.

Happy with her answer, he leaned over and kissed her. "I'm so glad you're in my life, Doc." The admission felt bigger than he let on.

He was falling in love with her, slowly and unmistakably. Each moment mattered more than the last. They hadn't said those three little words to each other yet, but they certainly felt them. For now, that was enough.

41

With the end of the cold, blustery winter and the wet, soggy spring, the warmth of May finally arrived. T-ball season came along with it. The Harris clan were all in with it, too.

A year had come and gone since the first victim of the Phantom had been uncovered. Things had been eerily uneventful for months. Lauren and Nick were hopeful that the killer had just lost interest or even died. Still, Lauren had a sneaking suspicion it was the calm before the storm.

The Harris family sat in folding chairs watching the T-ball game. The Saturday afternoon sun felt spectacular on Lauren's face as she watched Tommy clear the bases. She clapped supportively as Jill sat beside her. Nick was on his feet most of the game, shouting and coaching from a distance.

She smiled up at him, her sunglasses shielding her eyes. "He is such a good father," she said.

"Yes, he is," Jillian agreed. She leaned over to Lauren. "So, things are going okay with you two?"

With a confident nod, Lauren said, "Oh yes."

Jill lowered her sunglasses slightly to make eye contact with Lauren. "Please remember that Nick is a very sensitive soul. When he commits, he commits completely. There's no turning back for him."

"I feel the same way about him."

"I'm glad. I don't want to see him hurt."

Lauren felt a little uncomfortable. "I would never intentionally hurt him."

"I know." Jillian paused for a moment. "I still feel terrible about him and me. We just weren't ready, and there we were with a child, trying to figure out what we should do. I know now that we did what was right for both of us. And Tommy seems to be okay."

"I am totally supportive of the way you two co-parent. Tommy seems well-adjusted and happy."

"I'm trying so hard to make sure that Tommy knows how much we love him. We don't want to confuse him."

Lauren smiled. "You have gone above and beyond. Nick changed the moment he realized you were coming here. He felt so lost without Tommy."

"I am so thankful for your family, Lauren. It's meant more to us than I can explain."

Lauren smiled. "We are happy to have you in our lives, Jill."

Before she could say another word, her phone buzzed. She looked down at the number and then locked eyes with Nick. Then his phone vibrated in his pocket. She opened the phone and read the text message to herself:

I'm with the Michigan State Police. FBI field office advised me to contact you. Found a body in Sleepy Hollow State Park.

Lauren excused herself and walked to her car. She called the detective and gathered details about the scene. Once the game was finished, Nick met her by the vehicle.

"So we're going north?" he asked.

"Yes," she answered.

"The Phantom?"

"I believe so, yes."

Once they packed some bags, they headed to Michigan. Lauren watched out the window at the passing landscape, sadness overwhelming her at times.

"What's going on in that head of yours, Doc?" Nick asked.

"I thought he may have been done."

"We'll get him. Even if it takes time."

42

The five-hour drive put Lauren and Nick in town after 7:00 p.m. It would be getting dark soon, so they went straight to the forest to meet the Michigan State Police officers. When they arrived in the parking area, two officers met them and led them into the dense forest.

Sleepy Hollow State Park, located in Laingsburg, Michigan, was over 2,600 acres. The GPS coordinates led law enforcement right to the scene. That was one positive. The police were using VICAP. That gave Lauren some hope.

As she neared the trail, the familiar sickness swept over her. She looked around but didn't see the victim. The deeper they went into the forest, the brighter things became, illuminated by portable lights. Several forensic teams, clothed in white-footed jumpsuits, crawled around on the ground collecting evidence. Cameras flashed as photographs were taken. A man dressed in a blue-footed jumpsuit stood beside the grave with a clipboard and pen. He wrote frantically, glancing down at the body and then back to the clipboard.

Then she heard it. The voice of a young woman.

That's why he never leaves anything behind.

Lauren looked around, finally spotting the girl to her right.

He dresses in a jumpsuit just like those. He chased me at a different place in the forest and then dumped me here.

The girl vanished.

Based on what she could tell, Lauren felt that the victim must have had a strong personality. Victims with weaker constitutions sometimes had trouble coming through clearly. With those victims, she had always had to work harder to obtain information.

For a few moments, Lauren stood still. She tried to get her bearings. Nick walked ahead of her but turned back every so often. He noticed she kept lagging, her eyes darting all over the place.

"You all right?" he asked.

She nodded. "Yes. I'm fine," she replied as she followed him toward the man holding the clipboard.

Nick reached him first and shook his hand. "I'm Dr. Wells," he said.

"I'm Special Agent Nicholas Bennette, and this is Dr. Lauren Harris."

"The profiler," another man said as he stepped forward with his hand out. "I'm Detective Vincent Roberts with the Michigan State Police. I got a call this morning from the victim's stepmother. She received GPS coordinates in a text message."

Lauren knelt at the site and peered into the grave. When the victim revealed herself earlier, she had seemed gray, and Lauren couldn't make out the exact details of her face or body. As she looked down into the hole, she got her first real look at the young woman who had been so severely beaten and bruised. Burn marks circled her wrists, but her face had been perfectly preserved, likely washed and clean.

"This is Polly Melton. She's an eighteen-year-old freshman at Michigan State. She sent an email to her stepmom telling her she was leaving on a camping trip."

"Went missing on April eighteenth?" Lauren asked.

"Yep. Got a full-ride scholarship. Excellent athlete. She was a local celebrity, really. Came from nothing. Her bio mom OD'd. Dad married a local girl and then walked out on both of them. Stepmom raised her. That girl was into so much trouble when she was younger," he said, pointing at the victim. "Her stepmom and I had many lengthy conversations about her. Sad situation, really. But sports straightened her out."

Lauren studied the body for a moment longer.

"This fits what I noted in my initial profile," she said. "She had a strong personality."

"We will need her laptop for the crime lab," Nick said.

Lauren stood and walked away from the scene. She looked around again. Finally, she spotted the girl hiding behind an evergreen tree. As they made eye contact, Lauren felt as if she were being pushed through a tunnel. Gray surroundings closed in, followed by the sensation of hands being bound. Tremors of electricity coursed through her, the wires around her wrists sizzling against burning flesh.

She smelled the men's cologne again. The same mattress. This time, when she saw the killer, he wore a surgical mask. His eyes were clearly visible. They were a deep blue. His hair was covered with a surgical cap, and he wore scrubs. Then she felt a spoon come to her mouth and the taste of broth. No sound, though.

The vision shattered the previous obstacles. Lauren finally caught a glimpse of some facial features. The knowledge that he wore a jumpsuit was also very noteworthy. Why the scrubs, she wondered.

In her initial profile, she had ruled out a medical background. Perhaps she was wrong. Still, it didn't make sense that he hid his face. He killed his victims, so he was safe from being identified.

The apparition stood face to face with Lauren now. She reached out and touched Lauren's arm. The sensation sent Lauren back into the vision. She noted a musty smell. The room had small, narrow windows covered by thin sheers. The windows sat high, near the top half of the room. She was in a basement, maybe. Several fluorescent lights hung from the rafters. Bleach stung her nostrils.

As she stood still, her thoughts raced. She stared into Polly's milky, dead eyes. The detail she shared with Lauren was extremely helpful.

"Thank you," Lauren said in barely a whisper.

How do you know about the jumpsuit?

Polly's aura brightened, but she didn't speak. As she dissipated into thin air, Lauren was left with more questions than answers. She had never had such an intense interaction with a victim before. This was a first. She wondered if her gift was growing stronger. However, she assumed it was Polly's strong character that allowed the visions to intensify.

Lauren felt the warmth of Nick's hand on her shoulder. With a startled jerk, she turned. He stood with a puzzled expression on his face.

"You have got to tell me what's going on. You do this all of the time," he said softly. "Now you're pale, and you act like you're going to pass out. Are you okay?"

She nodded. "I'm fine, Bennette. I told you, this helps me gain clarity."

"I don't understand, Doc," he said.

"It's just a way to collect my thoughts."

He shook his head and folded his arms. "I don't buy it. I know you better than that now. You're not telling me everything."

"What don't you buy?" she asked.

"You have to tell me what's going on, Doc."

"Nothing is going on, Bennette. I just need to think," she answered, a hint of anger in her tone.

She removed herself and walked deeper into the woods. As she looked down at the forest floor, she considered telling Nick about her abilities. However, this wasn't the time nor the place. She trusted Nick, but she wasn't sure how he would react.

She heard footfalls behind her. She knew he wasn't prepared to let the subject drop. She turned to face him.

"I will talk to you about this later. I promise."

43

The FBI put them up in a hotel. They had plans to meet the medical examiner the next morning. She wondered what the autopsy would reveal.

Lauren sat at the desk. She wore her blue pajama shorts and matching tank top. She feverishly looked over the reports and notes, trying desperately to find some answers. The police in Michigan gave her a list of possible suspects, but it did not help. None of them matched the profile, and no one had the distinct blue eyes she had seen in the vision. One thing was clear. The police were desperate. Everyone knew how dangerous the unsub was. She hoped that the law enforcement agencies exercised patience. She had seen too many investigations botched out of desperation.

Quietly, she contemplated whether or not to involve the media. The unsub was an attention whore. Perhaps making a plea to the public through the media could work to their advantage. However, she could not offer a physical description of the unsub.

She glanced at the clock on the laptop. It was after midnight. She took her glasses off and rubbed her eyes. Turning in the chair, she looked at Nick, who was sprawled out on the bed watching the sports channel. He wore a pair of black cotton knit shorts and no shirt.

He must have felt her eyes on him, because he sat up and spoke. "I want you to be honest with me," he started.

"Okay," she said softly.

"Tell me what happened in the woods today. And not just today, but every single time we have gone to a crime scene. Something happens to you. You separate yourself from everyone else. When you come back, you look like you have seen a ghost."

He did not know how right he was. "You want to talk about this now?" she asked.

"I need to know."

She heaved a sigh and then stood and walked to the bed. She sat down beside him and scooted up to rest her back against the headboard.

A battle raged within. She had not talked about her abilities with anyone outside her family. She had talked to her mother a lot. Annie had encouraged her to develop her talents. No one else knew. She had hidden it from everyone else, even Chelsey and Selina.

Visions and voices meant emotional instability. For a nationally respected forensic psychologist, that would be career-ending. Her credibility would be completely lost.

Nick's tone turned harsh. "You are shutting down. I can see it in your face." He furrowed his brow as anger settled in. "Why do you do this, Doc? I still do not understand you sometimes." He waited for a response, but she did not offer one. He became more frustrated. "I have told you more about my military service than I have ever told anyone. I have trusted you with myself. Everything about myself. You still shut me out."

Tears stung her eyes as he chastised her.

"Please, Lauren. Talk to me. Tell me what is going on."

She looked down at her hands and picked at her cuticles. "I do not really know where to start."

"The beginning is always a good place," he encouraged as he

took one of her hands into his.

Closing her eyes, she swallowed hard. Nothing had prepared her for this kind of vulnerability. Yes, she had shared intimacy with Nick. She felt a deep emotional connection with him, but she was not sure he would understand this side of her. She did not fully understand herself.

Nick had taught her how to share herself with him. That was true. She had let him see the darker parts. She had cried in his arms after waking up from nightmares. She had shared those nightmares with him. He had understood. Would he truly understand this? Still, she had to try.

"Nick, I see those girls. Each of the victims. I see them. I see how they died. I feel what they felt. It is real to me."

"When we visit the crime scenes, we all feel it. That is perfectly normal. Of everyone I know, you of all people should understand that."

"It is different for me. My mother called me a sensitive. It is a gift."

He shook his head. "I do not think I understand what you are trying to say."

"I can communicate with the dead girls. They show me what happened to them. It is like I am living through it with them."

"So you can see a dead person?" The doubt in his voice made Lauren wish she had just refused to talk to him about it. This was exactly what she was afraid of. That he would look at her differently. That he might not love her anymore. That he would abandon her.

She pulled her hand away and put it gently back in her lap.

"Do not," he said as he pulled her hand back into his. "I am listening. I am not judging."

"I can only see someone if something terrible happened to them at the time of their death. It does not happen with everyone. That is why I have such a high success rate with solving cold cases."

"Is that what happened on New Year's Eve? Did you see Fenton's dead wife?"

She nodded.

"But you cannot see the perpetrator of the crime?" he asked.

"Well, not until today. Something different happened with Polly. I usually catch bits and pieces of each situation. Today, when the victim communicated with me, she told me that the man who is killing these women, the man who killed her, uses a footed jumpsuit like the crime scene investigators wear. She said that is why there is no trace left behind at the scenes. When I looked through her eyes, the man who killed her wore a surgical mask and scrubs. He had the most piercing blue eyes. I could not see the rest of his face because of the mask. The room was musky, and I think it was a basement, given the layout. And the cologne. The last two victims have remembered the smell of his cologne."

Nick nodded as he listened.

"When this happens, everything sharpens. Yes, I have to piece things together, but there are parts that are missing that I have to figure out on my own. I really do not know how else to describe this to you."

The shock in Nick's eyes was exactly what she expected.

"How long have you been able to do this?" he asked.

"Since I was a little girl. I solved my first cold case when I was six. It involved a little boy who had been murdered ten years prior to my birth. My mom had taken me to the park. I kept seeing a little boy standing by the swings, but no one else saw him. He was always so sad. When I talked to him, he told me that he missed his mom, and he asked me to help him. He showed me how he died, but I saw it through his eyes. Someone strangled him. When he showed me, I could not breathe, and I started choking. I felt the dirt as it fell on top of me. When I came to, my mom was kneeling over me. I had passed out. She asked me what had happened, so I told her everything. I described what he was wearing. We did not talk about it anymore. But when I was older, my mom told me that she had called the police with an anonymous tip. The boy's body was recovered in the ground beneath the swings. He was murdered, but the case remained unsolved. At least that is what my mom told me.

"As I grew older, I tapped into my emotions. I became more aware of them. I learned how to live with what I could do. My mom told my grandmother about my gifts right before she died. No one else knows."

Nick let go of Lauren's hand and stood. He walked to the balcony doors and opened them. He needed the fresh air. "I am not sure what to say, Doc."

"I did not ask for this, Nick. You are Catholic. You are a man of faith. Your belief system tells you to praise a mystical being that you cannot see and you cannot hear. All cultures believe in some kind of being. A higher power. We are taught to believe in things we cannot see. So if you are willing to believe in God, is it so far out of the realm of possibility to believe that a human being has the ability to see something that someone else cannot? To feel things that others cannot?"

"Catholicism is different."

"No. It is really not. You are taught to believe in a being that you have never met. According to your mythology, salvation comes as a result of believing that Christ was the son of God. That he died and rose from the dead. If you believe in that kind of a miracle, why is it so hard to believe in other miracles? I have been given a gift to help understand the grief of others and to provide a way to help the victims of awful, horrible crimes. To give closure to them as well as their families."

"It just seems like, like…"

"Like it is made up," she interrupted. "I know. This is exactly why I have not shared this with anyone. This is why I did not want to tell you."

He turned back to her and walked to the bed. He sat down again. "Doc, are you even religious? You know so much about religion and beliefs and culture, but do you believe?"

She shook her head. "I am not religious. Before my parents died, they taught me the value of being open-minded. I suppose their influence is what drew me to cultural anthropology. Mom told me that everyone held to a different belief system. Our family had been regular church-going folks. The sermons flew in the face of what I held dear in my heart.

"Mom also told me that sometimes God allowed things to happen that no one really understood, but that was okay because in the end, there would always be a reason. There would always be an answer. I held onto that when she and my dad died."

"I am out of my league here," he said under his breath.

The shame rested heavily on her. Fear caused her to tremble. "You do not have to understand. I know what I see. I know what I feel. I know that The Phantom's victims are trying to find peace.

They are trying to understand why they were chosen. Why they had to die. That is where I come in. That does not make it easy. It just makes it necessary."

"I would never break your confidence like that. I will not betray you."

Relieved, she nodded. "I appreciate that."

She got up and walked past him to the balcony. She stepped outside and shut the doors behind her. She needed to think. For the nausea to go away.

The doors opened behind her. She felt the warmth of Nick's body against her back. His arms wrapped around her. "Doc, listen to me," he whispered. "I think you are the most amazing person I have ever met. I am lucky to have you in my life. We have a great relationship. The professional partnership takes a lot of trust, as does our romantic relationship. We put our lives in each other's hands every single day."

Silence.

"If you say this gift is part of you, then I have to believe it. You have never lied to me. Again, we have to trust one another to ensure each other's safety. Your abilities actually explain a lot."

She turned to face him. "I use my education to solve crimes. I do take some of the information from the victims, but most of the profile comes from the science of profiling."

He touched her face and then stroked her hair. "I know how scary it was to tell me all of that. It took courage and trust. I appreciate that you opened up to me."

She tried to smile, but she could not. Tears stung her eyes again.

"There is one thing you have not told me. How did your parents die?"

She turned away and looked out over the cityscape. The memory of their death came rushing back. She secured her hands on the balcony railing as the wind blew her hair away from her face. "They were murdered," she answered.

"You solved it, did you not?" Nick asked.

Her back remained turned from him. "It was my first professional cold case. No one knew I was even working on it. If anyone had found out, they would have pulled me off it right away."

"What happened?"

"My father was the county prosecutor. He had dealt with small-town crime, of course, but there had been one case that kept him up at night. It had truly terrified him. I had heard him talk about it with my mom. From what I remember, he and my mother had received death threats. My mom and dad had also talked to my grandparents and my aunts and uncles about it. They had even talked about moving. My mom had refused, though. She said she was not going to let anyone force her out of the home and the community she loved.

"I stayed with Ingrid and Jim the night it happened. My parents had gone out for their usual date night, and when they arrived home, they were abducted. A hit had been put out on them."

Tears streamed down her face now, her cheeks hot with emotion and her eyes beginning to swell. "My parents were shoved into a van at gunpoint. They had been taken to a field in the adjacent county. There was evidence that my mom had been sexually assaulted. The report indicated that my father had been found tied to a tree with a gunshot to the head at close range. My mom had been found bound and gagged next to the tree. The authorities believed my mother had died first and then my father. Mom had been shot execution-style."

Nick turned and walked to the balcony chair. He sat down, trying to process the information. He leaned forward and put his elbows on his knees. He ran his hand through his hair and then sat back. The situation nearly struck him dumb. "I am so sorry, Doc."

Tears kept coming. "The man who had killed them got away with it for a very long time. I made it my mission to solve the crime and bring peace to my parents. The man responsible for their deaths had always been suspected, but there was always a lack of evidence, and his alibi had been solid, or so it seemed. The case went cold, but I was on a mission. I refused to give up.

"I spent hours in that field. I saw everything through my mother's eyes. I felt everything she felt. I never caught a glimpse of the killer's face, though. Always his hands. I memorized the shape of his fingers. The lines on his hands. That was all I had. Those hands. I finally confessed to my grandmother that I had been trying to solve their murder. I told her what I had seen. She believed me without question."

Lauren brushed the tears from her cheeks. "When I graduated from college, got my license, and put my life back together, I launched my own investigation. The lady you met at the Halloween party and that we went out with the day after, Jo, she helped me with the case. She followed the leads I gave her. She finally found who she thought committed the crime, and she arrested him. By that time, there were major advances in DNA technology. They ran the semen collected from my mother and the epithelial cells from the rope around my dad. It matched. I was still allowed to interrogate him. His hands. His hands were the same hands I had seen through my mother's eyes. Finally, I found peace."

Lauren took a deep breath. "He got the death penalty, and on the day of his execution, I watched as they strapped him to the chair and forced the electric current through his body. I watched life leave him. It was the most satisfying thing I had ever witnessed."

She had spent years working in and around prisons. She had gone with victims and their families when sentences were carried out, sitting beside them as they waited, bearing witness with them. It was never about enjoying death. It was about knowing the person responsible could never hurt anyone again.

For her, it meant finality. Accountability. Justice. Her parents finally had justice.

Her sobs intensified again as she shook against the intensity of the memories. Nick stood and rushed to her, taking her into his arms as she cried. He stroked her hair, trying to offer a comforting touch. "Oh my God, Lauren, I am so sorry."

She wept for the longest time, nestled into his embrace. Finally, she came to herself. The moon had shifted in the night sky. She had lost track of time. "It is over. And I am stronger for it."

Nick looked down at her and tilted her face, her eyes meeting his. "You are so special, Doc. And I cannot thank you enough for being in my life. For sharing these things with me."

"It actually feels good to share it with you," she admitted. With a deep breath, she exhaled slowly. "To tell you all of this has set me free in a way. I do not have to hide anymore."

44

Nick and Lauren stood in the medical examiner's office listening to the explanation of the findings. The ME spoke in a steady, clinical tone as she reviewed the report. They looked down at the lifeless victim. The Y-incision was barely visible at the top of the sheet.

The ME showed them the burn marks on the victim's wrists. They were severe. Polly had abrasions consistent with running into trees and branches. Her fingernails were nearly gone from where she had clawed at the plastic coffin lid. No DNA or trace evidence was able to be collected. However, the ME found something helpful.

As the ME pulled away the sheet, she pointed to a mark on the victim's inner thigh. "It's a bite mark."

Lauren bent down to take a closer look. "It is," she agreed. "Ted Bundy," she whispered.

"What?" Nick asked as he also leaned in closer.

"The unsub is copycatting," Lauren began as she stood up. "Ted Bundy bit some of his victims when he killed them. It was one of the things that led to his capture."

"Mmm," Nick said as he shifted his posture.

"Bite marks are as unique as fingerprints," the ME added as she walked to her desk and made a note in the file. "I took pictures of the marks, and forensics has already been here."

Lauren put her hand to her chin contemplatively. She studied the mark and the body from afar for a moment as she collected her thoughts. She walked away and paced. "The unsub has already copied Gary Ridgeway by placing objects in the victim's vaginal cavity. This time, he bit the victim. He is either getting sloppy, or he is truly copying the killers he admires."

"As I said, forensics has already been here. They swabbed the mark, hoping to get DNA. I don't think they had any luck, though."

"I will need copies of the photographs," Lauren said. "This information also needs to be added to the VICAP profile. And hopefully, forensics did find some trace that can be used," she added as she held up her hands, her fingers crossed in a gesture of hopefulness.

Nick walked closer. He hesitated, his jaw tightening as if he were weighing something. "What if there's more to this than copycatting?"

"I don't understand," Lauren said with a scowl.

Nick's unusual nervous expression caused Lauren's eyebrows to rise. He was visibly agitated and on edge. "What if this guy is doing all of this to send you a message? What if he is testing you to see if you can solve this? If he knows who you are and follows your research, he knows you are an expert on serial crimes. What if this isn't just about the victims? What if it has to do with you?"

The scowl on Lauren's face deepened. Although she wasn't exactly sure about the foundation of Nick's theory, it was a very interesting proposal. An unsettling feeling washed over her. She had mixed emotions. She was very proud of his developing analytical skills. Nonetheless, his theory was frightening for many reasons. Their eyes locked, and Nick's eyebrows rose expectantly as he waited for Lauren's opinion. Still, she couldn't find her voice. Seeing that he'd finally struck her speechless, he continued. "You know I could be right," he added.

She only nodded and then quickly turned to the ME. "Any personal belongings missing? Jewelry, perhaps?"

"It looks like she wore a ring consistently on her left ring finger, but the police didn't mention anything to me about it."

Nick pulled out his phone and texted the detective. He inquired about any missing jewelry. A reply quickly came through confirming that she always wore an engagement ring. When Nick shared the message with Lauren, she looked down at it, her arms folded and her thoughts racing. "He's still taking trophies," she added.

"And although we don't want to think about it, he may very well be targeting you." Nick folded his arms. "I'll die before I let something happen to you."

45

For the first time in her career, Lauren took a sabbatical from the Ellis Institute and from Wright State. She needed to throw her entire being toward figuring out and solving The Phantom serial killings.

The cases she had worked on didn't instill fear in her heart. She had always come at them with an iron will and had never been easily shaken. She'd always understood and accepted the risks. However, The Phantom case felt much different. Dire.

She wondered if Nick's theory was valid. Could The Phantom be trying to spark her attention? Although she tried desperately to put that prospect out of her mind, she found it difficult to do so. She wondered if perhaps Nick might be overreacting and pulling her into his paranoia. The idea that the killer might be more interested in her than in satisfying his own sadistic needs felt uncomfortably self-centered, even considering it. Still, the potential remained very unnerving. So, erring on the side of caution was the only solution.

Lauren spent an entire month researching and combing through the photographic evidence, trying to find some clue she could have missed. She read through forensic reports looking for things she could have overlooked. She even looked through some cold cases that were similar in nature, but she had never studied anyone who'd buried their victims alive.

The case finally hit the media. Along with making front-page news, many of the local media outlets focused on the case, tracking its progress or lack thereof. Lauren and Nick's faces were in front of the public daily. Although Lauren felt that giving The Phantom any media recognition was defeating the overall purpose, she knew that it would play to his ego. That could assist in breaking the case.

By mid-June, the pressure felt constant and inescapable.

As she sat on her deck in a pair of cutoff jean shorts and her black bikini top, she looked over more documentation. She heard the garage door slam and jumped a little. Then she heard Nick call to her, "It's just me."

"I'm out here," she called to him.

He turned toward the patio door, pulled it open, and walked out. With a smile, he looked down at Lauren. "Come on. Get up. Let's go," he insisted, waving his arms in an upward gesture.

"What? Where are we going?" she asked as she frowned.

He walked to an empty chair and sat down. "It's your birthday. Do you actually think we're going to sit around here and do nothing?"

"Nick, please, I don't want to…" she trailed off.

"Nope. I'm not taking no for an answer. Get dressed. We're going somewhere. I don't care if it's just to McDonald's. You can't sit around here and sulk on your birthday."

"I'm not sulking," she argued.

"Listen to me," he said, leaning close to her. "If I don't take you out for your birthday, you'll never forget it. Also, the possibility of me giving you birthday sex will be drastically reduced. You'll be so mad at me for not remembering your birthday, you'll hold a grudge."

She shook her head, a reluctant smile tugging at her mouth despite herself. "You know me better than that, Bennette," she said, with an eyebrow raised.

"Yes, I do know you better than that, but you still need to get your ass up and get dressed."

With faux anger, she put her laptop on the glass tabletop and stood. She glared at him playfully. "Don't talk to me like that."

He stood up, too, smiling sardonically. He leaned in close and kissed her nose. "Got you up, didn't it?"

She playfully swatted his arm. "Where are we going?" she asked.

"Ah, you'll see," he concluded as he turned and walked back into the house.

After following him in, she traipsed upstairs and pulled out a pair of jeans and a dark green V-neck short-sleeved shirt. She stepped into a pair of brown leather flip-flops and pulled her hair up into a messy bun. She heard Nick coming up the stairs. He stood in the doorway wearing a pair of jeans, flip-flops, and a tightly fitted brown graphic T-shirt.

"Let's go, Doc."

"Where the hell are we going?" she snapped.

"Such language from the birthday girl," he said sarcastically as he walked to her and kissed her forehead.

As they turned to walk out of the bedroom, both of their phones buzzed. Lauren's stomach fell, and a lump rose up in her throat. The date on the screen confirmed what she already knew. It was June eighteenth. She closed her eyes, wishing she didn't have to look at her phone. When she opened her eyes, Nick was staring down at his phone, shaking his head.

"Another girl?" Lauren asked, praying to be wrong.

"Afraid so," Nick answered. "Looks like we're going to Indiana for your birthday."

46

Nick and Lauren stood in the middle of Whitewater State Park looking down at the body of Stephanie Peters, a twenty-four-year-old social work graduate student at Indiana University. According to local law enforcement officials, she loved hiking, had a boyfriend, and close friendships.

For Lauren, the scene felt different. Although the team had been aware that the other victims knew the unsub, this scene indicated that the unsub and the victim might have shared a close relationship. Something more personal than opportunity, but still undefined. In Lauren's visions, she heard laughter between the unsub and the victim. She felt the tender kiss of the unsub, and the kiss was welcomed by the victim. Suddenly, the situation changed, and she felt pinned against something. Then the electrical shock.

The fear from the victim was different this time. The victim was genuinely surprised when the tables turned on her. It wasn't just the adrenaline driving the terror. It was the fact that the victim had trusted him with her whole heart. The emotional shock ran deeper than the physical pain. In fact, the feelings of confusion ran rampant, and the familiar smell of the musky basement and cologne drifted into Lauren's senses.

She stood quietly away from the scene as she absorbed all of the information Stephanie shared. The sounds of the park faded around her. Then she felt Nick's presence as he stepped closer, careful not to intrude.

"What do you see?" Nick asked quietly.

"She knew him," Lauren whispered. "This victim had a connection with him. A connection that mattered to her."

"Talk to me," he encouraged.

Lauren shared with Nick everything that she saw. She was hesitant, but still, she knew she had to have faith that he would understand.

Turning back around, Lauren walked to the plastic coffin and investigated it one more time. She noticed the bruising around the victim's wrists seemed worse than the others. There were even bruises around her neck, as if she had been choked. That was certainly an unexpected change. Still, that meant that the murder was personal to the unsub.

From what Lauren and Nick gathered from the forensics team, they had, once again, come up empty-handed. There was no trace. No boot prints. Nothing that would tie the unsub to the crime.

47

Nick and Lauren made the short drive back to the station to meet with the family. The boyfriend sat in the interrogation room while the victim's mother was kept in the family lounge.

When they walked in, one of the officers told them that the detective was leaning hard on the boyfriend. Lauren knew it was out of desperation, not suspicion. The situation made her angry. The profile she had carefully constructed was being ignored for the sake of convenience rather than fact.

Nick and Lauren stood behind the observation glass and watched. The boyfriend was grieving so intensely that he could barely form a coherent sentence. His shoulders trembled as he spoke, his hands clenched tightly together.

Nick leaned over. "You think this might be our guy?" he asked quietly.

Lauren shot him a disapproving glance. "Have you completely ignored everything about this crime? The detective is desperate. This man has none of the markers in the profile. I feel like I'm watching a defenseless animal being tortured. This is ludicrous."

As they continued observing, the detective slammed himself into the chair behind the metal table, planted his fists on its surface, and leaned into the young man's face. He repeated the same question he had asked ten minutes earlier.

"Where were you on the night of May eighteenth?"

"I already told you that I was at home." His voice weakened as tears streamed down his cheeks. "We got into a fight. She wasn't with me. She left earlier that evening."

"I've had enough of this," Lauren muttered under her breath.

She turned and briskly walked out of the observation room. Without waiting for permission, she knocked once and entered the interrogation room. Her eyes locked on the detective.

"Can I speak with you for a moment?"

"We're not done here," he said, pointing at Stephanie's boyfriend.

They stepped into the hallway.

"I need you to be rational," Lauren said evenly. "Have you even read the profile? This man does not fit any facet of it. He works as a waiter. He has no technical skills. He is not a suspect."

The detective's face flushed. "Who the hell do you think you are, coming in here telling me how to do my job?"

Nick heard the raised voices and stepped into the hallway, but before he could intervene, Lauren spoke.

"I'm Dr. Lauren Harris," she said calmly. "I authored the profile you are ignoring. You have been badgering this man for how long? His behavior and his demeanor do not align with the offender we are looking for."

"He has motive," the detective snapped. "They were fighting. He admitted it. The relationship was rocky. That is motive."

Nick stepped between them. "There's no need to shout. Let's slow this down."

Lauren did not back away. "Motive without opportunity does not make a suspect. That is basic investigative protocol. Did you take the time to review VICAP or the profile presentation?"

The detective fell silent, his jaw tightening.

"I'm going in there to speak with him," Lauren said. "You have already done enough damage."

She stepped past him and returned to the interrogation room.

Lauren paused, gathered herself, and entered. She offered the young man a gentle smile and sat across from him.

"Mr. Fry," she said, "I'm Lauren Harris. I consult with the FBI. I am very sorry for your loss."

"Thank you," he said quietly, nodding.

Lauren felt the familiar heaviness settle in her chest. The air in the room shifted. Stephanie stood near the corner, silent, her presence heavy with grief and regret. Lauren did not look at her directly.

"Mr. Fry, can you tell me about Stephanie?" Lauren asked. "What was she like?"

He swallowed hard. "She was the love of my life," he said. "She was a good person. Everyone loved her. I can't imagine anyone wanting to hurt her."

"Tell me about your relationship," Lauren said gently.

"The last three months were rough. We were having problems, like any couple does. I accused her of cheating."

"What made you think that?" Lauren asked.

"She changed. She pulled away. I thought it was something I was doing. She wanted nice things, and I couldn't always provide them." He broke off, burying his face in his hands.

Lauren sensed movement beside him. Stephanie knelt near him, resting her hand lightly against his arm. Lauren felt the weight of remorse and confusion but no answers, no explanations.

"What kinds of things?" Lauren asked.

"I saved for over a year to buy her a necklace. Sapphire pendant. She loved it. She wore it all the time. Even slept in it."

Lauren glanced toward the one way mirror. "What about an engagement ring?"

"She gave it back."

"Why?"

"She said she needed space. She stayed with her mom. She started getting texts late at night. She would leave without telling me where she was going. I never found proof, though. Never."

"Did you check her phone?"

"No. She kept it on her all the time. I figured she needed time. Then I got an email saying she was going canoeing with friends. I never heard from her again." His voice cracked. "Then I got a text with numbers. I didn't know what it meant. I called her mom. No one had heard from her. I knew something was wrong."

Lauren listened quietly.

"I was angry," he continued. "I was hurt. But I would never have hurt her."

"I believe you," Lauren said softly. "I am truly sorry for what you are going through."

She stood and left the room.

Stephanie remained behind, silent, her presence fading as Lauren stepped into the observation area.

Lauren met the detective's gaze. "I told you it wasn't him. Next time, read the profile. You'll save everyone time and spare innocent people unnecessary trauma."

48

In the fall, Tommy started kindergarten. Jillian started seeing someone who was immediately taken in by the Harris family. Brandon and Chelsey moved in together. Selina and Liam's relationship became a little unstable, so they became more on-again/off-again. For the most part, life moved forward and settled into new patterns, some steadier than others.

As the morning sun beamed in through the slits in the blinds, Lauren lay beside Nick as he slept. With her sheets drawn up to her chin, she observed the hues of brown and red in his thin beard. The silhouette of his body under the sheets made Lauren want to touch him. They made love before bed, but she craved his closeness.

She hadn't noticed that his eyes were open until he smirked. "What?" he asked.

"Just watching you sleep," she said with a reciprocating smile.

"Have you given any thought to moving in together?" she asked bluntly.

He opened his eyes again. With a quizzical gaze, he replied, "I didn't know I was supposed to be thinking about it."

"Well, I know we've never talked about it," she began, "but that doesn't mean that I haven't been thinking about it."

"I figured you might not be ready to talk about it," he said, rolling onto his side to face her.

"You're here most of the time anyway," she rationalized.

"That's true," he agreed, though his expression remained

thoughtful.

"Well, what do you think?" she inquired further.

Their eyes locked. His face grew serious as he put his palm on her face. He brushed stray hair away and smiled. "I think it might work," he answered after a brief pause.

"Then why don't you go ahead and cancel the lease on your apartment and move in with me? I'd love to have you in here before the holidays."

He sat up, steadying his weight on his elbow. He looked down at her and kissed Lauren's forehead. "Do you think you could handle me on a full-time basis?"

She smiled at him. "I think I could handle it just fine."

With a shy glance, he said, "You know you make me better, right?"

"What do you mean?" she asked, tilting her chin up.

"Being with you makes me better. I'm a better man because of you, Lauren," he said quietly.

"You've always been a good man," she replied quietly.

He shook his head. "It's you, Doc. It's all you," he concluded as he leaned down to kiss her expectant lips.

49

A week later, Nick began moving in with Lauren. Nick took over the empty room in the attic. He put up his baseball memorabilia, basically making the space into a man cave.

Lauren enjoyed the arrangement. He was a reminder that her life had taken a different turn. Things hadn't turned out the way she once imagined, but she no longer saw that as a failure. She had believed that she would never be able to grow close to someone. Now she knew she had simply been wrong. He had proved her wrong.

Lauren sat on the front porch swing, contemplating the newness of the situation with Nick. She found herself distracted, however, by The Phantom. He kept her guessing, and as the body count kept going up, so did Lauren's frustration level. The contrast between the quiet evening and the violence playing out elsewhere did not escape her.

There were still no solid leads. Disheartened, Lauren felt like she must be missing something. There had to be a clue that was right in front of her, yet she had to be overlooking it.

Nick opened the front screen door and sat down beside her. He put his arm on the back of the swing. She snuggled in close to him as the setting sun brightened the porch and the wind blew the gold, yellow, and red leaves onto the lawn.

Just as they started to relax, Lauren saw a sheriff's cruiser coming up the road. It struck her as odd. The sheriff rarely came to the lake community. The area had private security instead.

The car pulled into her driveway. The deputy opened the door and stepped out. It was Harold Marlin. He had given Lauren the news about her parents so many years ago. The sight of him tightened something in her chest.

Still snuggled up to Nick, she called out, "Good evening, Harold."

He tipped his black ball cap and nodded. "I'm sorry to bother you, Lauren," he began, "but I think there's something at the station you need to see."

A panic shot through her as she stood to her feet. With furrowed brows, she folded her arms. Nick stepped up and held out his hand. They shook.

"Special Agent Nick Bennette," he said gruffly.

With a polite smile, he gave Nick a moment of attention by saying, "I'm Harold. I've known Lauren since she was a tiny little thing." Then he turned his attention back to Lauren. "Anyway, I think you need to follow me in. When we got it in the mail, we all thought you'd be able to help us."

"Got what in the mail? Is everything okay?" she asked.

"Well…" he started hesitantly. "Um… you'll see what I mean."

"Let me grab a pair of shoes and a jacket," she said as she turned and walked into the house. She quickly reemerged wearing a pair of leather flip-flops and a windbreaker.

"I'm going with you," Nick said as he opened the front door and grabbed his tennis shoes.

"You're right, you are going with me. I have a feeling this is going to involve you anyway," she said.

He leaned down and slipped on his shoes. Nick grabbed the

keys to her black Lexus SUV from the hook on the wall beside the front door. Lauren was already in the driver's seat, so Nick settled into the passenger side.

While they drove into town, they didn't talk. The feeling of anxious tension hung in the air. Lauren's mind raced with possibilities as she white-knuckled the steering wheel. Finally, after twenty minutes, they pulled into the parking lot.

Once out of the car, Nick quickly took Lauren's hand in his as they walked in. The dispatcher, whom Lauren knew well, greeted them and let them back into the secured part of the building. Harold waited on them. Standing beside him was Andy Massie. Andy was a detective for the sheriff's office.

"What's wrong?" Lauren asked as she held tightly to Nick's hand.

"We got something in the mail today and we thought you should see it," Andy replied. "It was addressed to you. We think it might be related to those Phantom murders you've been working on for the Feds."

Andy turned and directed Nick and Lauren into his office. He held out a piece of paper enclosed in a plastic evidence bag. Lauren took it into her grasp and examined it. Symbols were written on the paper, and Lauren immediately realized what she was looking at. A chill traced its way up her spine. "The Zodiac," she said.

"I don't understand," Nick said. "The Zodiac?"

"Between the years 1966 to 1974, the Zodiac killer sent more than twenty written letters to the police," Lauren explained. "Many of those letters had ciphers just like this. To this day, some of those ciphers still haven't been translated. The Phantom is copycatting the Zodiac."

"But why would this be sent here and not directly to you?" Andy asked.

"Because it's *for* me," she answered. "He wanted it to go through you. The Phantom is challenging me."

Nick turned away and put his hand on the back of his neck, frustration and fear mixed together. "So he *is* targeting you." He sighed heavily and turned around to face them again. "This just gets better and better, Doc," he said under his breath.

"We must figure out what this says," Lauren said. "I'm going to fax it to my team."

After scanning the document and emailing it to Travis, Nick and Lauren left.

During the drive home, neither said a word.

Lauren pulled into the garage. She started to open her door, but Nick quickly grabbed her wrist. Startled, she turned her head and looked at him.

"Lauren, this is too personal. You have to go somewhere that's safe. Get off of this case," Nick said, his voice tight rather than raised.

"That is absolutely out of the question. There's no way I'll let him scare me into abandoning this case," she argued.

Nick shook his head. "You are so damn stubborn!"

"No. I just won't be bullied."

"I don't give a shit about this case if it means putting you in danger. Hell, I'll take myself off of the case. Lauren, use your head!" Fear edged his words.

"I am using my head," she retorted. Then her features relaxed. "Everything's going to be fine." Even as she said it, she knew the case had crossed a line.

"The hell it is!" he exclaimed.

"There's no point in yelling."

"You mean everything to me. I love you."

The words hung between them, unexpected and raw. They both looked at one another, realizing that those words had never been spoken between them before. Nick quickly recovered. "I will not stand by and do nothing. We're getting a security system in this house."

"I already have one."

"And you don't use it?"

"My dad had it put in."

"Well, then freakin' use it!" Nick said, his eyes wild with fury.

"If it makes you feel better, I will call to have it activated."

"Well, it does make me feel better." He turned his head away from her for a moment as he tried to compose himself.

She shifted in her seat. Pulling away from his grasp, she touched his cheek tenderly. "I'm going to be fine, Nick. It's going to be alright."

50

Sitting in the study, Lauren typed on the desktop. Despite how calm she tried to appear to Nick, she was extremely unsettled. She was upset and anxious. The effort it took to keep herself steady left her drained. Finding very quickly that she couldn't concentrate, she decided to venture out and sit on the dock for a while. Maybe being around the sounds of the lake would center her.

Wearing a pair of gray leggings and an old college sweatshirt, she grabbed a blanket off the back of her father's leather chair in the corner of the study. She wrapped it around her shoulders, slipped on a pair of rubber-sole house slippers, and went down the stairs. The sounds of a football game came from the living room TV. Not wishing to disturb or distract Nick, or answer questions she wasn't ready for, she crept into the kitchen and out the sliding glass door.

Down the long flight of wooden stairs, she went to the dock. The sounds of the lake against the shore as some boats passed in the distance somehow reassured her. Only slightly. The trees against the backdrop of the gray fall sky reminded her that winter was well on its way.

The phone ringing in her pocket startled her. She quickly pulled it out and saw that it was Jo calling. She flipped it open, but before she could say hello, Jo shouted, "I'm getting married!"

"That's great!" Lauren exclaimed. "I am so happy for you!"

"I want you to come," Jo said. "I want you to be a part of the wedding! It'll be next month."

"November? That's fast." She paused for a heartbeat. The word next month lodged uncomfortably in her mind. "But of course I'll be in it. Just email the details."

It was quiet for a moment. "Lauren, what's wrong?" Jo asked. "I can tell there's something wrong."

Lauren sighed. "This case is really getting under my skin," she admitted as she ran her hands through her hair.

"You still haven't gotten anywhere on it yet?"

"No," she replied with a disappointed tenor. "Things keep getting more bizarre."

"You'll figure it out. You are one of the most brilliant people I know. If anyone can put this puzzle together, it's you."

"Thanks," she answered quietly. The words didn't land the way they normally would have. She quickly changed the subject. "So where is the lucky groom?"

"Oh, he's traveling again. More colleges needing help with their computers, I guess. He is usually gone throughout the entire spring and summer. October is when things begin to die down. Then he's at it again in April. He makes enough money to take the winter and early spring off."

"That's good. I bet it's pretty lonely when he isn't around."

"Yes, it is. But we talk nearly every day." Jo continued. "So, how are you and Nick?"

"We're good. He moved in, and we're doing well."

"Good. I am so glad you're happy."

"I am," she agreed with a nod. She wanted that to be true without qualification. "He is a good man."

"Well, listen, I need to get going. My shift starts in an hour. I just wanted to share the news with you and give you a heads up."

"Congratulations again. I'll be waiting for that email."

Lauren ended the conversation feeling very pleased for her friend. The feeling faded faster than she liked. Suddenly, the phone rang again. This time it was Travis from the lab.

"Hello, Travis. Have any news?" she asked.

"You're not going to like this," he said cautiously.

The lump in her throat made it difficult to speak. Fear gripped her as she waited.

"So, I've analyzed the cipher. It is a direct message to you. I am going to fax it to you. I also sent it on to be cataloged as evidence. The paper is quite common. No big deal there. The ink isn't unique either. The handwriting is also a dead end. I wish I had better news for you."

"It's okay. I'll wait for the fax." Her voice sounded steadier than she felt.

"I'll send it right now."

Lauren hung up and walked up to the house, her stomach clenching as she wondered about the message. For the first time, she didn't feel curious. She felt braced.

She pulled the sliding door open and then walked upstairs. She heard the fax ringing and then heard Nick get up from the couch. She knew he'd be following her up the stairs.

She took the paper off the fax machine. Nick peered at the results over her shoulder. The message read: *I thought you were smarter, Dr. Harris.*

Her breath came shallowly as the reality of the message sank in. Her pulse quickened, sharp and insistent. She read further: *I am the Phantom. I am the bringer of justice. When I come, I take souls. I have been called to take yours.*

Lauren put the paper on her desk and walked to the leather chair, the blanket still wrapped around her shoulders. The fleece, however, was no match for the chill running down her spine.

Nick's face lit up with anger. "Fuck," he said under his breath. Then he sat down on the leather ottoman. "You are going to listen to me," he started. "I am not going to argue about this. I want the security system back on by Monday. I am going to have an agent posted here around the clock," he said, pointing toward the front yard. His voice was tight, controlled, and barely holding. "I won't take no for an answer. Make sure you carry your gun with you all of the time, okay?"

Lauren shook her head. "You don't understand, Nick. If this guy wants me, there will be no stopping him."

"Bullshit! We can take precautions!" he shouted as he stood and paced. "You're going to continue with your leave of absence, too."

"Now, wait a minute," she said as she stood up. Her voice wavered before she steadied it. "I'm not going to quit living my life just because some psychopath has picked me out of a crowd. This could go on for decades. I'm not going to put my life on hold."

Nick walked to her and grabbed her shoulders. His eyes filled with determination as he looked into hers. "I cannot lose you."

"You won't," she insisted. The words felt more like hope than certainty.

"Well, I'm not taking any chances!"

51

Lauren stood beside the hole in the ground and peered down into it. Chanon McDaniels was a twenty-two-year-old student at West Virginia University, and Beech Fork State Park in Barboursville was where she met her end. She was the eighth victim.

Lauren walked away feeling completely helpless. The activity around the scene made her long for a solitary moment. Her eyes filled with tears as she walked to the nearby stream. The spirit of the woman stood beside her, her reflection muddled by the water rushing over the rocks.

Turning her head toward the ghost, she felt a cold touch on her arm. Suddenly, Lauren was taken to another place. She no longer stood by the stream, but instead found herself in a musty basement. A strong odor of bleach hung in the air. She noticed a light in the corner. It hung from the joist above. Lauren walked toward it. Hanging on the wall were newspaper articles and clippings regarding the murders. What she saw next turned her stomach.

Lauren saw pictures of herself plastered all over the corkboard. Some of the photos were taken when she and Nick had been out. One stood out among them, nonetheless, and sent a shiver down her spine. The photograph showed Nick and Lauren wrapped in a blanket, sitting on her living room couch. The Phantom had been close enough to get that shot.

Terror and panic gripped Lauren. She felt her heart rate speed as she trembled. She must have been gasping loudly for air, because when she woke from her vision, she was resting in Nick's arms. She was still beside the stream, but Chris and Lisa were also kneeling next to her. The sound of rushing water crashed back into her awareness, cold and unmistakable.

"Doc," he whispered.

She slowly opened her eyes. "What happened?" she asked as she struggled to sit up.

"You collapsed, Lauren," Lisa replied. "So take it easy standing, okay?"

"I… I don't know… what happened…" Lauren stammered.

"Have you eaten anything today?" Chris asked as he stood.

"I don't remember what I've eaten today," she replied as Nick helped her to her feet.

"You had better take her back to the hotel," Lisa suggested. "She's probably dehydrated. There's a nasty flu going around, too. She could be coming down with that. Feed her, too, Bennette."

Exhaustion tugged at her as they made their way to the SUV and then to the hotel. After a shower and some food, Lauren lay down on the bed and drifted off while Nick typed up preliminary notes on his laptop.

Lauren stood beside the stream again. Chanon looked at her. "I can't do this right now," Lauren whispered.

"It won't be long," Chanon said.

"I don't understand," Lauren replied.

Lauren stood on the lawn of a college campus. Students rushed about. She made her way into a building, books in her hand and a backpack weighing her down. She shoved the door open and walked up a flight of stairs. She found the office she needed to go into and turned the knob. She pushed open the door and greeted the receptionist sitting behind the desk. She saw a man in the corner, hunkered down, connecting wires to a very large server. He had blond hair, but his back faced her, so she didn't see his face.

Then, strapped to the bed in the musty basement, she felt the electricity coursing through her and smelled burnt flesh. Agony and terror overwhelmed her as she screamed, "I don't want to die!"

Just as quickly as the dream started, it ended with Lauren sitting up in the bed, her chest heaving and Nick sitting on the side of the bed.

"Doc," he said as he brushed away the tears from her cheeks, "tell me what's happening."

Instead of explaining the dream, she threw her arms around him and sobbed. He held her for what seemed like a very long time. Finally, her breathing calmed and she stopped shaking.

"Just lay with me," she begged.

Nick stripped down to his boxers and a white T-shirt and pulled the covers away. He slipped into bed beside Lauren and pulled her into his arms. With her head resting on his chest, she drifted back to sleep.

The next morning, Lauren and Nick went to the M.E.'s office. Everything matched the other victims, even a bite mark. Once again, however, no trace was found. The Phantom truly had the upper hand.

52

Nick planned an impromptu trip to Key West. They were right in the middle of hurricane season, so the rates were terrific. It was easy for him to see that Lauren's exhaustion was seeping into other areas of her life, so he hoped that being away for a week might help her recharge her batteries.

Basking in the sun, Lauren rested in a beach chair under an umbrella. Nick walked in from the water and plopped down on the empty beach chair beside her. He stood, water dripping from him onto the sand. He dried off with the large beach towel and then sat down in the empty beach chair beside her.

He felt her stare and looked in her direction. She smiled. She turned in the chair and put her feet on the hot sand. With her elbows resting on her knees, she beamed. "You are quite the specimen," she blurted out. "I rather enjoy looking at you. I don't know how you find time to work out."

"You hear me every morning running on the treadmill. I have to stay in shape. Gotta keep you comin' back for more," he joked.

Her countenance turned serious.

"What is it, Doc?" he asked curiously.

"I've never told you that I love you," she said sadly. "I owe you an apology for that."

"You don't owe me an apology. I know you love me," he said.

"It's not fair that I don't say it, though. You tell me that you love me all of the time. You have changed my life, Nick. You told me once that I made you a better man. You should know that just your loving me makes me a better person. I'll always be grateful for that."

Nick raised an eyebrow. Accolades like this weren't Lauren's style. "Doc, what's wrong?"

"Why should there be something wrong?"

"Because this is very unlike you."

She looked down at the sand, hiding her eyes behind the sunglasses. "I just think you should know how I feel about you, especially if something were to happen to me." Tears ran down her cheek.

He lifted her chin with a finger. "You listen to me," he said softly. "I don't want you to think like that. I know things have been crazy lately. I won't let something happen to you. Do you understand me?"

She nodded without a word.

"And I love you, too," he said, drawing near to kiss her lips. "Always will."

53

The first weekend in November marked Jo and Skylar's wedding. Lauren had been preparing for the wedding from afar. Jo had given her the dress specifications, and Lauren had purchased it along with shoes and accessories.

With a full weekend of activities planned, Lauren and Nick arrived at the DoubleTree in Columbus on Wednesday night. The bridesmaids booked a spa day on Thursday. Friday would be the rehearsal dinner. Saturday would be the wedding.

The wedding party was enormous. There were nine bridesmaids and nine groomsmen, two flower girls, and a ring bearer. Jo and her family had spared no expense for the special day. Skylar's family also seemed excited.

The rehearsal dinner took place at the nearby country club. Nick and Lauren shared a table with Jo, Skylar, two groomsmen, and a bridesmaid.

Lauren took a drink of white wine. She tried to keep her thoughts in the present moment, but her mind kept wandering.

Skylar waved his hand in front of Lauren's face. Her eyes focused, and she smiled.

"You okay?" he asked curiously.

"Oh, yes. I'm fine," she answered.

"She's been tired a lot lately," Nick interjected.

Skylar nodded. "Jo told me that you still haven't tracked down that killer. He's up to his eighth victim?"

Lauren nodded.

"We're really not supposed to talk about it," Nick interrupted.

Lauren ignored him and continued. "This case is going to be the death of me," she blurted out as she took another drink of wine.

"Don't say that, Doc," Nick insisted.

"Why do you say that?" Skylar asked as he turned his body toward Lauren.

"The killer truly is a ghost," she answered. "He leaves no trace. Nothing useful."

Skylar pursed his lips. "That must be terribly frustrating for a brilliant person like you. To have some psychopathic killer outsmart you? It seems like he's always just one step ahead of you."

Lauren gave a defeated nod.

"Oh, I'm sorry," Skylar continued. "I didn't mean anything by that."

"Of course not," Lauren replied.

"I read in the Columbus paper that he sent a letter to the cops," he continued.

"Yes. Quite disturbing," Lauren replied.

"Doc," Nick chided her. "I'm going to have to insist you stop talking about this," he said grumpily.

"I don't want to get anyone in trouble," Skylar added as he looked at Lauren and then Nick. "I didn't mean to pry."

"I know," Nick answered. "It's just that this whole thing sort of takes it out of her. And the investigation is still active, so we can't technically talk about it."

With a nod and a smile, Skylar said, "I completely understand. It's just all over the news. Kind of hard to ignore, I guess. Everyone's talking about it, and every campus I visit... well, everyone's pretty shaken up."

"We'll get him," Nick said confidently. "He'll screw up. They always do."

54

Everyone met at the church around 2:30 in the afternoon. By 3:30, Jo and Skylar were making their way to the altar. After a beautiful and very long ceremony, Lauren stood in the receiving line. She shook hands with old friends and smiled at new acquaintances. Finally, everyone left the church and made their way across town to the reception.

As they entered the large venue, the bridesmaids and groomsmen walked in and sat behind the long table. As Lauren looked out over the crowd, she estimated that there were at least 200 guests in attendance. It was by far the largest wedding and reception she'd attended. It didn't even compare to Josh and Lucas's weddings, and the entire town had been invited to those.

Cheers filled the room as Skylar and Jo entered the room. Lauren was so proud of Jo. She had finally found happiness. A soulmate to share her life with.

The evening went on. Chatter and laughter filled the air as the live band played. The dance floor quickly became crowded with people, and the line at the open bar was overwhelming. Finally, after dancing and drinking for several hours, Lauren and Nick decided to leave the reception. As Nick went to get the car, Lauren gathered up her things and headed over to Jo and Skylar to wish them well.

Jo stood first, offering a warm embrace. She pulled away, beaming with joy. "You're leaving?" she asked with disappointment in her voice.

"Yes, I'm afraid so. It's really late," Lauren said with a smile. "Way past my bedtime," she said with a wink.

"I am so glad you could be here with me," Jo said sweetly.

They embraced again. "I am so very happy for you. You deserve the absolute best. It was a beautiful wedding," Lauren said as she broke the embrace.

Next was Skylar. He stood and stuck out his hand. Lauren shook it and nodded. Then they embraced. An unexpected scent of a familiar cologne drifted in the air. She stopped, frozen by fear. She came to her senses and quickly pulled away, trying to cover for her reaction.

"Lauren, what's wrong?" Skylar asked. "You look sort of sick."

She felt sick, but shook her head nonchalantly. "Oh, I've had too much wine. It seems that the older I get, the less alcohol I can handle."

"Do you need me to go get Nick?"

"Oh no," she protested. "I'll be fine."

Jo stood, concerned by the situation. "Let me walk you out," she offered.

Lauren nodded. They walked arm in arm out the door. Once they reached the foyer, Lauren turned to Jo. "If you don't mind my asking, what cologne does Skylar wear? I'm trying to get some ideas for Nick," Lauren said.

"Oh, he wears Acqua di Gio by Armani."

Lauren nodded and then took Jo's hand. "Take care of yourself, Jo. I want you to call me the moment you get back from your honeymoon. I want to hear all about it."

Jo beamed. "I'll call you. I promise."

Lauren walked out to the parking lot, the astonishment nearly bringing her to her knees. Still, she stayed steady. Skylar's cologne couldn't be a coincidence. Was it possible? Was he The Phantom? He was always so interested in the case. Always making comments about how much smarter the killer seemed to be than Lauren. He had blonde hair. From what she could remember of her visions, he also had a similar build.

Nick drove up. He stepped out and opened the passenger-side door. Lauren didn't move, the shock still rattling through her like a jolt of lightning. She searched her mind for an alternative explanation, but she came up empty-handed.

Nick helped her into the car. He got back in and observed her. "Doc, I'm worried about you," he said.

Their eyes met. The horrifying reality she needed to share with him nearly choked off her air supply. She couldn't find the words.

As they drove out of the lot, he continued. "What the hell is going on?"

Lauren wasn't ready to share her theory. It just sounded too crazy. She couldn't process any of the possibilities. So, instead of answering his question the way she wanted to, she said, "I'm just too drunk." She left it at that, realizing that one of her best friends may have married a serial killer.

55

Once away from the wedding and safely at home, Lauren began contemplating all of the possibilities surrounding Skylar. She tried to think of explanations that made sense; things that would exonerate him. As a professional, she couldn't accuse him of anything. She had no evidence pointing in his direction. There was absolutely nothing to indicate that he had been killing women.

Although his sporadic work schedule raised her suspicions, it just wasn't enough. True, he had open access to all of the college campuses associated with the victims. His job allowed him to travel.

Telling Nick would be pointless. The only thing she had to rely on were her visions. That wasn't enough to make a case. So, Lauren tucked it away and tried to go back to solving the crime through scientific means. She combed through the evidence and reports repeatedly, hoping something would stick out—something that might lead to Skylar. She prayed it didn't. She knew how devastated Jo would be.

Lauren lay awake, looking at the slivers of moonlight dancing on the wall. She then stared at the ceiling. Nick slept peacefully beside her. The ringing phone caused her to jump. She looked over at the clock. It was 4:03 a.m.

Nick's cell rang next.

"That can't be good," she whispered.

She leaned over and answered the call. It was the on-call worker at the FBI. She and Nick were being summoned to Jefferson Lake State Park. Riley Portman's body had been discovered.

The drive to Richmond was grueling. Lauren and Nick were

utterly exhausted as they pulled into the station. They were met by Trevor Frazier. Chris and Lisa hadn't arrived yet, so Frazier offered for them to wait. Lauren didn't want to. She wanted to go to the scene before any more time passed.

In the car, Frazier explained that Mr. Portman's response to the GPS message had been delayed. The device had been malfunctioning. Still, the message came through eventually. Because of the publicity surrounding the case, Mr. Portman immediately contacted Frazier.

Riley was a student at Ohio State University. She was nineteen, preparing for her sophomore year in the general studies program. According to Frazier's conversation with Mr. Portman, she hadn't chosen a major yet but was leaning toward veterinary sciences.

Frazier pulled off the side of the road. Other police cars also lined the shoulder. Lauren stepped out, an uneasy feeling causing her to stop for a moment. As she scanned the area, there was no sign of Riley's spirit.

Nick followed Frazier and Lauren through the thick trees. The spot wasn't very far off the road. This meant something entirely different to Lauren. She felt it in her bones, but she needed confirmation.

The yellow crime scene tape came into view. Just outside the perimeter stood Riley's thin, pale ghost. Her long black hair draped over her shoulders like a shroud. She was hunched over, her shoulders slumped forward.

Turning her attention to the hole in the ground, Lauren knelt. The shock of the scene rattled her. There was no plastic coffin. Riley's lifeless body lay in a shallow grave, forensics brushing the dirt from her body.

Lauren looked up at Nick. "He was in a hurry," she said.

"What do you mean?" Nick asked.

"This doesn't fit the MO. There's no plastic coffin. Doesn't make sense."

"Unless she almost got away," Frazier interjected.

"True. That would mean that The Phantom wouldn't have been able to complete his ritual. He had to stop her, and that took priority over the dramatics," Lauren agreed.

She looked back down at the body. There were many consistencies with the other victims on almost every level. However, some differences stood out. Riley's entire body was bruised. Typically, the lacerations and abrasions were fairly superficial and related to running through the woods. The marks Lauren observed were much worse. There were deep gashes in the skin. Some of the victim's skin just wasn't there, especially on the extremities.

Lauren stood and allowed the team to continue to work the scene. She made her way under the tape toward the road. Riley stood waiting. Her presence was ominous and enraged. Through her thoughts, she said, "I'm pissed."

Riley's head rose and her dark brown eyes met Lauren's. Lauren found herself in darkness. She heard the sound of a motor, a car engine, perhaps. As she felt around, there was a latch. She pushed it, and the trunk lip popped open just far enough to study her surroundings. She saw the yellow lines on the road. She heard other cars passing. She saw headlights. Obviously, Riley was in the trunk of a vehicle.

Then a sudden jolt, and Lauren felt herself tumbling onto the hot pavement. Despite the pain of the road rash, she stood and looked around. She ran up the highway, hoping to flag down a car.

She needed help.

Tires screeched. She looked behind her just long enough to see the car she had tumbled from coming to a stop at the side of the road. She ran into the woods, hoping the trees might provide some safety. She had a significant head start on him.

Hope rose up inside of Lauren as she looked through Riley's eyes. Her feet pounded against the forest floor. Her breaths came quickly as she raced forward, determined to survive.

Looking back, she tried to see if he was chasing her. When she turned around, the thud of a tree to the face dizzied her. Falling and tumbling forward a few feet, she steadied herself and spat out pieces of bark.

Suddenly, Lauren realized she was standing outside of Riley's body and watching the unsub. He had slammed the car door and was sprinting into the woods. Wearing a dark hoodie, Lauren couldn't make out features. Then she was back inside of Riley as two large hands grabbed her ankles. She kicked and screamed, hoping to loosen his grasp. Then another dizzying blow to her head. The warmth of blood ran down her face. She tried to stand but lost the battle and fell to the ground, the hazy disorientation making it impossible for her to get back on her feet.

Then she felt him jump on top of her. As he straddled her, he pinned her arms against her body. She couldn't move. She felt his hands wrapped in her dark hair and the blows to the back of her skull as he slammed her head against the ground. The disorientation worsened as the coppery taste of blood seeped into her mouth. Then everything went dark again.

Quickly, Lauren came out of the vision. Riley's ghost stood directly in front of her, their eyes locked. *Bastard still took the time to clean me up, though,* she said telepathically.

The vision explained why the burial was different. It also explained the large areas of skin that were missing. She had almost escaped The Phantom. He had to improvise, too, and make decisions on the fly. That explained why there was no coffin this time. Riley was already dead when the unsub put her in the ground.

Lauren's thoughts immediately jumped to Skylar. Could he do this? Was he capable of such a horrific thing? His stature and general physical build fit, but how many other men fit the physical qualities of the unsub?

After walking back into the woods to the crime scene, she knelt again. Another vision. She smelled the mildew in the basement. Then she saw a man standing in scrubs and a surgical mask. His blue eyes pierced her mind. She felt the binding around her fists and ankles. The cologne faintly hung in the air.

The ring. She looked down at her hands. He was taking the ring. She shook her head in protest. With a hand on Lauren's shoulder, she entered this reality once more.

"You okay, Doc?" Nick asked.

Lauren stood to her feet and turned to him. "This one is much different," she said quietly. "This one almost got away."

56

Back at the station, Riley's best friend, Becki Nixon, waited to speak to the detective. Becki had been the last person to see Riley alive.

Lauren sat in the family lounge with Becki as Nick stood behind the glass observing. Becki was rather heavyset, with short, mousy brown hair and fair skin. Her eyes were red and swollen from crying. Her hands gripped a bottle of water tightly. She shook slightly, the anxiety obviously getting the best of her.

Lauren leaned forward and rested her elbows on her knees. She folded her hands and pursed her lips. "Miss Nixon, I am so sorry for your loss. I know you two were close."

"Like sisters," Becki answered as her voice trembled. "I'm an only child. I needed Riley." The emotions choked her and stole her voice. She put her head in her hands and sobbed, the bottle of water tumbling to the floor as she leaned forward.

Lauren put her hand on Becki's back, hoping to provide some comfort.

"I told her not to go!" Becki shouted as she quickly recovered.

"Go where?" Lauren asked.

"On that fucking camping trip!" she shouted.

"Tell me about that," Lauren encouraged.

"Riley is not the outdoorsy type," she said adamantly. "When she said she was going, I told her she was fucking crazy. The only reason she was going was to impress some guy she'd hooked up with."

"Did you ever meet the guy?" Lauren asked.

"No," she replied. "Riley wouldn't bring him around anyone. I kept telling her he was either married or had a girlfriend. A guy that doesn't want to meet your friends and your family is hiding something," Becki bit out.

"How did they meet?" Lauren asked.

"Through school," she answered as she fidgeted. "She worked in the admissions office. I guess the guy came to install computer stuff all of the time, and they started talking."

"Did she ever give you his name?" Lauren asked.

"No. She refused to tell me anything about him. That was odd. She always told me everything. We didn't have secrets."

"What else can you tell me about the relationship?" Lauren asked.

"Well, about a month and a half ago, she told me that he invited her to go camping. I kept trying to tell her not to go because I knew she hated stuff like that, but she wouldn't listen. In fact, we argued the day she left."

"Did she tell anyone else she was going camping?" Lauren asked.

"She called and emailed her folks. She told them she'd be back but didn't say when. It had been two weeks, and no one had heard from her. I knew something had happened to her." Sobbing again, she tried desperately to hold herself together.

"Did you ever notice a vehicle when he came to pick her up? Did she mention anything about his car, perhaps?" Lauren asked.

She shook her head as she brushed away the tears. "They always met someplace. He never came to pick her up."

"Is there anything else you can remember? Anything that might help us?" Lauren asked.

She shook her head. "I can't remember anything else. I'm sorry."

Lauren thanked her and then excused herself. She walked to Nick, who still stood on the other side of the wall.

"Another dead end," he said defeatedly.

57

Nick and Lauren stood in the M.E.'s exam room. They waited to hear the findings of the autopsy. When they did, however, neither of them was surprised. A bite mark had been found again. Forensics took swabs, hoping to find trace DNA.

"Blunt force trauma to the head is the cause of death on this one," the M.E. said. He turned Riley's head to the side. A large crushing wound could be seen on the back of the skull. "There's also evidence that she tried to escape. And boy, did she fight hard," he continued. He pointed to the defensive wounds. "We also got lucky with trace. Forensics found several fibers in her hair and all over her body. They are testing them as we speak. I think she was stuffed into the trunk of a car, just based on what I saw. What I can say for sure is that she fell out of the car at high speed. See the wounds on her elbows, knees, hands, even her forearms. She tucked and rolled when she escaped. I found particulates in the wounds, and those have also been sent to forensics for analysis."

"Can we get a picture of the bite mark?" Lauren asked. "I'd like to compare it to the films we already have."

"I'm a step ahead of you. I've already got it here in the file," he said as he handed her a packet.

Lauren took a last look at Riley's face. She hoped that the tiny pieces of evidence left behind might be the break they needed.

58

During the four-hour ride back home, Lauren became immersed in her thoughts. Her preoccupied countenance must have worried Nick. He began asking questions to start a conversation, but Lauren hushed him. She told him she wanted to sleep and did her best to retreat into the quiet recesses of her mind.

They pulled into the driveway. A sheriff's cruiser sat in the way. An officer stood beside the vehicle. Both Nick and Lauren nodded at the officer as they exited the vehicle. They made their way past him. Lauren unlocked the front door, and both of them went inside.

After a shower and settling in for the night, Nick and Lauren cooked a quick dinner and then retreated to the sofa for some TV. As they sat on opposite ends of the couch, their legs wrapped around each other, the warmth of the soft blanket on top of them offered a little normalcy. Instead of watching the TV show, however, Lauren held the latest victim file in her hand. She combed through it for clues.

Feeling Nick's eyes on her, she glanced up in his direction.

"You going to tell me what the hell's going on?" he asked as he muted the television.

Lauren slid her glasses on top of her head and took a deep breath. There was no use trying to keep him in the dark any longer. They didn't keep secrets from one another, and he always knew when something was amiss. "Nick, I think I may know who The Phantom is," she blurted out.

His face hardened, and his eyebrow raised skeptically. "How?"

"In my visions, I always smell cologne. When I left Jo's

wedding, I hugged Skylar. It was the exact same smell. In the visions, I've always been able to see the killer's eyes. I've never really looked at Skylar's eyes, though. Still, I think it's very possible that The Phantom and Skylar could be the same person."

"Any proof?" Nick asked.

"No, but that's what we're working on, right?"

"Absolutely," Nick agreed.

"I think he really messed up this time, though," Lauren continued. "With the fibers from the trunk of the car, we can get the make and model. That should narrow things down slightly. If the fibers match a car belonging to Skylar, then we've got him. We can get a warrant to search the car."

Nick nodded. "True." He squinted. "There's more?"

"I am going to go to Jo. I'm going to do as much fact-finding as I can. I'm going to figure this out before anyone else has to die," Lauren said with conviction.

"You do realize that we have his handwriting," Nick asked.

Her mouth dropped open. "From the cipher. Yes. That's perfect."

"We still need probable cause to collect a writing sample from him, though. Your visions aren't going to be enough."

"I know that, too. And if I pick anything up from Jo and Skylar's, it won't be admissible."

A grave expression colored her face, and tears welled in her eyes. Nick moved closer to her, her legs across his lap. He reached out to her and touched her cheek. "Hey, hey, Doc. Listen to me. We're going to get this guy. We've been patient this long, right?

You've got to hang in there. I've learned to trust your judgment, and if you think that Skylar is our guy, then I believe you. But we need solid proof."

She nodded. "Well, I will get it. I swear I will."

59

Lauren sat at Jo's kitchen table with a cup of coffee in her grasp. She put the mug to her lips and took a sip.

The quiet of the house was almost deafening. The ticking of the clock on the kitchen wall gave off an unsettling vibe as Lauren looked at Jo. "Where's Skylar?" she asked curiously.

"Always working," Jo answered as she took a drink of coffee. "I'm so glad you decided to visit me. I get sort of lonely when Skylar's gone. But the hospital is usually calling me for something."

"Did you have a nice time on your honeymoon?" Lauren asked kindly.

"Oh yes. Rio was beautiful."

Lauren examined Jo for any new jewelry. Perhaps Skylar gave some of his trophies to her. If that were true, it would break the case wide open. The evidence would be in plain sight and fair game for the authorities. Still, Lauren didn't see anything.

"So when are you and Nick going to tie the knot?" Jo asked curiously.

"Oh no. No knots for me." Lauren shook her head resistively.

"Well, why not?"

"I'm just not the marrying kind," she answered lightly.

"Nick seems to be a very good man."

"Oh, he is," Lauren agreed. "I just don't think I want to get married. To anyone. Ever."

"You may change your mind," Jo said as she put the coffee back down on the table.

"I highly doubt that I will change my mind," Lauren argued. Changing the subject, Lauren feigned discomfort. "Do you mind if we go sit in your living room? I think I've overstretched doing yoga. I need a softer place to sit."

"Sure," Jo said accommodatingly. They stood from the table and went to the living room. Lauren sat down on the sofa in front of the large picture window. Hanging above the fireplace was a beautiful painting. It depicted a farmhouse in the snow. There were knickknacks scattered about, too. Jo and Lauren shared similar interests in antiques and primitive décor.

Unable to take her eyes off the painting, Lauren stood and walked to it. She gazed at it, almost spellbound by the print. Suddenly, a flash of one of the victims entered her mind. She saw the basement and smelled the musty odor.

Pointing to the painting, Lauren said, "This is just absolutely lovely."

"Oh, thank you. That's actually Skylar's family farm."

"He has a farm? Where?"

"It's in southern Ohio. His grandparents owned it when he was growing up. His parents inherited it. When they moved to Florida, they left it to Skylar. That's actually where he lived when I met him. Of course, when we moved in together, he didn't stay there anymore. He still keeps it up, though."

"Does he farm the land?"

"Oh goodness gracious, no. He doesn't have the time," Jo replied with a smile. "But he does lease the land to other folks. No one lives in the house right now, but he is constantly there, it seems. It constantly needs repair. There's an old barn that he is working on restoring, too. It's just a lot of work. I know it makes him feel closer to his grandparents, though. He says he has a lot of good memories there. So I don't protest about it too much."

"Has he ever taken you there?"

Jo thought for a moment. "You know, he never has. I never really asked to visit, and he never offered."

Lauren tried to hide her suspicion. Still facing the painting, she continued in a happy tone. "Where in southern Ohio is this place, Jo?"

"I think it's in Minford."

Lauren nodded. "I know exactly where that is. It's about forty-five minutes to an hour from Shawnee State Forest, where my family and I used to visit quite frequently."

"Didn't The Phantom bury a body there?" Jo asked.

With an open-mouthed nod, still fixated on the painting, Lauren replied, "Yes. He did."

Lauren wondered if Jo might be in on the murders. Could she be lying to cover for Skylar? Surely not. Lauren had known Jo to always be an honest, moral person. She was a doctor, for Christ's sake.

She continued as she turned and went back to the couch.

"That serial killer has the college campuses practically shut down," Jo continued. "Everyone is panicked."

"I can imagine," Lauren said with a nod. She picked at her cuticles as the doubt took over. Skylar certainly had the opportunity to commit the murders, but she felt shame for wondering if her close friend might be a part of it. Was it plausible?

The phone buzzing startled both of them, and they jumped slightly. A text message came through from Nick. It read: Fibers match a late-model Ford Taurus. Concrete matched the highway near where the body was found.

"Everything okay?" Jo asked.

Lauren looked up with a closed-lip smile. "Oh yes. Everything is fine." She rebounded quickly. "Can I take a look at your garage? I'm thinking about doing some updates to mine. I'm wondering if I can get some ideas from looking at yours. I know you recently did a remodel of that space."

"Sure," Jo said, jumping up from the couch.

They walked through the house to the garage. Lauren stood in the middle of the room, pretending to admire the newly renovated area. Only Jo's car sat in the three-car attached garage.

"So does Skylar drive your car or his own when he goes to the universities? I know your car is probably a lot better on gasoline since it's newer," Lauren inquired.

Jo shook her head. "No. Skylar prefers to take his own car. Between us, we have three cars."

"I didn't know that."

"Well, there's mine," she said, gesturing toward the Ford Excursion. "And then he has his work car that he takes to the farm. It belonged to his parents, but they signed it over when they moved. Then we bought a new car within the last few months."

"I see," Lauren nodded, still trying to appear nonchalant.

"His parents' car is a clunker. I'm ashamed he still has it," Jo said with a chuckle.

"What sort of car is it?"

"Mmm," she said as she rubbed her forehead, trying to recall the make and model. "I know it's a Ford. That's all the man buys. I can't think of the name of it."

Lauren waited as Jo tried to come up with the information. "Where is it?" she asked curiously.

"Well, like I said, he usually drives it to the farm. It's probably there in the barn. Honestly, I think he keeps that car for sentimental reasons. It's really not in the best shape," Jo said, amusingly.

"But I thought you just said he uses it to go to the farm."

"Well, yes and no. He usually drives the Excursion to the farm, and then when he runs errands and works with the people who lease the land from him, he drives that hunk of junk around."

Lauren laughed candidly, trying to keep the mood light. Inside, she felt like screaming.

"Does Skylar ever talk to you about his interest in The Phantom? Each time we've met up, he's always so fascinated by the situation. Always asking about the investigation," Lauren added.

"He says he thinks you'll never catch the guy," Jo replied. "He thinks that if the guy has stayed under the radar this long, you'll probably never figure out who's killing those co-eds."

"And what do you think?" Lauren asked curiously.

Jo folded her arms, but not in a defensive posture. She contemplated the question for a moment and then replied, "I've seen you work, Lauren. You've solved the unsolvable. I know that it's a matter of time before you figure it out. You are the only person I've ever met who could solve a cold case in less than a year. Most detectives spend decades on one case."

Lauren pursed her lips. "Will you do me a favor?"

"Anything," Jo replied.

"The next time Skylar says anything about The Phantom, will you remind him that I'm smarter?" she concluded with a wink and a smile.

60

The Thanksgiving holiday rolled around. To change things up a bit, Lauren and Nick offered to host dinner. They were excited to have everyone over for the day.

The weather was still warm, so the children ran around outside, belly-flopping in leaves and enjoying the last bit of warmth before the snow began to fall. The adults took advantage of the nice weather, too, by sitting on the patio, socializing and eating.

Jill brought her boyfriend, Kevin, and his sixteen-year-old daughter, Rachel. He and Rachel were the only new faces among them, and they were not exactly new. Everyone had gotten to know them over the last couple of months, but the holiday was the first big event he was able to attend.

Oddly, Brandon and Chelsey kept to themselves. The tension in the air was almost tangible. Lauren, nevertheless, did not want to pry.

Finally, after a couple of hours, Brandon stood to his feet, taking Chelsey's hand in his. She stood beside him, her head on his shoulder. He cleared his throat and put one hand in his jeans pocket. The adults quieted as the children's laughter carried on the wind.

"We have an announcement to make," Brandon began.

"We're pregnant," Chelsey said with a shrug and a toothy smile.

The cheers mingled with the clapping made Lauren smile as she stood and made her way to Chelsey. She embraced her. Chelsey's small frame trembled against Lauren. With a scowl, Lauren pulled away and met Chelsey's gaze.

After Nick congratulated them, Lauren made an excuse for Chelsey to come inside with her. They walked through the house and onto the front porch, where they sat in the swing together.

"You're going to be a mom," Lauren said.

"Scary, huh?" Chelsey said as she dropped her gaze and fidgeted.

"If it's what you want, right? I mean, that's all that matters."

"I figured Mom and Dad would blow a gasket because we're not married," she remarked.

"Your parents are more open-minded than you give them credit," Lauren argued.

"I'm not ready for this," Chelsey said as tears filled her eyes.

"From what I gather, no one ever is," Lauren replied. She took Chelsey's hand into hers. "Aren't you happy about this?"

"I'm just afraid," she admitted with another half-hearted shrug.

"Are you going to finish school?"

"Yes. I can't quit now. I only have a year left."

"That's a wise decision, Chelsey."

"Brandon wants to get a job with the FBI. He is hoping Nick can help him. Brandon is supposed to talk to Nick today," she added.

"Don't forget that your family isn't here to judge you. We're here to support you," Lauren reassured her.

As Lauren put her arm around Chelsey's shoulder and pulled her in close, she hoped that she could provide some sort of comfort to her. She truly wanted things to work out. However, Lauren knew that the battle ahead would be a tough one for the young couple.

Becoming a parent had never been on Lauren's radar. She had always assumed she would be alone. If she was honest with herself, she could not imagine being a mother. She truly wished the best for her niece and Brandon, but taking on the role of a parent was not for her.

61

As the day grew older, everyone went their separate ways. The exhaustion from spending the holiday with the family overwhelmed both Nick and Lauren. They both felt a little frazzled.

"How's a bath sound?" he asked as he walked up the stairs to the second floor.

"I think that sounds fantastic," she replied as she followed him up.

They undressed, and Lauren ran the water into the garden-style tub. She felt the warmth of Nick behind her as he brushed her hair to the side and kissed the crook of her neck. She smiled as a sense of satisfaction settled on her.

Nick took her hand and helped her step into the water. He followed. As they settled in, their legs weaved together, the heat from the water soaking into their pores. Lauren rested her head on a bath pillow as Nick admired her. Feeling his stare, she asked, "What?"

"The whole thing with Brandon and Chelsey got me thinking," Nick admitted. "Do you know we've never talked about having kids or getting married?"

"We've never had to talk about it," she answered as she kept her eyes closed.

"Do you ever think about having kids with me?" he asked bluntly.

She raised her head and opened her eyes. "Honestly, no." From the scowl on Nick's face, Lauren knew she'd hurt his feelings.

"It's not you, Bennette. It's me," she added, hoping to lighten the mood. "I just never thought of myself as the mothering kind. I never really saw myself having children."

"Ever?"

"Well, I never really saw myself in a long-term relationship either, but here I am."

"So, how do you feel about children now?"

"I like children. I love my nieces and nephews. I think Tommy is an amazing little boy. I think children can add value to a couple's journey," she replied.

"What about having children with me?" he asked, still probing.

"Nick," she said with seriousness in her tone, "what are you asking? Just come out with it."

With a heavy sigh, he rolled his eyes slightly and then made eye contact with her. "I want to know if you love me enough for a bigger commitment."

"Isn't what we have enough?"

"It is for now."

"Well, then why fix something that isn't broken?"

"So, you don't want marriage or kids?" he asked as his tone changed.

Lauren sighed. "As I said, I haven't given it much thought. I am quite happy with our relationship the way it is. I think what we have is very stable and healthy. I am very satisfied with the current state of affairs. Aren't you?"

He shook his head and looked down at the water. "I guess I just thought that the ultimate way to show you how much I love you and how committed I am to you would be to ask you to marry me."

"But you don't need to. I don't need that from you. I know you are loyal to me. I know we are committed to each other. We don't have to be married for you to prove that."

"Did you ever think I want marriage? That I might need a commitment like that from you?"

"Why do you feel that way?" she asked.

"Because I grew up believing that if you loved someone, you married them. You had kids with them. You made a life with them. A family."

There were no words. She didn't respond.

He quickly got up and grabbed the towel off the floor. He stepped out and dried off. After wrapping the towel around his waist, he walked out and closed the bathroom door behind him.

Lauren could see he was upset with her, but she didn't really understand why. She stayed in the tub a few minutes more and then drained the water. She grabbed her cotton pajamas from the hanger on the door and slipped them on.

The bedroom was empty when she walked in. She heard the sound of the television in the living room, so she walked down the stairs and into that space. Nick sat on the couch watching a basketball game. He wore his plaid pajama pants and a black V-neck T-shirt.

Lauren walked around the back of the couch and then sat down on the opposite end. Her body situated on the edge of the couch, she examined Nick for context clues. "I've made you angry," she began.

"I'm sorry."

Nick glanced at her briefly. "I'm not angry. I'm more disappointed than anything. I've been the only one in this relationship who's given any thought to a lifetime commitment with kids," he explained. "I know you. So, I should have guessed that it hadn't crossed your mind."

"That sounds so awful. It's not like that," she protested.

He shifted his weight and turned to her. "Do you understand how much I love you? How much I want you?" He paused as he waited for a reaction. She sat stock-still, so he kept going. "Do you understand how lost I'd be if you weren't in my life?"

"Why are you so preoccupied with this? Is it because of Brandon and Chelsey?" Confusion colored her expression. "You have me, Bennette. I don't need a ring or a piece of paper for that. I don't plan on going anywhere. There is no one on this earth I want to be with."

"I want more."

She shook her head. "What more could you want? And I'm not capable of more right now. I'm sorry," she admitted. "I love you. I know that with everything that I am. I hope that's enough for now." She paused and narrowed her gaze. "I know why your anxiety is getting the best of you."

"Why's that?" he said with venom in his tone.

"It's Skylar." Lauren waited for confirmation, but Nick didn't provide any. "Everything will be fine. There is an officer constantly posted outside the house. And I think you forget that I'm quite strong and an excellent shot."

"But you challenged him."

Confused, she tilted her head. "I don't understand."

"You told me that when you met with Jo, you told her to tell Skylar that the next time he brings up The Phantom being smart, you wanted her to remind him that you're smarter. You challenged him. He's going to rise to that challenge. I just know it."

Lauren listened silently as he kept on. "I'm a Catholic. I don't see things the way you do. I don't have visions. Even though I gave you a hard time about it when we first met, I do believe in intuition. I value it. My intuition tells me something terrible is going to happen. Don't ask me how I know, because I have no proof. I just know."

Lauren scooted closer to him and placed a gentle hand on his knee. She smiled serenely. "Nick, I'm very careful. I have taken extra precautions, especially after the cipher we received."

"I don't want to lose you," he said as his expression became more intense.

"You aren't going to," she said as she reached for his hand. "If something does happen to me, then go after Skylar with everything you've got. Jo told me he has a farm in Southern Ohio. I know if he takes me, that's exactly where I'll be. Once Jo realizes who he is, she'll help you find me. Just remember that. We have some evidence now. Use it."

"Come here," he said tenderly as he opened his arms to her.

She sank into him and put her head on his chest.

"I love you, Doc. Sometimes too much, I think."

"I don't think you can ever love anyone too much," she concluded.

62

Lauren sat at her desk in the study, typing on the computer. It had been a gorgeous Sunday, and she had spent the day writing, working diligently on a second novel. Now it was eight o'clock in the evening. Nick had been gone since before 5 a.m. He had been called to another scene on an unrelated case.

She looked at the photo of them sitting in a five-by-seven frame on her desk. It had been taken during one of the family gatherings. She couldn't believe this was her life. She never dreamed she would find someone who loved her the way Nick did.

As her fingers tapped the keys, she paused for a moment to check her outline. Suddenly, she heard the thud of a car door outside. She wondered if Nick might be arriving home, but he usually pulled into the garage.

She stood and walked down the stairs. The first floor was still empty, with no sign of Nick. She walked onto the porch to make sure the officer was still there. The horror of what she saw caught her completely by surprise. The officer was slumped over against the driver's side window. Then a hard blow to the back of her head came, and everything went dark.

A loud noise startled her awake, and disorientation clouded her mind. Then the shock of electricity surged through her body, and she convulsed. Her teeth chattered, and her head ached. The smell of singed hair and the sound of voltage deafened her.

The electrical current stopped. She tried desperately to catch her breath. As she scanned the room, the horrific reality of her situation settled upon her. She was in a small concrete room with no windows. She could only see one door. This wasn't the room she'd seen in her visions.

She looked down at herself, taking account of her physical well-being. She wore a pair of black lace panties and a matching bra. She wasn't wearing this when she was knocked out.

The sound of someone breathing caught her attention, and she turned her head. A figure with broad shoulders lurked in the shadows. As he came into the light, all of her suspicions were suddenly realized. Skylar smiled at her as he sat on the side of the bed. The smell of Armani cologne drifted to her nostrils, and her stomach sank.

Before she could speak, Skylar put a finger to her lips and hushed her. She jerked away and ignored his gesture. "I knew it was you," she slurred, still trying to recover from the electrical shock.

"You people are all about certainty. Your egos won't let you be wrong," he said as he stood and paced, obviously agitated. "You didn't tell anyone about your suspicions about me. Otherwise, I'd be in jail."

Lauren knew that letting him talk was the best way to survive. Arguing with him would only make him angrier. She had one goal right now, and that was to live. She wanted the opportunity to run, just like Riley. Staying quiet and agreeable was the best way to accomplish that.

When she didn't respond, he approached her angrily, placed his hand under her chin, and squeezed, forcing her mouth into a distorted O shape. "So quiet, Lauren?" he bit out. Then he let go and turned away from her.

"Nothing really to say, is there?" she replied.

"Do you know how long I've had my sights set on you?" he shouted, wringing his hands anxiously as he paced back and forth.

She shook her head, tears welling in her eyes. She didn't want to cry. It would make her seem weak. So she stayed silent.

"I've been tracking you for years. Years!" he yelled. "I watched your friendship with Jo, and because you seemed unattainable, I went for her. Even she rejected me at first, but I kept going, kept on her, and finally she broke. She let me into her life. She dated me for a long time without sharing it with you, but I got to know you quite well through her. I also got acquainted with the folks at BCI and the State Police. I have friends in high places, too, you know. Travis, your friend in tech support, he was my mentor. He didn't even know he was helping me master the art of deception."

"Why me, Skylar? Why am I so important?" she asked, desperation in her tone.

"Well, you inspire me, Dr. Harris," he said as he crossed his arms and leaned against the cinderblock wall.

"How?"

"Your case studies are absolutely fascinating. You walked out of situations you should have died in. Then, to read the case study about your parents, that topped it all off for me. I knew that I had to get your attention somehow. You didn't get it, though. Even after I started taking the girls on the eighteenth, you didn't get it."

"My birthday?"

"Yes, you stupid bitch!" he exclaimed as he lunged toward her and slapped her face. "I started in the spring, preparing to celebrate your birthday in June. I had to be perfect for you."

Lauren felt more confused. It was now December. He had never killed during the winter months. Besides that, Skylar simply wasn't making sense. However, she knew from years of work in the field that it didn't have to make sense to her for it to be completely rational in his mind.

He walked to the bed and sat down. "I've waited a long time for you, but when Jo told me what you said to her about The Phantom, bragging about how you were smarter, well, that just felt like an open invitation."

He leaned in and kissed her collarbone. She closed her eyes, attempting to block out the sensation of his lips on her body. "Every time I've slept with Jo, I've seen your face. Now that I have you, I'll show you that I'm better than Nick."

She felt his finger slowly move down her stomach and to the top of her panties. "I've watched you kiss him," he whispered. "I've watched you with him. I know I'm better than him."

He pulled away slightly, hoping to see fear in her eyes, but she defied him and hardened her expression. Her eyes slowly moved to meet his. "You may take this body, but it won't be me. You can rape me. You can beat me. You can even kill me, but someone will avenge me," she said softly. "That's what I've done my whole life. I've given a voice to those who can no longer speak. Someone else will do the same for me. I have faith in that."

Rage flared in his eyes as he stood abruptly and flipped a switch. A jolt surged through her, rattling the shackles against the metal frame, before everything plunged into darkness.

63

It seemed like an eternity had passed when her eyes struggled to open again. She lay flat on the bed, still shackled. Her ankles were also bound by metal restraints. She was spread-eagle on the dirty mattress underneath her.

She closed her eyes again and saw Nick's face in her mind. She thought about how he'd confessed his love to her. Guilt rested heavily on her shoulders. She could have at least tried to understand where he was coming from. He loved her enough to marry her. He wanted children with her. And all she could do was defiantly disagree.

The memory of how unreceptive she'd been pained her. Tears fell from her eyes and into her hair. She had left everything undone. She was no different than any of the other victims. They had left things undone, too. All she wanted right now was the opportunity to make things right with Nick. She wanted to take him in her arms and tell him how sorry she was. She realized that she might never see him again. That thought made her nauseous.

Opening her eyes once more, the sensation of cool hands on her ankles shifted her attention. Then she felt Skylar's lips on her calves and then her outer thighs. She had wondered how long it would be until the assault. Now, faced with it, she steeled herself as Skylar hovered over her and pushed her panties to the side.

Immediately, she separated from her body. She shut her brain down and went to another place. It didn't matter, though. She still heard her own cries, and she still felt the pain of the violation. Thankfully, it ended quickly, until she felt the sharp bite, teeth sinking into the inside of her thigh.

Things quieted for a moment. She closed her eyes, proud that she'd made it through the rape. Then she felt searing pain where he had bitten her. She screamed as the agony intensified. "Oh my God," she shouted. "What the hell are you doing?"

"Salt," he answered dispassionately.

He bit her so hard that he broke the skin. Now he mashed a handful of salt into the bite mark as a form of torture. Sweat poured from her body as she began to hyperventilate. Then came the electricity again. A part of her longed for death. Still, she had to fight. She had too much to lose.

After several hours of torture and rape, Skylar propped her up against the headboard again. Her body limp with fatigue, she barely held her head up. Hunger and dehydration started setting in. She was losing track of time, too.

He sat down on the side of the bed with a bowl of soup in his grasp. He put the spoon to her lips, and she swallowed, wondering if it was poisoned.

Before he put the next spoonful of liquid to her mouth, she looked at him with rage in her gaze. As strongly as she could, she asked, "Why nourish me if you're going to break me?"

"Well, if you haven't got your health, you haven't got anything," he answered.

Lauren tried to rely on her training and her understanding of the criminal mind. He was undoubtedly brilliant but walked the fine line between genius and insanity. She wanted to understand his needs and desires to build rapport and trust. Still, his need for power and dominance would outweigh anything she could possibly do to ensure her survival.

64

Lauren lost track of time as she remained in the confines of captivity. Skylar nourished her with food, walked her around the basement to keep her active, and gave her water to drink. At gunpoint, he allowed her to bathe. She was permitted to relieve herself a few times a day.

He raped her repeatedly. He electrocuted her. He bit her again and again and then poured salt into the broken skin, always dressing her injuries afterward.

Lauren quickly realized that two entirely different people lived in Skylar's body. He was truly a Jekyll and Hyde. The less dominant personality was calm and understanding, nurturing even. The violent personality emerged for the torture and abuse.

When left alone with her thoughts, Lauren remained restrained. She cried a lot and thought about her parents. She was thankful they'd died. Living through her disappearance and murder would have surely killed them.

Despite Lauren's criticism of religion, she prayed. She wasn't sure what she prayed to, but the sentiment was what mattered to her. She missed her family. She was thankful for all of the time she'd spent with them.

She thought of Nick. She wanted to feel his arms around her. She longed to hear the soft baritone of his voice. The conversation they'd had haunted her. She wanted to take it all back.

Sometimes the anger swelled inside her, and she screamed as loudly as she could. Although she knew no one would ever hear her, the release made her feel better. The rage she felt toward Skylar was immeasurable. She couldn't believe this was her fate. However, she realized that the other victims likely felt the same way before they'd died.

Her wrists were cut from the shackles. Occasionally, she pulled hard at them, the metal digging even deeper into her flesh. She played out every single scenario in her head that might lead to her freedom. Nevertheless, she came up empty every single time.

Each time Skylar took her to the bathroom or allowed her to shower, she thought about overpowering him. She knew exactly how to defend herself. She was biding her time, though. She knew a perfect time would present itself. She just had to remain patient.

65

Skylar walked through the door with a bottle of water in his hand. Taking the key hanging from a chain around his neck, he unlocked the shackles and replaced them with zip ties, just as he always did.

"Are you thirsty?" he asked.

She nodded.

"I brought you some water," he said kindly.

Relief swept over her as she realized the more compassionate personality was present.

He put the bottle to her lips and let her drink. She drank as much as she could and then took a breath. "Thank you," she said.

He touched her face with the palm of his hand. "You truly are beautiful, Lauren."

She smiled in response.

"I need to wash your face. Today's the day," he said as he stood and put the bottle of water on a small wooden end table. Strolling to a cabinet, he opened the metal doors, a loud clanging sound echoing through the room. He pulled out a washcloth and then closed the doors.

"What is today?" she asked.

He walked toward the sink in the room and began running water over the cloth. "It's time," he replied as he shut off the water and walked back to the mattress. He sat on the side of the bed and began cleaning Lauren's face.

"Time for what, Skylar?" she asked curiously.

"It's time to hunt," he answered as he smiled sardonically.

Knowing exactly what he meant, she tried to remain calm. She didn't want him to think he'd rattled her.

He finished cleaning her face and stood. He walked to the sink again and neatly hung the cloth over the bowl. Making his way back to the end table, he grabbed the bottle of water and then walked back to the mattress. "Take one more drink and then we need to go. It's getting late," he ordered.

He put the bottle up to her lips again. She drank as much as she could. Her chance to escape was coming, and she needed to be hydrated.

Zip ties still binding her, Skylar stood her to her feet. The concrete was cold against her bare feet. He guided her to the door and opened it. Darkness surrounded them, and the sounds of the forest were louder than usual.

She saw the dark-colored Ford Excursion with the double doors gaping open. Skylar scooped her up into his arms and then placed her inside and slammed the door shut. She didn't beg. She didn't talk. She simply waited for the chance to run.

As he drove further into the night, Lauren lay silently in the back. She brushed her face and head against the carpeted trunk, hoping to pick up fibers and to leave skin cells behind.

She felt the vehicle come to a stop and heard the car door slam. A few brief moments passed before Skylar opened the back. Behind him, stars lit up the sky. The harvest moon hung brightly in the night sky. The smell of fresh pine drifted in the air.

Wearing lab gear and shoe covers, Skylar picked her up again and carried her deep into the dark forest. The leaves crunched as they went further and further in. Finally, he put her down. She looked up at the moon, trying to estimate what time it was. Most of all, she was trying to figure out what direction she should run. Which way would lead her toward the highway?

Lauren listened as the leaves crunched under his feet. She strained to hear water. She had hiked many times in this very forest, but never when it was dark. She knew her way just fine in daylight, but she was incredibly disoriented. There were no distinct clues for her to even guess where she might be in the vast forest.

Still gazing up at the sky, she felt his stare and turned toward him. The sociopathic monster had emerged once more. He set her on her feet and cut her restraints. She stood in her bra and underwear as the moonlight danced on her skin.

With a blank look, "Run, bitch," he said in a whisper.

Without being told twice, she turned abruptly and ran as fast as her weakened legs could carry her. She dodged trees but felt the branches scraping against her skin. The leaves and the forest floor felt muddy and slick as she sprinted forward. Several times she lost her balance and fell, tumbling farther into the darkness. She recovered quickly, however, and finally caught the sound of running water nearby. She made that her goal. Get to the water.

Suddenly, she felt the hair on her head pull taut. Unable to stay steady, she fell backward into Skylar's arms. He threw her to the ground and ripped her panties from her body. He penetrated her again as she screamed for mercy. He quickly covered her mouth and held her wrists tightly to the ground. She struggled to get loose, the dampness of the ground aiding her in slipping one of her hands from his grasp. She scratched him, hoping to make contact with his skin. She wasn't sure if she did.

Angered by her own physical weakness, she kicked, but it was to no avail. He was stronger than her, even at her best. Still, she kicked as much as she could and thrashed hard against him. Enraged by her defiance, he pinned her again and went at her harder. She felt her insides ripping as he thrust himself into her again and again. The pain made her wonder if she might split in two. When he finished, he grabbed a handful of her hair and beat her head against the hard ground, knocking her unconscious.

66

She opened her eyes, surrounded by darkness. The only thing she could compare it to was when she had cave-dived in college. It had been the most intense darkness she had ever experienced. She ran her fingers over her body, feeling her clammy skin. He must have put her panties back on because she was wearing them. She felt the smooth surface under her and instantly knew there would be a lighter somewhere within reach. Finally, she found it and flicked it, the small flame illuminating everything.

Dirt surrounded her on every side. Just as he had done with his other victims, Skylar buried Lauren alive. She didn't know how long she had been unconscious or how much more time she had to breathe. Either way, she knew her life would end if her team didn't find her.

She felt something else against her skin. It was a piece of paper held tightly against her bra strap. She held the light close so she could see it. She opened the paper and read it. "Smile. He's watching you," was written on it. Her gaze narrowed as she held the lighter. She didn't understand the message.

The heat from the flame burned her thumb, so she let it go out. She peered into the darkness and finally saw a red blinking light right above her. Skylar had built this coffin very differently than the others. The main chamber was where Lauren lay. On top of it was another compartment. It housed a camera. That meant either he was watching her, a feed was being sent to her team, or both. Still, someone out there was looking at her, watching her die.

As she lay in the deafening silence, she realized that her capture wasn't just about her. It was about her team, and most of all, it was about Nick. She knew that Skylar was playing a game. He always had been. In this game, Nick was also a victim. It was the ultimate way to show that he was in control. Simply sending GPS coordinates wouldn't render Skylar's intended reaction. Filming her death, making it seem she was within reach, was the ultimate torture.

She knew not to hyperventilate once the realizations had sunk in. Instead, she closed her eyes as tears fell from the corners of her eyes and into her hair. Frustration and rage welled up inside her, and she screamed as loudly as she possibly could.

67

Nick turned onto the street, anxious to see Lauren. He hated getting called away from her on a weekend. He looked at the clock in the car as it turned over to midnight.

He spotted the sheriff's cruiser in front of the house, but there was no movement. He pulled into the driveway, fully prepared to confront the officer on duty, especially if he was asleep in his car.

His feet hit the pavement, and he started toward the vehicle. As he approached it, he realized something wasn't right. Then he heard sirens in the subdivision as they grew closer. The shock made his heart sink to his knees.

Blood pooled in the lap of the deputy. He'd been shot in the temple. Nick suddenly felt as if he had been hurled into a scene from a horror movie. He knew exactly what had happened.

Another cruiser sped toward the house and skidded to a stop. The sheriff's deputy jumped out and ran to Nick.

"We gotta find her. He took her," Nick began.

"Hey, buddy," he started, "let's just calm down for a minute and go inside."

"We can't go in. It's a crime scene. We have to get a team out here, and they have to go through the house to see if there's any evidence first." His thoughts raced. "I gotta call... I need to call Lisa... and Chris... and her family." He paced. "Damn it to hell!" he shouted.

In his moment of weakness, he dropped to his knees on the front lawn. Tears streamed down his face as helplessness covered him like a shroud. The reality he now found himself in caused him to shake. A thousand horrible scenarios rushed through his brain. One thing was certain. Lauren was in incredible danger, and right now Nick was powerless to save her.

Within an hour, a forensics team descended on Lauren's house. Chris, as well as others, combed for evidence. They were joined by state and federal teams as well. They were desperate to find something that might point them in the right direction.

Nick waited outside with Deputy Skiver. He gave a statement as to his whereabouts that day. He also recalled the last time he spoke to Lauren. Leaning against the Suburban, he waited to see if the teams had any luck in their quest to collect evidence. When he saw Chris walking out the front door shaking his head, Nick knew they were no closer to finding Lauren.

"Nothing?" Nick asked.

Chris pursed his lips. "Not a damn thing, Nick," he replied. "I'm sorry. There's not even a sign of a struggle. I'm not sure how he got past her or the security system. He must have knocked her out, because she'd kick his ass otherwise."

"I can't just stand here and do nothing."

"You have to tell her family," Chris said as he put his hand on Nick's shoulder.

Nick stared blankly into Chris's face. "I know who did this," he said quietly.

"Who?" Chris asked as he scowled.

"Skylar Collins."

"How do you know that?"

"Lauren figured it out," he replied. "We collected fibers from Riley's body that matched a late-model Ford Taurus. Lauren said that…" Nick stopped himself. He realized he was about to refer to a dead person as a primary witness. He couldn't reveal Lauren's secret. "Skylar is The Phantom."

"You'd better get some proof fast," Chris concluded as he started toward his car. He threw his kit into the passenger-side seat and closed the door. He locked eyes with Nick. "If you don't find evidence, then we have absolutely nothing to go on."

68

At 1:30 a.m., the Harris family gathered at Ingrid's. Cora and Holly stayed home with the children. Everyone else sat in the living room, anxiously waiting for Nick to tell them why they were all called out in the middle of the night. Chelsey and Brandon stood by the picture window, watching the sheriff's cruisers circle the block.

"What is going on, Nick?" Jim demanded gruffly.

"Lauren's been taken," he replied.

The collective gasp felt deafening. Instantly, Annie was brought to tears as Morgan held her close.

"What do you mean that she's been taken?" Ingrid asked.

"The Phantom took her. I had to go out on another case really early yesterday morning. I got home a little after midnight. The deputy who was posted in front of the house was shot in the head. Lauren's been taken. The forensic teams couldn't find any evidence of a struggle, and no trace was collected. I don't know where the hell she is, but I promise you, I will find her," he decreed as the tears welled in his eyes. "I will not rest until I find her," he vowed.

By 2:30 a.m., Nick was on the phone with Travis, discussing options to trace her cell phone or any other electronic devices she may have taken with her. Although she'd left her laptop behind, Nick hadn't found her cell.

He realized he didn't have a warrant yet. Still, he asked Travis to pull everything he could about Skylar Collins.

By 3:30 a.m., Nick phoned Selina and Lisa. He debriefed them on the situation. It was all hands on deck. He knew that the clock was ticking. The longer Lauren stayed missing, the less chance she'd be found alive. The only comfort he had was that Skylar kept his victims alive for a little while before he killed them.

With the house finally cleared, Nick settled back in as best he could. The clock chimed 4 a.m. as he stood in front of the fireplace. Every once in a while, he paced. Brandon watched the teams still working to collect evidence from the cruisers out front. Chelsey sat on the couch, feeling rather helpless.

Finally, Brandon turned to Nick and walked to him. With a gentle hand on his shoulder, he said, "Brother, you've got to get some sleep. Staying awake isn't going to find her any faster."

Nick shrugged as a helpless expression colored his face. "I can't sleep without her beside me anymore."

Chelsey stood and walked to them. "Listen to me," she said as she made eye contact with Nick. "Lauren's a fighter. She's had to be. She's strategic, too. She will be alive. She won't let this psychopath kill her. She'll fight."

"She may not have the chance to fight," Nick said sadly.

69

Nick had been up for over twenty-four hours. He started drinking coffee around 5 a.m. to stay alert, but the adrenaline coursing through his veins did the rest.

It was 9 a.m. as Nick stood in Travis's workspace in Columbus. Lisa and Chris stood beside him as Travis researched Skylar Collins.

"You know without a warrant, none of this is admissible," Travis said as he typed frantically.

"Yes, I know," Nick answered. The clear annoyance caught everyone's attention.

"I just can't believe he'd do this," Travis admitted. "He has always been such a nice guy. So helpful."

"I'm telling you, he's our guy," Nick replied. "I just need probable cause for a warrant. I think the fibers are a good start, but I feel like the prosecutor and judge will want more."

"Well, from a personal knowledge base, I can tell ya that Skylar is a hacker. That means he's smart enough to cover his tracks. He's probably covered his tracks."

"The bastard has to have a driver's license, Social Security number, taxes," Nick remarked. "Find it, Travis. Find what I need."

"I have to hack into whatever he's done. That takes time."

Nick turned on his heel and threw his hands up. "She doesn't have time!" he shouted.

Lisa stepped in. She put her hands on his shoulders in an attempt to calm him. "Nicholas, you have to hold it together. I think maybe we should put another agent on this."

"Are you kidding me?" he asked, his eyebrows raised, his arms now folded.

"You're too close to this," she said.

"I have followed this son of a bitch for over a year. I've seen how he kills. Lauren understood why. Our partnership is what made this work. We wouldn't even be here right now if it wasn't for her profile and the work we've done."

"It's also what got her taken," Chris interjected.

Nick turned to him. His eyes filled with fury. He pointed at him and lunged forward. "Are you blaming us? You think Lauren somehow caused all of this?" he exclaimed.

"I cannot work with you screaming, Nick," Travis shouted. "You've got to go away. Get some distance. This is going to take some time."

Lisa walked out of the room with Nick. "You have got to sleep," she said.

"I can't sleep," he admitted. "All I keep seeing in my mind are those girls and how they looked when we found them. I don't want to see her like that. I can't." Tears fell from his eyes as he pinched the bridge of his nose.

"We're a good team," Lisa encouraged. "This is what we do. We solve crimes. We'll get this guy, too. I know we will. The fibers should be enough for a warrant."

"I want more. I want to be sure I can nail his ass to the wall," Nick argued.

"Let Travis do what he does. He'll find something."

"But will she be alive when we do?" Nick asked.

70

After sitting down on the couch just outside the lab, Nick gave in to his exhaustion. He drifted off into a dreamless sleep, but he was shaken awake. Travis stood in front of him. Nick sat up and rubbed his eyes.

"How long have I been out?" he asked.

"It's 11:30," Travis replied.

"At night?"

"No, in the morning."

"Did you find anything?" Nick asked.

"I found a registration for the Ford Taurus. It's in someone else's name. A Velma Collins of Minford, Ohio."

"Who's Velma Collins?" Nick asked.

"Looks like his grandmother. I had to hack into several programs to even find it. She owned a Taurus. I think maybe she died and didn't transfer the title."

"Then how does he drive it? How's the registration still good?"

He shrugged.

Selina burst through the door at the end of the hallway with Liam trailing behind. She rushed to Nick and threw her arms around him. The sobs came in an uncontrollable pattern as they held the embrace.

Once she composed herself, she pulled away, with Liam draping his arm around her shoulders. "Have you figured anything out?" she asked.

"We're working on it," Nick answered.

Liam took a backpack off his shoulder and gave it to Selina. She unzipped it and pulled out some clothing. "I brought you a fresh set of clothes," she said.

"How'd you get into the house?"

"Lauren gave me the security code."

He gave a half-hearted smile and took the clothing from her. "Thanks."

"There are toiletries in the backpack, too. I knew you would probably want a shower, and I also knew you wouldn't leave the lab."

"I appreciate it."

"Hey, man," Liam added, "if there's anything we can do, you tell us. We'll do it."

"Thanks," Nick said as he pursed his lips. "I think I'll go get that shower. Maybe grab something to eat."

"I can go pick something up for you," Liam offered.

"That'd be great."

As Nick stood in the shower at the lab, he closed his eyes, letting the hot water cascade over his body. With his hands against the shower wall, he hung there, drenching his hair. He tried not to think about the possibilities. He just wanted Lauren home with him. To feel her in his arms again. He couldn't afford to panic. He had to stay calm and focused for her.

The day grew older, and after drying off and dressing again, Nick, Liam, and Selina spent the rest of the day combing through case files, trying to find something he may have missed. They sat at the large metal table with files strewn all over.

Travis burst through the door. "You won't believe it!" he exclaimed.

Nick stood expectantly.

"Skylar transferred the title of the car into Jo's name yesterday. It takes twenty-four hours to upload. That's why it didn't show up this morning."

"So the car's registered in her name now?"

"Yes. I already called Cindy with Trace and Iris with the Federal Crime Lab. They reran all of the tests, and they can confirm with certainty that the fibers in evidence match the vehicle that is now in Jo's name. You have to run with this, Nick. We don't have time to wait on more evidence. This will be good enough to at least allow you to question her. Maybe not get a warrant to search the car, but this seems pretty solid to me."

Nick grabbed his jacket from the back of the chair and put it on. "It gives me a way in for sure. I don't need a warrant either. I can just have a conversation with her. Anything in plain sight is fair game."

Liam stood. "I'm going with you," he said. "This is my case, too."

71

Liam and Nick stood on the front porch waiting. They heard footfalls inside growing louder as they neared the front door. It swung open, and Jo greeted them with a smile. "Hey, guys," she started. "Come on in. What's up?"

They nodded and walked into the foyer. "Lauren's missing," Nick blurted out.

"Oh my God," she said as her eyes widened. "Come in, please. Sit down," she said, motioning toward the living room.

Nick glanced around. He desperately wanted to find something that might lead them to an arrest warrant.

"What happened?" she asked as she sat down on the couch.

"Not sure," Nick answered.

"Do you think it's The Phantom?" she asked.

Nick settled into an empty recliner, leaning forward with his forearms resting on his knees. He clasped his hands together, striving to project an air of patience. Liam sat down on the far end of the couch.

"We think so," Liam answered as he nodded.

Nick cleared his throat. "Jo, where is Skylar?" he asked candidly.

"Well, he was here yesterday. I had to meet him so he could sign his grandmother's car over to me," she replied lightly.

"Why did he do that?" Liam asked.

"I really didn't question it," Jo answered with a shrug.

"Why didn't you question it? Isn't that strange?" Nick asked, a clip in his tone.

"I… I really didn't think about it. He wanted to do it, so we did."

"Do you do everything he asks you to do?" Nick bit out.

Jo furrowed her brow defensively. "Nick, I'm not sure what you're implying…" she trailed off.

Liam quickly intervened. "Have you seen Skylar since?"

"Well, no. He's working," she replied.

"Where?" Liam followed up.

"I think he was going back to Portsmouth. The university's server keeps crashing. He said he could have taken care of it remotely, but he wanted to deliver good customer service and go in person."

"So, he left when?" Liam pressed.

"Oh, he's been gone since last Wednesday," she answered.

"Let me get this straight. He drove all the way back up here to transfer a title and then left again?" Nick asked.

"Oh no. I went to him. The car stays at the farm in Minford."

"What farm?" Liam asked, confusion in his tone.

"He has a farm in Minford," she replied. "He keeps the car there. He drives his other vehicle to the farm and then uses the Taurus for local travel. Says it's better on gas."

Jo bent over to pick up a piece of lint from the large oriental rug. As she did, a stunning diamond-cut necklace with a sapphire pendant slipped out of her collar.

The image of Stephanie Peters instantly flashed in Nick's mind. Stephanie, a twenty-four-year-old graduate student, had been found at Whitewater State Park. Nick recalled her boyfriend mentioning a necklace he had bought for her, a piece of jewelry that had not been recovered from the scene. During the investigation, Nick had come across a photograph of Stephanie wearing that exact same necklace.

"Where'd you get that necklace, Jo?" he asked.

"Skylar gave it to me," she said as she sat back up and touched it gingerly.

Nick pressed further. "When?"

"I think it was May."

The timeline matched.

Nick's eyes shifted to Jo's hands, now trembling. On one finger, she wore an antique ring. He remembered speaking with Betsy Mullins's family, the Morehead State student from southern Ohio. A photograph in her case file had shown the same ring. It was a perfect match.

"When did you get the ring, Jo?" Nick asked.

"Skylar gave it to me on our honeymoon."

The timeline was off, but everything else made sense. The necklace, the ring, and the fibers were certainly enough for a warrant.

Nick excused himself as Liam kept Jo occupied. He walked outside and made the necessary calls. Within thirty minutes, a forensic team was dispatched, and the county sheriff delivered a warrant to search the home.

Another warrant would be executed in Scioto County. It would allow the farmhouse to be searched, and the Ford Taurus would be seized. The next step was for Nick to locate Skylar and bring him in for questioning.

When the team arrived, Jo was completely caught off guard. Shocked and angry, she stood silently in the driveway alongside Liam and Nick. She knew exactly how this process worked, and it was clear to Nick that she was deliberately exercising her right to remain silent, even though no arrest had been made.

Chris exited through the front door carrying empty evidence bags. He stopped in front of Jo and glanced at Nick and Liam.

Nick turned to Jo. "We're going to need to take your jewelry into evidence."

"What?" she asked angrily, her arms folded in defiance. She shook her head. "I don't understand any of this. You haven't told me a damn thing. We're having a conversation, and the next thing I know, we're standing out here while a forensics team goes through my personal belongings. I'm watching friends, people I've known for years, tear my house apart, Nick. What the fuck is going on?"

With little sympathy, he met her gaze. "We believe that your husband is The Phantom. He's been stalking and killing women. Hunting them for sport."

Her eyes filled with horror. Disbelief blinded her as the pigment of her face turned bright red. "Skylar? Are you joking?"

"This is definitely not a joke. He has Lauren. He's probably torturing her right now. This very minute. But I can't go get her because I have to follow procedure. Tearing your house apart and taking your jewelry is part of that procedure. The jewelry you're wearing belonged to two of the victims. So hand it over."

"I don't believe you. You're lying," she bit out.

"Oh, I wish I was. And you don't have to believe me. The warrant I have says I can take the damn jewelry. It doesn't belong to you, Jo. It belonged to two women that your husband killed," Nick concluded sharply.

Her eyes drifted toward the house. The number of people coming in and out was staggering. Then she looked at Chris. Unapologetically, he held open an evidence bag.

"Drop the ring in," he demanded. She did as she was instructed.

"Now the necklace," he said. Jo reached up and unfastened it. She dropped it in the bag.

The team was able to take both Jo's and Skylar's toothbrushes and hairbrushes to analyze DNA. Another warrant would allow for a bite sample to be taken from Skylar when they found him. Their next step was the drive to southern Ohio.

72

Nick and Liam stayed at the same hotel where Nick and Lauren had lodged during the investigation of Betsy Mullins's murder. Unable to sleep, Nick pored over the case files. A dark, primal part of him imagined grabbing Skylar by the throat and choking the life out of him.

Still, he knew he needed to try to sleep. So he gave up and lay down on the bed. He closed his eyes and thought of Lauren. He missed her. Her blue eyes and soft brown hair tugged at his memory. The way the sun hit it when they were venturing on the lake brought tears to his eyes. He worried that he would not see that vibrancy again.

He prayed for her safe return. He prayed that she would be able to recover once she was found.

Liam burst into the room. "We got it!" he exclaimed. "The warrant for the farmhouse. We've got it. Let's go!"

They drove to a rural part of the county about forty five minutes away from downtown. As they pulled off the county highway and onto a dirt lane, a rundown farmhouse appeared in the distance. The Taurus sat outside.

With the forensics team, they entered the residence. The house was empty, and local law enforcement cleared the scene. As Nick walked from room to room, there was no sign of life. The basement also had no clear signs that Lauren had been there.

Once the car was placed on the tow truck, it was taken back to the lab. Chris would be able to collect samples and compare them to the evidence they had already collected. Nick and Liam drove back to Columbus as well. They were both anxious to see what Travis could pull off the hard drive they had taken from Skylar.

As Nick sat on the sofa in the lab, his head in his hands and his elbows on his knees, he sighed discontentedly. "Why didn't we find her at the farmhouse?" he asked as he stood and began to pace.

"Maybe he has more property somewhere. A place we don't know about," Liam replied.

Nick walked down the hallway and into Travis's lab. "Pull up property records for the farmhouse," Nick demanded.

Travis followed the instructions, and blueprints appeared on the screen. Beside the main property was a square marked with precise dimensions.

"What's that?" Nick asked as he narrowed his gaze.

"It looks like an outbuilding," Travis answered.

"What?"

"There's an outbuilding on the property somewhere. Didn't you find one?" Travis asked.

"There was no fucking outbuilding," Nick answered.

"Yes, there is," Travis followed up. "If it's in the county records, it's there somewhere on the property."

"That farmhouse is surrounded by dense forest. Our team looked over the entire area. There's no outbuilding," Nick insisted.

"I'm telling you, there is. You all need to go back. It's got to be deeper in the woods. Maybe you all didn't go far enough," Travis refuted. "You need to go back and look in the woods. There's a building somewhere on the property," Travis stated.

The phone vibrated in Nick's pocket. He pulled it out and flipped it open. "Bennette," he answered.

He heard Chris's voice on the other end. "I found hair matching all of the victims in the trunk of the car."

"Lauren's?"

"No. But I found particulates in the tires that matched all of the crime scenes."

"He's using the other vehicle," Nick said. "He's still there on the property somewhere. He knew we'd never find him," Nick muttered. "Chris, we've got to go back to the property. We've got to do a grid search in the woods. There should be tire tracks from the Excursion there. If you can match the tire tracks, I can get a warrant to arrest him."

Nick hung up and looked down at Travis. "Find the records for…" Nick began.

"Already on it," Travis answered as he pulled up the information about the Excursion. The BMV database showed that it was registered to Skylar.

Liam, Nick, and the state and federal team members converged on the property once more. With flashlights in hand, the large group walked the property grid. Chris worked on making casts of the tire tracks.

Suddenly, a voice shouted in the distance, "Over here!"

Nick sprinted toward the sound. Someone stood nearby, their flashlight aimed at the ground. Adrenaline surged through him as he stopped, bracing himself for what they might uncover. Could this be where she was buried?

The patch of grass before them looked noticeably out of place. Moments later, Liam arrived, surveying the area alongside Nick. Testing the ground, Nick stomped on the grass. It sounded hollow.

"There's a latch," Liam said, kneeling down and running his gloved hands over the surface.

Nick crouched beside him, and together they lifted the concealed door. Beneath it lay a storm cellar. They descended carefully into the underground space, finding themselves in a small, reinforced concrete room.

The walls and floors were solid concrete, and a separate room branched off from the main area. It was equipped with a sink and a tub, its stark functionality unsettling. In the center of the main room stood a metal framed bed. Shackles hung ominously from the headboard.

Liam left and yelled for Chris. Nick stayed behind and walked to the bed. There were blood stains on the mattress. He did not realize that Chris was standing beside him.

"Don't touch anything, Nick," Chris said as he came down the stairs.

"I won't."

Chris got a black light out of his kit and asked Liam to shut the fluorescents off. He scanned the area and found semen stains on the bed. Nick's stomach turned. He quickly ascended the stairs and walked into the darkness, steadying himself against a tree. The thought of anyone violating Lauren made him nauseous, and he fought hard against the bile rising in his throat.

Nick felt Liam's hand on his back. "Chris is collecting samples. Once anything is matched to Lauren, we've got him."

73

Nick stood outside of Chris's lab, pacing. Then he saw Travis round the corner with a horrified expression on his face.

"What's wrong?" Nick asked.

"You need to see this," Travis said quietly. "Come with me."

Nick followed him to the workspace, where Liam, Selina, and Lisa stood in the center of the room. Selina was crying uncontrollably, and Liam was doing his best to console her.

On the screen in front of them was an image of Lauren's face, rendered in black and white. There was no sound. She appeared lifeless, her eyes closed. The frame showed only a portion of her upper body, adding to the haunting stillness of the scene.

"What the hell is this, Travis?" Nick asked.

"I got an email from a good friend of mine. It had a link with it. We exchange shit like this all of the time. When I clicked on it, this popped up," he replied. "I think Skylar hacked into his account and sent this. I'm running a trace on the IP address, but I think he's covered his tracks again."

Nick choked back emotion as he looked over at Lisa. "Is she dead?"

"No," Lisa replied with a confident shake of her head. "Her chest is moving, Nick. She's breathing."

He followed up. "Is this a live feed?"

"As far as I can tell, yes," Travis answered. "I'm also searching for the uplink so I can track it. It's encrypted, so it's going to take some time for me to break through."

"Jesus Christ, she doesn't have time!" Nick shouted. "She's right there," he said, gesturing toward the screen.

"How long do we think she's been there?" Chris asked, looking at Travis.

"From what I can tell, the feed has been online since about three a.m."

"Which means we have less than twenty four hours to find her," Chris added.

"That's when the oxygen will run out according to our experiments here in the lab," Lisa said with a nod.

"If it's dark, how are we able to see her?" Nick asked.

"He's using a night vision camera," Travis answered.

Chris's phone buzzed. He looked up and smiled grimly. "It's a text. The seminal and vaginal contribution matched Lauren and Skylar. The blood is also Lauren's. We've got him."

"Let's go get this bastard. I want his head on a platter!" Nick said as he turned and stormed out the door.

74

Liam and Nick stood in Jo and Skylar's living room. She sat on the couch, arms folded, a defiant air about her.

"Has he contacted you?" Nick asked.

"No. You took my phone, remember?" she replied venomously.

"We need him here, so call him," Nick said as he looked over at Jo and then eyed the landline on the end table.

"He didn't do this!" she shouted as she stood to her feet.

Nick met her toe to toe, anger seething beneath his calm exterior. "He did do this, Jo," he said evenly. "We found his little hideout in Minford. His DNA is all over it. We found her blood. He is The Phantom. So, you're going to pick up the goddamn phone and call him here."

"I will not set him up," she said, setting her jaw.

"You will get him on that fucking phone. You will tell him to get his ass home. When he gets here, I'm going to arrest him, and I'm going to find Doc. She's your friend, too. Remember? Your husband is a serial killer, Jo. Are you really going to risk going to prison for him? Aiding and abetting? Obstruction? Evidence doesn't lie."

Tears welled in her eyes. Her bottom lip quivered. "He's my husband, Nick."

"I don't care who the fuck he is. He's got the love of my life stuffed in some plastic box God knows where, and time is running out for her."

"A box?" she asked, confusion crossing her face.

"He linked a live camera feed to the lab so we can watch her die. Do you want to be a part of that?" he asked.

The astonishment on Jo's face was unmistakable. She walked to the landline phone and picked up the receiver. She told Skylar to come home right away because there had been an accident. He promised he would arrive in just a few hours.

The police cars departed, and Liam stayed with Jo while Nick went back to the lab. Liam promised that when he arrested Skylar, he would bring him in. Chris also stayed behind, planning to seize the SUV for analysis.

Back at the lab, Nick sat in front of the computer screen, watching Lauren. She appeared to be asleep, or at least she seemed to be. Beside him, Travis worked diligently, typing as he tried to break through the encryption.

"Has she woken up at all?" Nick asked.

"No. He's either drugged her or knocked her out pretty good," Travis replied.

"Travis!" Lisa scolded.

"Sorry," Travis muttered. "I can be a little too blunt sometimes."

Nick turned his attention back to the screen just as Lauren's eyes began to flutter open. She reached for a lighter and flicked it, the small flame casting light around her. Her eyes darted in panic as she took in her surroundings.

Lisa stepped closer to the screen and pointed. "What is that?" she asked, indicating a piece of paper tucked under the strap of

Lauren's black bra.

Nick shook his head. "I don't know. None of the other victims were left with a note."

They watched as Lauren's fingers brushed against the paper. She pulled it out and unfolded it, flicking the lighter again to illuminate the words. Her expression darkened as she read the message, her brows furrowing. Then her eyes locked onto the camera lens.

A few tense moments of silence passed before the flame went out. Suddenly, Lauren screamed, but just as quickly as she lost control, she regained her composure. She closed her eyes for a moment, then opened them again, her gaze steady and focused.

She held the paper up to the camera, revealing the message.

"Got it," Travis said, taking a screenshot.

Nick squinted at the screen, trying to read the note, but tears blurred his vision. Lauren dropped the paper and pressed the palm of her hand against the lens.

Nick placed his hand on the screen over hers. In that moment, he imagined the feel of her soft skin beneath his palm. His shoulders sagged as he dropped his head, overcome with emotion, and wept.

Travis moved to another station and enlarged the message. After printing it for handwriting analysis, he carefully placed it in an evidence bag and handed it to Nick.

A look of horror crossed Nick's face as he read the chilling words.

"Smile. He's watching you."

Lisa's jaw dropped. "My God," she whispered.

"Sadistic bastard," Nick muttered, turning his attention back to the computer screen.

Lauren lay still, taking shallow breaths.

75

"He's here," Selina said as she walked into the lab. "Security just texted me. They're in the parking garage. They're coming up right now."

Nick pushed the chair out from under him and stood. He walked to the interrogation room and waited. The door opened as Liam stepped in with Skylar handcuffed. He sat Skylar behind the metal table and then stood in the corner, allowing Nick to take the lead.

"Wow, Nick," Skylar said. "You look like shit, man."

Nick had not shaved, his stubble slowly taking over his face. His shirt was untucked and his tie loosened. He was disheveled, and he could not care less.

Nick sat down across from Skylar. "Tell me why," he began.

"Why what?" Skylar asked.

"Why her? Why Lauren?"

"I have no idea what you mean," he answered smugly.

"I know I can pin at least two murders on you because of the trophies you took. The jewelry that belonged to those girls. I also know I've got you for Lauren's abduction because we matched your DNA. Then there are the fibers from your car. Dude, you're finished. Tell me where she is," Nick bit out.

"Well, the Taurus isn't my car. It was never my car. And now it's Jo's."

"You're actually going to drag her into this?" Nick asked as he leaned back and crossed his arms.

Chris knocked on the interrogation door, and Liam opened it. He handed Nick a piece of paper and then left the room. Nick peered down at the paper briefly. "Here's a warrant to take a dental sample. You bit your victims, which was the dumbest thing you could have ever done. If your bite radius matches the ones on the victims, you're fucked."

"I want a lawyer," Skylar said with a shrug.

"Lawyer or not, you have to give us the sample. It's a warrant signed by a judge."

Liam stepped out of the room and returned moments later with a forensic dentist. Once the sample was collected, Nick leaned forward, resting his arms on the cold metal table, his fingers interlocked. "You could save yourself a lot of headache if you just confess. Tell me where she is," Nick suggested.

"I said I want a lawyer," Skylar demanded firmly.

Nick leaned over the table, his hands pressed against its surface, his shoulders squared in an intimidating stance. Locking eyes with Skylar's clear blue gaze, he said coldly, "No lawyer's going to save you from this."

"Are you sure you want damaged goods, Nick? I mean, Lauren was the best fuck I've ever had, but she put up quite a fight. I'm sure she's torn to pieces down there now and up here," Skylar said as he put his index finger to his temple.

Nick grabbed Skylar's shirt and jerked him up. He shook him violently. "You son of a…" he began as Liam quickly intervened. He pulled him off Skylar.

"Tell me where she is!" Nick shouted as Liam struggled to keep them apart.

Skylar leaned forward. "I can see why you couldn't resist her. She is a ten out of ten, Nick."

Nick lunged forward again, knowing if he got a hold of him, he would kill him. Liam wrapped his arms around him, keeping him from endangering the investigation.

"Come on, Nick. Let's walk," Liam said as he pulled him out of the interrogation room.

The door slammed behind them. Nick and Liam stood just outside the door. They heard fast footsteps approaching and turned to see Chris running down the hallway with papers in his hand. "Lauren's hair and skin are all over the back of his SUV."

Nick wanted to kill Skylar. He knew if he got his hands on him, he would. So Liam took the lead. He turned the doorknob and pulled, walking in and sitting across from Skylar. Nick watched from the tank.

"Skylar, why is Lauren's hair in the back of your SUV?" Liam asked.

"Maybe we had sex back there. Maybe I was having an affair. Maybe she was cheating on Nick," Skylar replied.

"I really need you to be honest here, man. It will be the difference between life in prison and the death penalty. There is truly no way out of this for you," Liam said.

Skylar shrugged.

"The bite marks on the other victims," Liam continued confidently, "are going to prove that you killed them. The others that were not bitten, we will have to work on that a little harder. But the fact that hair matching all of the victims was found in the Ford Taurus means you had them in the trunk. Now why would you put anyone in your trunk? You were so sure we would not catch you that you did not even clean out your car. Who the hell does that?" Liam asked as he threw up his hands and laughed.

"I'm not saying anything," Skylar said.

"You won't have to because the evidence speaks for itself," Liam concluded as he stood and walked out of the room.

Nick waited in the hallway, arms folded, shaking his head. "We're holding him."

"You bet we are," Liam agreed. "We're going to take all of this evidence to the DA, and they're going to charge him. A jury will undoubtedly convict."

A woman in a lab coat approached them, handing Nick a file folder. He opened it to review the bite analysis, then turned and walked back into the interrogation room, his demeanor noticeably calmer. Sitting down at the table, he laid the folder in front of him and opened it. Inside were the bite analysis and photographs from the autopsies.

Nick carefully placed the transparent overlay of the bite marks onto one of the photographs, aligning them perfectly. He glanced up at Skylar, a hint of satisfaction in his voice. "Well, would you look at that? It's a match, Skylar."

Skylar sat silently.

"We got you, you son of a bitch."

"But you don't have her," Skylar said quietly, his eyes meeting Nick's.

"Give us time," Nick said confidently. "The members of this team are brilliant. They've worked with Lauren their entire careers.

They will figure out where she is with or without your help. Then she'll get the chance to confront you. To testify. To watch the lethal injection go into your arm knowing that you're going to burn in hell."

"Good luck, Agent Bennette," Skylar said pompously. "I'm smarter. None of her team can match me when it comes to computers. That's why every college in the Midwest hires me to work on their systems. I'm a genius, and that's why you'll never be able to hold her or touch her or talk to her again. She'll be mine forever now."

Nick stood, gathered the file, and glared at him. "We'll see, won't we?"

"Go to hell, Nick," Skylar bit out.

"You first," Nick said as he turned and walked out of the room.

76

Nick sat at one of the workstations in Travis's space. He watched the computer screen as Travis worked diligently to break into the feed. As the hours passed, however, hope diminished.

Lauren's face was a constant reminder that they were failing. She opened her eyes occasionally. Everyone could see she tried to take shallow breaths to conserve oxygen.

Frustrated and angry, Nick stood and walked to the middle of the room. He folded his arms, wrapping them around himself, wishing he could do more. He prayed for a miracle. He wanted to find her. Hold her. Touch her. Comfort her.

Then Lauren's mouth moved, grabbing everyone's attention. Nick walked back to the workstation and sat down, Selina standing behind him.

"I can't read lips," Nick said.

Selina pursed her lips. "I can."

"What's she saying?" Nick asked as he glanced up at Selina.

Tears fell from Selina's eyes. "She says she knows it won't be long. She knows we're watching. She says that Skylar is the one you should be after." Selina paused and then kept going. Her voice trembled as she fought back emotion. "She says that she loves you, Nick. That she always has, even if she didn't show it." Selina brushed the tears away. "She says she wants you to go on with your life when she's gone. She wants you to be happy and to find love again."

Nick's bottom lip trembled as the possibility of never finding

Lauren settled over him. His eyes filled with salty tears. He touched the screen and traced the shape of her face. "Don't give up, Doc," he whispered.

"She says that she will always be with you and she's sorry."

No longer able to remain composed, Nick dropped his head and sobbed. Selina moved to his side and knelt. She rubbed his back in an effort to comfort him.

The door flew open, startling everyone in the room. Liam rushed in. "He's dead," he blurted out.

Nick turned his head, still wiping the tears from his face. "Who's dead?"

"Skylar's dead," Liam went on.

Selina and Nick stood, astonishment and disappointment in their expressions.

"Are you serious?" Selina asked.

Liam nodded, an exasperated expression on his face. "He hung himself in his cell at county this morning."

"Are you fucking kidding me?" Nick shouted.

"He's gone, Nick."

"Any hope of finding her died with him!" Selina exclaimed.

Nick turned back to the screen. Lauren's face was still in the frame, her mouth no longer moving, but her eyes darted about. The timer in the top right corner of the screen counted down the hours and minutes she had left.

"Now what do we do?" Liam asked as a hopeless expression

colored his face.

"I can't just stand here and watch her die," Nick insisted.

"What choice do we have?" Liam asked with a shrug.

"The particulates might be our only hope. If Chris can narrow down the soil samples, we might just be able to trace her location."

77

Nick stood beside the medical examiner at the county morgue. He peered down at Skylar's body. The bastard had managed to escape the consequences he deserved. The families would never truly have closure. Everything was left completely undone. Skylar had exercised the ultimate control over the entire situation.

After the drive across town, Nick stepped off the elevator and into the forensics department. Chris waited at the end of the hallway with a smile on his face.

"I have good news," he called.

Nick briskly walked toward him. "I hope so, Chris."

"I have separated the soil samples from the SUV tires."

"And?" Nick asked.

"I can narrow down the last place Skylar went. Some of the soil matches the Minford farm. Others match highway pavement. Another sample matches the soil from the crime scene with Betsy Mullins, the girl found in Shawnee State Forest."

Nick's eyes lit up. "We can give this to Travis. It might help him narrow down the feed since we have a precise geographic area. This is great, Chris," he concluded as he took the papers from his hand and walked back to Travis's lab.

Travis and his team were still at their computers, trying to break into the encrypted feed. Nick handed the papers to Travis.

"We know where she is," Nick said. "She is somewhere in Shawnee State Forest."

Travis began keying in the information. Nick glanced at the computer displaying the live feed of Lauren. She was crying now. The expression on her face told him that she had lost all hope of being rescued. The lens seemed to shake as she pounded her fists against the top of the coffin.

Travis looked up at Nick and pointed to a large map on the screen. "All of these are satellite feeds of the area. I've been able to hack into all of them except one." He pointed to a specific section. "This is the one I can't get into. That's the one we want."

"So where's it coming from?" Nick asked.

"Well, that's the problem. I can tell you that it's coming from southern Ohio, but I can't tell you exactly where. I don't know whether it's in the forest or on the farm or in a freakin' dungeon on the property. The only thing you can do is take the knowledge you have about the soil and go. Personally, I think he buried her in the same vicinity as Betsy Mullins. I think that area is probably familiar to him. He wouldn't pick a place that wasn't."

Liam spoke up. "She also used to camp there with her family. So he could have buried her someplace that means something to her."

"We'll take two teams," Nick said. "One will focus on the area where Betsy was found. The other will focus on the area where Lauren and her family used to camp. I'll need to get in touch with Ingrid to see if she can give me a location."

"I will keep trying to break into the feed," Travis added. "I'll also keep an eye on Lauren. Call me when you get to the park. When she hears something, she'll react, and I can let you know when you're close."

78

Liam drove as Nick spoke to Ingrid. They agreed to meet at Shawnee State Forest to assist with the rescue efforts. So, after what felt like an eternity in the car, they arrived in the parking area. It was nearly 1:30 p.m. The lot was filled with vehicles.

Nick spotted Ingrid, Lucas, Josh, Brandon, Truddy, and Doug standing next to their cars. "Park there," Nick said, pointing in their direction.

As he opened the door and stepped out of the car, Ingrid approached him. "What do you want us to do?"

"I need you to show me where you camped when Lauren was a kid. Was it the same place every year?" he asked.

Josh spoke up. "It was the same place, but I'm not sure if we could find it. A lot of this has changed."

"We have to try," Nick said as he dialed Travis.

The volunteers, forensic teams, law enforcement, and K-9 units split into two groups. One team walked toward the area where Betsy was found. The other team followed Lauren's family into the woods.

The K-9 handlers provided Skylar's scent to one dog and Lauren's scent to the other. The handlers led the way, with the dogs pulling them in the same general direction. Lauren's family followed closely behind, but eventually, they lost sight of the handlers and the dogs.

The deeper they walked into the woods, the poorer the cell service became. Nick eventually lost connection with Travis.

In the distance, Nick heard someone shout, "Here!"

Nick's heart pounded as he sprinted toward the sound of the K-9 handler's voice. When he arrived, he saw the dog lying on the ground, panting heavily, while the handler knelt beside it, gripping the dog's collar tightly. "What'd you find?" Nick asked.

"The dog picked up Lauren's scent and alerted here," the handler said, pointing to the ground under the dog.

Nick glanced down and noticed blood staining some leaves. Moments later, the other dog raced toward them, signaling that it had also picked up Skylar's scent.

Nick knelt to get a closer look. He gazed up at Ingrid and then looked around. "This area familiar at all?"

"Not really," she answered, shaking her head.

"Let's keep going with the dogs," Nick directed.

The dogs ran ahead, plunging deeper into the forest. With every step, Nick felt his hope fading, especially when the dog tracking Lauren's scent lost the trail. However, the dog following Skylar's scent stayed on course, leading them toward a darker, denser part of the forest. The others hurried closely behind.

The dog stopped abruptly and alerted to a specific spot where the ground had been recently disturbed, bare dirt with no grass or leaves. Suddenly, the walkie-talkie on the handler's hip crackled to life. Travis's voice came through, shouting, "I think she hears you. Start calling for her!"

"Lauren!" Nick shouted.

Travis's voice came through on the walkie-talkie again. "The feed is gone!"

Nick grabbed the device from the handler's belt and spoke into it. "What the hell do you mean?"

"I think the feed was on a timer," Travis replied.

"Are you fucking serious?" Nick said angrily. "Now we're going in blind!"

Nick handed the device back to the handler and sank to his knees. He began digging with his hands.

Liam called to other members of the team. "We need shovels over here!"

A swarm of officers descended on the site, shovels in hand, attacking the earth with relentless urgency. Nick ripped off his suit jacket and hurled it aside, his movements fueled by desperation. Snatching a shovel from a nearby officer, he joined the frenzy, carving through the mud and soil, shouting her name with every thrust. Dirt sprayed in all directions as the volunteers pressed on with unyielding determination.

Suddenly, Nick's shovel struck something hard. He froze, heart pounding, then struck again to be sure. A hollow clang confirmed it wasn't just his imagination. "Stop!" he shouted, leaping into the hole. Tossing the shovel aside, he clawed at the dirt with his bare hands. His fingers brushed against a wire, sparking a moment of dread. Was it a bomb? Then he uncovered a camera, and beneath it, Lauren's face came into view. Her wide eyes locked onto his, her lips moving in silent, frantic words, muffled by layers of soil. "Oh my God," Nick said under his breath. "Doc, hang on!" he shouted.

The forensics team pulled Nick out of the hole and began digging down further around the plastic coffin.

"We need a blanket," Nick shouted as he stood with his hands on his hips, trying to catch his breath.

Liam handed Nick a towel, his hands trembling as he wiped away the dirt caked on his skin. A volunteer approached, offering a blanket. Nick took it without a word, clutching it tightly in his arms. Turning away from the chaotic scene, he stared into the shadowy forest. His breath hitched as he caught a fleeting glimpse of something inexplicable.

A group of women stood silently among the trees, their faces hauntingly familiar. Nick's stomach tightened as recognition washed over him, the Phantom's victims. They stood in a solemn cluster, their expressions filled with urgency, as if waiting for something. But why could he see them? Glancing back at the others on the scene, he noticed no one else reacting. No one else seemed to see them.

A voice, soft and achingly familiar, broke his trance. It was her. The love of his life, calling his name. His head whipped around, but the apparitions dissolved into the air, vanishing one by one like smoke in the wind.

Without hesitation, Nick sprinted toward the sound of her voice. Time seemed to twist and stretch, each step agonizingly slow. The world around him froze. Her family stood like statues, the volunteers immobile. It was as if the universe itself had paused, leaving only Nick and the sound of her voice. Nothing else mattered. He had to reach her. He had to hold her.

Diving into the gaping hole, Nick landed on his knees. His hands trembled as he pulled Lauren free, his arms wrapping around her trembling body. He threw the blanket over her fragile frame, feeling her cold, clammy skin against his.

Her breaths were ragged, her body convulsing with sobs that tore through the silence. She kept her arms tucked tightly against herself, as if trying to hold the pieces of her together. Nick pressed her against him, his grip unyielding, as if to shield her from the horrors of the world. "I've got ya, Doc," he whispered, his voice raw with emotion. "I'll never let go. You're safe now."

She couldn't speak, her sobs racking her fragile body as Nick rubbed his hands over the blanket, desperate to warm her. Unable to do anything else, she clung to his shirt, her fingers gripping the fabric so tightly it threatened to tear.

"Oh, my God," he whispered, his voice breaking. "I'm here. I'm not letting you go. It's over. It's all over."

The medical team approached with a stretcher, their presence pulling Nick's focus for a moment. He glanced at them, then back down at her, cupping her face gently in his hands. Her wide, petrified eyes locked on his, filled with fear.

"They've got to take you to the hospital," he said softly.

"Don't leave me," she pleaded through her sobs, her voice trembling.

"Never," he promised. "I'll be right there with you."

He wrapped her securely in the blanket, then lifted her into his arms, cradling her like the most fragile treasure. Ignoring the stretcher, he carried her out of the forest himself. Each step was steady and purposeful as he moved toward the waiting ambulance. Climbing inside, he gently placed her on the gurney.

Even as she began to calm, she refused to release his hand, her fingers laced tightly with his. He knelt beside her, his gaze never leaving her face.

"I didn't think you'd find me," she whispered, her voice barely audible.

He leaned closer, brushing a hand across her tear streaked face. "You should know by now," he murmured, "I don't give up that easily."

Her lips quivered, a new wave of emotion threatening to overwhelm her. "I was so scared that"

"Shh," he interrupted gently, his fingers threading through her hair. "Lauren, don't go there. You're here. You're safe. You're going to be okay." His voice softened to a whisper as he pressed a tender kiss to her forehead. "I'm never letting you out of my sight again."

79

Lauren stared out the window of her hospital room. She felt like the luckiest person in the world. She hadn't been able to stop crying since they'd found her.

Nick walked into the room, his clothing stained with mud. She turned toward him with a smile.

"Hey, Doc," he said as he walked to her and pulled a chair over to the side of the bed.

"Hey," she replied weakly.

"You doing okay?"

She nodded. "I'm okay."

"You're pretty banged up," he said, brushing a strand of hair from her face.

"Nothing is broken that won't heal," she said confidently. She put his hand on her lower abdomen. "Doctor says I can still have children."

Nick's eyes filled with tears as he nodded, still stroking her hair. "That's good," he said quietly.

"I'm sure they'll give you some scrubs to change into if you ask," she said sweetly, taking note of his appearance.

"I just wanted to get up here with you."

He took her hand in his and kissed her knuckles. "I thought I'd lost you," he admitted.

"You told me not to think about those things," she whispered.

"I don't know what I'd do without you, Doc," he replied.

"I owe you an apology, Bennette," she said as she looked down at his hand on hers. "I am so sorry that I hurt you when you asked me about marriage and children. I had plenty of time to evaluate what was important and all of the things I'd do differently if I had a second chance. I'm going to make good on all of that. I want you forever. I want to have children with you, a family. I want to spend the rest of my life with you."

He beamed. "Doc, are you asking me to marry you?"

"I think I am," she said with a grin.

"You know I will," he said as he kissed her knuckles again.

She paused and looked out the window again. "Did you get him?"

Nick shook his head.

"Why not?" she asked.

"We had him. All of the evidence was there. He hung himself in his cell."

"Coward," she whispered. "And Jo?"

"She protected him."

"Did she know what he was doing?" she asked.

"No. I don't think she did. She just couldn't believe he was the monster he turned out to be."

"I'm glad he's dead," Lauren said.

"I just wanted him to have to face you when you made it out alive."

"Nothing can undo what's been done. I am sorry that the other victims didn't get justice."

He nodded. "Me, too. He killed himself before we had the chance to find out where he'd put you." Nick paused. "Remember when you told me that your team was brilliant? You were right."

"They came through for me, didn't they?"

"With flying colors."

Lauren began to weep again. "Thank you, Nick," she said as her voice shook. "Thank you for being who you are. For being a gallant hero. You've saved me in absolutely every possible way."

"I will always save you," he answered. "There's someone else you need to thank, though."

With a furrowed brow, she said, "Who?"

"If it weren't for the K 9 units, we would have never found you."

She nodded. "I will make sure that I give a financial contribution to the unit. I'll also schedule a ceremony to honor the dogs and their handlers," she concluded.

"I think they'd appreciate that," Nick agreed.

Nick stood and stretched, exhaustion finally catching up with him. "I'm going to find a nurse," he said quietly. "See if they'll let me grab a shower."

"Okay," she replied softly.

When he stepped into the hallway, the room felt suddenly too quiet.

Lauren slid her legs over the side of the bed and stood slowly. The tile pressed hard against her feet. She walked into the bathroom and stopped in front of the mirror.

Bruises bloomed along her forearms in shades of purple and yellow. Raw burns circled her wrists beneath layers of gauze. Beneath the thin hospital gown, she felt the lingering ache deep in her muscles when she shifted, the kind that did not come from impact alone. She lifted her hand and traced the edge of the bandage absently before dropping it to her side as a tightness crept into her chest. Her breathing shortened before she realized it was happening.

She leaned forward, gripping the sink, forcing herself to inhale slowly. Counted breaths. Just like before.

A sound echoed down the hallway. A cart rolling. A door closing. Her muscles tensed instinctively, her heart racing as if she needed to prepare for something that never came.

Nick stepped back into the room. "Doc?"

She straightened quickly and turned toward him. "I'm fine," she said a little too fast.

He hesitated, then nodded. He did not ask again.

Lauren climbed back into the bed, pulling the blanket around her shoulders. Exhaustion settled over her more heavily than before. She stared at the ceiling, aware of every sound and every movement in the building around her.

She closed her eyes, unsure how long it would take for her body to believe what her mind already knew..

80

Before a crowd of federal and state officers, Lauren stood at the podium. Cameras flashed, and microphones filled the room as reporters leaned forward to catch every word. In the front row, Lauren's family sat together, their faces a mix of pride and relief. Behind them sat the members of her team, a quiet show of solidarity. Onstage beside her stood the K-9 handlers and the dogs who had played a vital role in her rescue.

Lauren cleared her throat and glanced at her notes. "Ladies and gentlemen," she began, her voice steady as the room grew silent, "I'm here today to thank everyone who contributed to my rescue. My team. The FBI. The Ohio State Police. BCI. County law enforcement. Each of you played an essential role in saving my life."

She paused, her eyes scanning the room before motioning for Nick to join her at the podium. He rose, walking to her side. Lauren turned back to the crowd, her expression softening. "The efforts of the human team deserve recognition," she said, "but we cannot forget the officers on four legs." Turning to smile at the handlers and their K-9s, her voice thickened with emotion. "It's because of you that I'm standing here today. You saved my life, and that's a gift I can never repay."

Tears glistened in her eyes as she continued. "While I can't put a monetary value on what you've given me, I am donating one hundred thousand dollars to the Central Ohio K-9 Training Program and another one hundred thousand to the Federal K-9 Training Program. Thank you for bringing survivors home to their families and for your unwavering dedication to service."

With a gesture toward the handlers and dogs, Lauren began clapping, leading the entire room in a standing ovation. Nick walked over to a table and retrieved a set of medals and plaques. One by one, Lauren presented each handler with a plaque, shaking their hands with heartfelt gratitude. Finally, she knelt before each dog, placing a medal around their necks as the crowd erupted into cheers.

Epilogue

By mid-January, Lauren's life had begun to settle into something resembling normalcy. She had started therapy to help her recover from the trauma, and while her physical scars were healing, the emotional wounds would take much longer to close.

Lauren and Nick were learning how to be intimate again. Nick, as always, was patient and understanding, giving her the space she needed. But Lauren was harder on herself, struggling with guilt and self-criticism. From her own training, she knew emotional healing couldn't be rushed.

Months passed, and soon it was July. Lauren stood on her deck, looking down at the large white canopy where the guests were gathered. Rows of white folding chairs were filled with friends and family.

She adjusted the hem of her white sundress as the warm summer breeze brushed her skin. Her eyes scanned the crowd, and she spotted Selina standing near the front, next to the officiant.

Jim, standing beside her, nudged her gently. "Ready?" he asked with a grin.

Lauren nodded, looping her arm through his. The violin quartet began playing the wedding march, and as she took her first steps down the aisle, her heart swelled with anticipation. This wasn't just a ceremony. It was the beginning of a new life with Nick.

Morgan began the ceremony, reciting the traditional vows. When he reached the pivotal moment, he paused and turned to Lauren. "And do you, Lauren Gail Harris, take this man, Nicholas Thomas Bennette, as your lawfully wedded husband, to have and to hold, from this day forward, in sickness and in health, for richer or poorer, until you are parted by death?"

"I do," she said, her voice steady, her heart full as she gazed into Nick's eyes.

"Then, by the power vested in me by the great state of Ohio, I now pronounce you man and wife..." Morgan grinned, looking at Nick. "Hey, Nick, you can kiss her now!" he added with a playful laugh.

Nick pulled Lauren into his arms, and as their lips met, time seemed to slow. For a brief moment, the world fell away. When they pulled apart, Lauren smiled up at him, her heart soaring. The resistance she had once felt, the lingering fear and doubt, was now a fading memory. Nick had shown her a happiness she never thought possible. A path she hadn't known she could walk.

He had opened her eyes to a deeper joy, teaching her that just because something was beyond her understanding didn't mean it lacked value.

Lauren, of all people, should have known this. After all, she had spent years seeing things others couldn't, guiding those who had no voice. And through everything that had happened to her, she remained determined to bring peace to the families of victims, just as she had promised herself.

As she stood there, looking into the eyes of the man she now called her husband, she felt a deep sense of gratitude. The weight of everything she had endured, the trauma, the pain, felt small in comparison to the future she was now stepping into. With Nick by her side, there would be no limit to their happiness. Together, they would face whatever came next, hand in hand, knowing they could overcome anything.

When their time on this earth came to an end, when their eyes closed for the final time, she knew they would reunite in the light, together, forever. Death wouldn't be the end. It would be the beginning of something even greater. And Lauren knew, without a doubt, that she would live the rest of her life to the fullest, cherishing every moment, with no regrets, only the deepest gratitude for the love they had found, and the future they would build together.

ABOUT THE AUTHOR

Tracee Ford, known as the "Smart Mouth Writer," has been telling stories her whole life. She is an award-winning novelist whose work explores the intersection of love, belief, and the unseen forces that shape human lives.

Her debut novel, *The Fine Line*, received a Five Star Reader's Favorite Award. Her second novel, *Idolum*, was also honored by Reader's Favorite and nominated by the Paranormal Romance Guild for Best Romantic Suspense. *Through Glass Darkly* later earned first place for Best Paranormal Romance (General), and the *Between Worlds* series received additional recognition from the Paranormal Romance Guild.

Beyond fiction, Tracee has walked many creative paths as a playwright, director, and puppeteer. Her lifelong interest in the paranormal, paired with lived experience, informs her exploration of trauma, belief, and the quiet moments where ordinary life brushes up against something more.